GEORGINA JEFFERY

The Jack Hansard Series

Season Two

Coblyn Press

For my husband

Contents

Acknowledgements

My heartfelt thanks go out to all the friends and beta readers who read the imperfect drafts of these episodes as they were written, offering valued advice and feedback on the story as it unfolded.

Likewise, I'm grateful to everyone who picked up the first book – and this one. I'm not one for lingering on trite-sounding sentiments, but it's always worth saying (and saying again) that your support means the world to me. I hope my words continue to entertain, and I seek always to do you proud.

Special mention goes to two contest winners from the *Season One Launch Party*: Laura Gallant and Charlie Gallant, who contributed the 'Potion of Height' and 'Claritea', respectively in their entries. Both creations appear as cameos in this book as items in Hansard's stock.

The story so far . . .

Since striking a deal with Ang to find her missing kin, Jack has suffered the crotchety Welsh coblyn as his travelling companion. On the trail of the missing coblynau, Jack and Ang soon encountered a strangely invisible thief, nicknamed Quiet Eyes.

They discovered Quiet Eyes was employed by a mysterious and malevolent entity called 'Baines and Grayle' - but were unable to uncover who they actually were or what their motives for kidnapping coblynau might be.

So, in a bid to gain more information, Jack accepted a deal with Quiet Eyes to retrieve a legendary phoenix egg from a hidden dimension for her.

After an explosive showdown, Jack and Ang made it to safety with one phoenix egg in their pockets, while Quiet Eyes also kept hold of one egg to present to her employers – for who knows what nefarious purposes...

Episode 1: Digital Sorcery

O n the outskirts of the city of Manchester, a daring escape was about to unfold.

It began with a chair.

Tied to this chair was a humble, hard-working merchant of simple means and honest ambitions. Myself: Jack Hansard, infamous dealer of miracles, enchanted artifices, and the Finest Occult Goods in all of the British Isles.

By my side, and also tied to a chair, was Ang. Ang was a coblyn. At less than three feet tall, the rope-to-captive ratio on her was rather excessive. Her grubby waistcoat and moleskin trousers, just visible under the mound of rope, were still sprinkled with pastry crumbs from her last meal.

Both of these chairs (and their unlucky occupants) were situated within an abandoned warehouse.

Ang broke the silence first.

'What was it I said to ye before about this idea, Hansard?' she announced to the musty air.

'You said it was a bad one,' I replied. Water dripped onto our heads from the shabby tin roof, which was now more corroded than corrugated. In the dim glow of a single light bulb we could see blackened brick walls that were crumbling under decades of dirt and slime.

'And what was it you said to me, *gwas?*' Ang continued.

'I said, "Don't worry, I'm sure he'll be happy to see us."'

'I ought t' wallop you one.'

'Lucky you're tied up, then.'

She squirmed against her restraints. 'When I get outta this chair, *gwas . . .*'

'Oh, shut *up*, both of you.' This came from the other corner of the room. Our captor watched us from his perch on a three-legged stool. It was a small stool and he was a tall man, so he sat awkwardly hunched over with his knees reaching for his ears. He shifted uncomfortably. 'It's nothing personal, you understand. But I could do without the chatter.'

I shrugged as best I could with both hands tied behind my back. 'I know how it is. Good price for us, is it?'

'It'll pay for a new set of wheels, I'll tell you that,' he said. Above him, the yellow light bulb flickered erratically, suspended from a wire thrown over a rusted beam. It created a rather capricious circle of light in the murk of the warehouse, at times lending a frenzied glow to his features, and at others dimming so that we could barely make each other out.

'What kind?' I asked conversationally.

'Quality Transit van, I reckon.'

I was hurt. 'You sold me out for a *van*, Steve? I'm worth more than that. A Range Rover, at least!'

'Dunno, mate. You ain't got much in the way of assets.'

This was regrettably true.

The bulb flared back to life again, casting wonky shadows of us over the otherwise empty floor.

I could feel the heat radiating off Ang as she stewed in sulking silence next to me. She hadn't said a word to Steve since he'd caught us in his little trap. It was an ingenious hex he'd used, a chain of sigils that framed the doorway like an invisible noose. It'd knocked us both out before I could finish saying 'hello'.

Must have cost him a bundle to put together. It was nice to know we were worth the effort.

'Who's the buyer, may I ask?' I said.

Steve scratched his mop of hair. 'Some bloke you swindled when you were last here. Sold him a potion of height, or something?'

'*Ha!*' Ang jerked in her seat. She strained to turn her head so she could harpoon with me a glare. 'That's why we're in this mess? What were the catch, ye bloody *ffwl?*'

'It did exactly what it said on the tin,' I replied, all innocence. 'One measure of height, to be applied as liberally as the client desired.'

'Which way?' Ang said acidicly.

'Hmm?'

'Ye heard. Up or down?'

Steve grunted a chuckle and provided the answer for me. 'Well, he weren't much taller than you, miss. So I'm guessing he didn't get it in the direction he was hoping for.'

'He should have paid more attention to the small print,' I said.

I tapped my heels on the bare concrete, staring into the shadows. There were plenty of holes in the warehouse walls for something small to sneak through if, say, that was part of your cunning escape plan.

A soft blue light flickered briefly outside one of the broken windows behind Steve's back.

I clicked my tongue and caught his eye again. 'How's the wife?'

He stopped mid-stretch. He'd been about to see what I was looking at. 'Oh, you know. Has to look after her old mum a lot these days, but she's fine. The travel gets her down a bit. I said we should look for a nursing home but she's having none of it.'

'That must be rough,' I said with sympathy.

'Eh. That's life.'

Ang hummed a sound of irritation in her throat. She didn't see the point in making pleasant with an enemy, but Steve and I went way back. You've got to expect a bit of friendly backstabbing in this business. Besides, for every minute I could keep Steve's attention focused on me, the more time we had for Ang's bluecap to find a stealthy point of ingress into the warehouse.

A few tense moments passed as Steve twisted on his stool. The blue glow disappeared from my line of sight.

'How's business on the charms front?' I asked. 'Going strong?'

Steve perked up, just slightly. It did wonders for his posture. 'Not bad, actually. Reckon it's the current socio-economic political climate, an' that. Lot of people on edge these days, looking for a lifeboat to cling onto. Fear makes people superstitious as anything.'

'Oh? You're getting more common customers than usual?'

'Like you wouldn't believe, Jack. Dunno how, but even the lady at the corner shop knew about my stock the other day. Asked about charms to keep immigrants away. I said there's no such thing!' Steve hunched forward again. 'You ask me, world's gone bonkers. Why's everyone so bothered about geography all've a sudden?'

On this I had very little to contribute. If I were a conscientious person (I'm not) I might have been a touch ashamed by how little I knew of current global politics. I was in the habit of switching channels when the news came on the radio, and I bought newspapers only for the odd crossword and to wrap valuables in. If I really couldn't avoid it, I might see some of the headlines trailing across the bottom of a TV screen while waiting to collect a helping of fish and chips.

So I settled for a vague, 'People are funny creatures,' in response.

But our host was on a roll.

'There's funny and then there's mad,' said Steve. 'D'you know what the big craze in charms is, these days? Digital charms. *Can you send me a lucky rabbit's foot by email, please?* Or, *A ward to cleanse my social media feed of bad energy.* Forget protection from evil spirits. It's against spam and viruses now.'

I listened to all this politely, as uncomfortable with modern technology as I was with modern politics.

Steve clearly caught the glazed look in my eye. 'This is all Greek to you, right? Do you even own a smartphone yet, Hansard, or you still using that old brick?'

'Flip-phones are still cool, I'll have you know.'

'No, mate. They aren't.'

''s ridiculous, anyway,' Ang said without lifting her chin. 'Protectin' from things that ain't even real.'

'Now wait a minute.' Steve rose from his stool and suddenly his height gave him menace. 'I may say it's mad, but I didn't say it's not real. D'you know how many malevolent forces like to hide in hard-drives, these days? Or on the bloody cloud. I tell you, we should thank our lucky stars that some ancient primeval curse hasn't downloaded itself onto every bugger's phone already.'

'Maybe it has, and that's why people are glued to them,' I said light-heartedly.

It was the wrong time for a quip. Steve walked forward and bent low into my face, expression dark. 'Don't even joke, Jack.' He reached into the depths of his bomber jacket and for a split-second my mind said *knife*, but my eyes quickly corrected with *phone*.

Steve held the glossy silver screen up and snapped a photo of Ang and me in our respective chairs. 'There,' he said. 'Should've done that earlier.'

The flash had startled me, but my smile didn't waver. 'Souvenir pic, is it?'

Steve shook his head and gave an exasperated sigh. 'You ever look at yourself, Jack? I don't like this techno-digital-multimedia-always-online-always-connected evolution, but that's the way people live these days and I've had to adapt. That's what you never got the hang of. Adapting.'

He pulled back and waved at our dilapidated surroundings – and the markings of his magic trap around the doorway. 'It's why you're here, mate. You've got a good brain on you, but you don't join the world enough to put it to use. I could see that, back when we first met. I thought, "There's a bright spark, but he'll never last. Too lost in his own world to look out for his own skin."'

Ang showed sudden interest. 'How long you known 'im?'

Steve glanced at her, then gave me an appraising look as he sat back down. We'd both been a lot younger, once. The bags under his eyes mirrored my own. 'You were with that lass, then, weren't you?' His mouth screwed up in thought. 'Cora, wasn't it? Some ten years ago at least, I'd've thought.'

'More,' I corrected.

'Really? Damn. *She* was a bright one. Knew what she wanted *right* away. I remember you hanging back, with this dopey grin on your face while she cut the deal. Tourist, I thought. Wonder if he knows what he's getting into.'

'I almost certainly didn't,' I said.

'You never had vision,' Steve went on. 'Not like that Edric Mercer. Now there's a man with *vision*.'

He sprung upright again, with a sense that the sudden surge of boyish excitement might put him at risk of toppling over. 'Have you heard the latest about that brilliant bastard? He went and captured a *phoenix*, Hansard. A bloody phoenix!'

I assume Steve didn't pick up on how my affable grin hardened into something substantially less friendly. 'Did he, now? That seems unlikely.'

'Damn near impossible, I'd think,' said Steve. 'He ended up fighting a god over it. But he blew that bastard into the abyss and walked out of the smoke without a scratch. And he took out half of the British Museum, with it! What a legend.'

'That's not how I'd tell it,' I muttered.

Steve snorted. 'Course you wouldn't. You'd start by lying your heart out, Hansard. And if Mercer's involved you'd call him a phony.'

'That does sound closer to the truth, yes.'

He chuckled to himself, as I apparently wasn't in on the joke. 'You'd like to think so. You ain't never gonna come close to Mercer's world though, Jack.'

That's what you think, I thought.

I caught Ang's eye. It held a warning. *Don't ye dare.*

What did she take me for? Prideful enough to blow open Mercer's obviously contrived and overly self-congratulatory account of how he in fact *did not* capture a phoenix, at all, whatsoever? Wouldn't dream of it.

I, uh, couldn't quite let it go, though.

So I cheerfully blurted out a retort. 'I expect Mercer's proud of his new pet, is he? Been flaunting it everywhere, I imagine?'

'Oh, no,' Steve replied. 'He didn't get to keep it. Because the phoenix got all used up.' He nodded his head with faux authority, clearly eager to have an excuse to impart this thrilling gossip himself. 'Mercer used its regenerative abilities during his fight with the god. They say he died and came back to life! And then the phoenix turned back to ashes afterward.'

I swore under my breath. Mercer had an explanation for everything, the smarmy git.

'And I suppose he hasn't mentioned Quiet Eyes or Baines and Grayle,' I grumbled. *Or the part where I technically saved his life.*

'Eh?'

'Oh, just some individuals of apparently no relevance.'

The parts Mercer had decided to omit – or downright fabricate, in fact – were in my view the best bits. Surely the plucky underdog who tricks his way into the phoenix's nest makes for a more interesting story? And what about the eggs? We *hatched* an Egyptian deity, and the phoenix *killed* it! (At least, we think that's what happened . . .)

And now there were two phoenix eggs left in the world. One of them was in the possession of Baines and Grayle, an entity who we still – for all our digging – knew nothing about.

And then there was *our* phoenix egg. The one we'd stolen back at the last, thrilling second.

Usually, the egg was nestled safely in the bluecap flame of Ang's lantern. But today it was stowed somewhere else about her person. This was because today, Ang's lantern was unlit.

I felt a reassuringly cold gust over my bound wrists. The rope went slack.

About time.

Now we just had to figure out what to do about Steve.

He was still talking excitedly about Mercer, another story of his past exploits – stealing a chariot from the sun-god or some similar nonsense. Mercer could have that effect on people. In our circles he was as close to a celebrity as you could get. Forget fast cars and loose women: racing Pegasuses and wooing tree nymphs was more Mercer's style. He was the guy everybody wanted to be.

Except me. I'd *hate* to be anything like Edric Mercer.

Damn, I was distracting myself from the matter at hand. As Steve's yarn wound down, I caught sight of the bluecap racing low along the far wall. Steve stretched again, about to turn towards it.

I cleared my throat loudly to catch his attention and pretended to inspect the ceiling. 'Your chap's taking a long while. Paying for this holding time, is he?'

Steve rolled his shoulders with a frown. 'So long as he pays up at all, I don't care much. At least it's dry.'

A bony elbow jabbed my stomach. Ang inclined her head toward the main door. Hovering over the light switch was her flickering bluecap.

She raised an eyebrow.

I nodded.

The light went out.

Steve yelped. '*What the*– Jesus Christ, that made me jump. Hold on a tick, I'll check the fuse box.'

Ang and I froze, both mid-rise from our seats. The shadow of Steve turned, completely unawares, toward the door.

Where the bluecap still hovered.

'Well, now,' I heard him say. 'What's this little fairy light, then?'

I took my chance and leapt forward.

I did *not* try to hit him about the head, because 1) this is not a very reliable method of knocking someone unconscious, and 2) I didn't really want to hurt him. Steve was just a guy who wanted a new van. It's all business, in the end.

So I tapped him on the shoulder–

'*Eh?*'

–and swept his legs from under him with his own stool.

'Ang, run!'

'Hansard you *prick*–' Steve groaned.

'Nothing personal!' I shouted behind me.

We slammed the door and rushed out into the night. There was a faint sound of scrambling behind us, but we soon lost ourselves in the maze of derelict industrial estate. We skidded past rusted shutters and rotting brick walls until we found a suitable alcove. We stepped inside and simply . . . faded into the background. Sometimes it's better to stand still in shadow and listen for the sound of frantic footsteps to simply pass you by.

I unfocused – both a mental and physical process. I allowed myself to relax, and blur with the scenery. Ang, as an uncanny being in her own right, slipped into this state effortlessly. We stood motionless, our combined presence merely a smudge against a damp wall. We watched Steve come rumbling by. The confusion was plain on his face.

'I can see you!' we heard him shout hopelessly, further down the alley. Poor bloke. He was doing his best.

Eventually he was out of sight, and earshot.

'Shall we find the car?' I said brightly.

'S'long as we find food, too. Am famished, *gwas*.'

'We weren't tied up for that long, for goodness' sake.'

'Felt like f'rever.'

'Well it could have been shorter if you'd got that bluecap working faster.'

The ghostly blue flame slipped out of hiding from under Ang's waistcoat. She unscrewed the cap on her lantern and it slid inside – looking rather more solid than before. If you looked closely, you might see the shape of an amber egg now sheltered inside it.

'Don't like it, *gwas*. Shouldn't be usin' bluecap for this work.'

'It *is* a treasure-seeking spirit,' I pointed out.

'Aye. Underground, maybe. Not through men's pockets.'

'But it's proven my point, yes? That bluecap of yours is a brilliant asset for obtaining new acquisitions.' I stepped out of the alcove with a preliminary peek both ways down the alley. No sign of Steve. I started down the narrow path to our left, where streetlights beckoned at the end of the gloomy row of derelict warehouses.

'Dunno. Seems like cheatin',' Ang said, falling into step beside me.

'Nonsense. We're just making the most of our resources.'

'Aye. It were too easy though, is what I'm sayin'.'

'You shouldn't complain about things going smoothly, for once.'

She arched an eyebrow. 'Ye sayin' that getting caught and tied up was things goin' smooth?'

'It's smooth for *us*.' I felt for the little USB stick that Ang's bluecap had deposited in my pocket and held it up under the light of an orange streetlamp. 'Probably a tidy profit on this.'

'So we're stealin' now as well?' Ang continued sourly.

'You might say Steve deserved it. He *did* try to sell us off.'

'Aye. And I s'pose ye didn't know he would do that. Did ye.' Ang's tone told me that it wasn't really a question. Her eyes bored upward into my chin. I expected her to give another sharp remark, but instead she simply sighed. 'Look, *gwas*. We're partners now, ain't we? I should get more of a say in how we're doing business. I've gone along wi' this'un, but I gotta say that outright stealin' don't feel right to me.'

I stopped in my tracks. 'Didn't I explain this all to you?'

'No.' She tilted her head. 'I has noticed, *gwas*, that ye tends to make long and fancy plans in yer head, an' oftentimes fails to enlighten me of them. Sometimes I thinks ye have whole conversations just wi' yerself.'

I mulled this over, well aware of the look on her face as I internally scrutinised her words. It's a lonely lifestyle, driving up and down the country hauling unlawful goods (unlawful only because there are no laws to govern them). The varied types of underground society I was prone to mingling in were hardly welcoming: most people I encountered were too shifty to be trusted even as distant business associates, let alone as friends.

But Ang, despite being Welsh, and a coblyn, and a devourer of pastries, had proven herself to be just that – a friend. And she was right. I had promised we'd be partners in this business. I hadn't been upholding my end of the deal very well at all.

'*Gwas*,' she said flatly.

'Right, right, I was just thinking. Sorry, is what I mean. Let's get to the car, and then I'll fill you in. How about that?'

Ang scuffed her feet along the ground in a grumpy sort of acceptance and we turned the next corner.

'*Stop right there!*'

I whirled round. Steve emerged from the shadow of an alley, huffing and panting. His lankiness was deceptive: he was not a fit bloke.

'Careful Steve, remember your heart,' I said, backing up. 'Don't go giving–' I grasped quickly for his wife's name, '–Catherine another fright like that.'

Steve doubled over in front of us, hands on his knees. 'Hansard, you bastard. You just needed to *stay put.*'

'Sorry. I didn't want to.' I ignored the logical compulsion to flee and prodded the question at the forefront of my mind. 'How did you catch up to us? We were long gone.'

Steve wiped sweat from his brow with one hand and waved the other which was holding onto the silver smartphone. It cast a brazen white glow over the murky brickwork.

'Scrying spell, *motherfucker,*' he said.

'What, on your *phone?*' I was incredulous, yet fascinated. 'You have an app for that?'

'Nah. The spell's embedded in the hardware. Actual silver casing, right. Crushed quartz grafted into the SIM card. And a spot of code written by yours truly. It's a beaut.' He held up the screen proudly, where a simple circle of blue pixels pointed right at me, as though I were true north on a compass.

'But surely the spell needs something that belongs to us, to track us down?' I said, edging forward.

Steve tapped twice – and a photo of Ang and myself tied to two chairs popped onto the screen. 'They say a camera captures a piece of your soul,' he said.

'Sounds unlikely.' I peered at the image. I was in need of a haircut. 'Great craftsmanship, though. Very cunning. Wouldn't expect anything less of you, Steve-O.'

His chest puffed with pride. 'This's what adapting looks like,

Hansard. No scrying crystals for *me*. Right. Now you know I can find you wherever you are, mate. So how about you just come on back with me and save us both the hassle.'

I liked Steve. He was a fairly genuine bloke. Simple goals, well-earned pride in his work, but not arrogant about it. He had the same heart as a car mechanic who would point out all the bits of an engine to you if you showed even a sniff of interest, regardless of your actual knowledge of how all the bits of metal and wire fitted together. Steve certainly wasn't made for deviousness, or for thinking like a devious person.

Unfortunately for him, I was.

'What's that button there?' I craned my neck, stepping even closer. 'And how do you switch the spell from one person to another? You can't attune a crystal to more than one thing at once, even I know that. Have you got more spells on there? What if you wanted to reprogram it with a different kind of scrying magic?'

'Ah, slow down. And don't touch that. It's all in the interface.' Steve juggled the phone, flipping onto a foreign menu screen covered in occult symbols, while my hand inched up toward it. 'That's the bit I built an app for. Doesn't work without all the embedded hardware, mind. I'm trying to make up kits, but it's expensive as hell. Not profitable at all. But the app part is easy because it's just buttons to adjust the– *Hansard you bastard!*'

Ang sprinted to catch up with me. 'Gettin' sick o' this runnin', *gwas*.'

'We'll cut down.' I grinned and clutched Steve's phone tightly. Poor sod. He wasn't even *expecting* the swipe.

We slowed to a jog before long as Steve's angry puffing faded behind us. In retrospect, we could've just outrun him again, regardless of any fancy digital scrying spell.

My car came into view. Just another nondescript car in a nondescript car park outside a nondescript industrial estate somewhere in the middle of Manchester. I like nondescript. The fewer details people can remember about where you've been, the better. I turned Steve's phone off and slipped it into one of my many coat pockets.

Ang slumped into the passenger seat, retrieving a half-eaten sausage roll from the glove box. She munched noisily on it until I'd driven us clear of the estate. I knew when she'd turned to stare at me by the smell of spiced pork wafting over the gearstick.

'All right, so I knew he was going to double-cross us,' I said.

"A friendly business meet', ye called it,' she leered back. 'Acquirin' new products? Ye told me we was jus' going to talk. The bluecap plan was only fer backup!'

I feigned dismay. 'Ang. Do you really see me peddling the kind of products Steve makes? Magical USB drives don't exactly look right next to crystals, potion bottles, and hex bags. It doesn't fit the, you know, aesthetic.'

'Oh, ye has an aesthetic now.'

'It's not *traditional*,' I huffed. 'What's next? Curses delivered by email? Miraculous remedies on a microchip? I mean, a scrying spell on a phone for goodness' sake. You might as well just hack someone's GPS. It's boorish and it's *boring*.'

'Why go to any trouble fer this doodad then? Ye gots it safe, right?'

'Of course it's safe.' I patted a pocket. 'This isn't for me. Or for us, rather. This is me repaying a personal favour. So it's uh, personal. Not business, is what I mean.'

I made a show of straining to read the road signs as we crawled a labyrinthine route into the suburbs of Manchester; in reality, avoiding the question in Ang's stare.

'What's on the computer stick?' she said to the side of my face.

I gave a half shrug. 'I don't know.'

'And who's it fer?'

'A friend.'

Her head thudded back against the seat. 'Ye promised to explain, *gwas*.'

And I'd hoped the added excitement might have dulled her memory. But I knew Ang better than to expect her to drop a line of questioning.

'He's a friend I owe a lot of favours to, all right? Don't ask me what for, because I'm not having that conversation now. Just understand that I'm happy to owe this guy favours, and I'm happy to *pay* them, too. So when he asked me to get this USB gizmo off Steve, well. I didn't see the harm.'

Ang was quiet for a moment. 'Are you sayin' I got dragged along an' tied up an' made to sit in a cold warehouse an' used me bluecap for thievery, all so you could run a personal *errand, gwas?*'

'Not if you put it like that. Look, this is important to me–'

'*Bluecap* is important to *me*. Don't ye dare be askin' to borrow it for yer own gains again.'

She swivelled sideways with arms and legs crossed and chin sunk onto her chest. I was treated to a periphery view of her grey curls sticking out from under the back of her flat cap.

My fingers drummed the steering wheel angrily. What did she mean, 'for my own gains'? What did she think my entire business operation was *for*?

'Let's see it, then,' she said to the window.

'What?'

'This stick ye had me runnin' after. I wants t'see it, at least.'

'Oh, very well. It's nothing special.'

I slowed the car while I fumbled for the little data stick, and passed it over for Ang to inspect. It had a plain black case and was about as long as her thumb. It still amazed me what you could fit onto such a small amount of metal and plastic – how easy to possess and to lose a whole library's worth of incriminating information. The days of floppy disks and two- or three- part programs didn't seem all that long ago.

Ang turned it over with nimble fingers, tracing the shape of the protruding metal and then holding it up to squint down the barrel, as it were, end-on.

'What's inside?' she asked.

'I don't know,' I said truthfully. 'And it's none of my business.'

'That's unlike you.'

Though I was focused on the road, I caught sight of her scrambling through the glove box. 'What on earth are you doing? Don't you dare lose that!'

'Relax, *gwas*.' She held up a stubby black plug – my battered but trusty USB car adapter, and the only reliable method I had of charging my ancient phone.

I raised an eyebrow. 'You can't plug it into that. It won't do anything.'

'Why not?'

'The car isn't a computer. It can't read flash drives.'

'But it fits. Look.' She plugged the USB stick into the port with a sullen 'told you so' expression. I don't always read Ang's wizened features correctly, but I got the distinct impression she was being childish on purpose.

So I spoke back like a parent to a child. Which, in retrospect, was a rather large mistake. 'Yes, very well done, the shapes match, you're very clever. But, you see, it's not going to *do* anything because it's not actually plugged into anything like– *don't plug it into the car!*'

Too late, Ang had already rammed it into the cigarette lighter. I lunged to grab it. There was a horrid *pop* and an acrid smell of burning.

And I wasn't in the car any more.

* * *

I didn't exactly wake up. It was a near-seamless transition. One moment I was inhaling the odour of scorched plastic; the next I was staring down an immaculate, glittering green corridor.

'Uh-huh,' I said. At a certain point, you stop being astonished by impossible transformations of reality.

I stared at my left hand, where a black scorch mark marred my palm. It didn't hurt.

Somebody was snickering.

'All right, I'll bite. What's this about?' I said to the empty corridor.

'*How does it feel to be trapped, mortal?*' an ethereal voice hissed. '*Welcome to my prison.*'

'Nice to be here. Lovely place you have. Very . . . smooth.' I peered at the walls as I said this. Geometric silver lines etched the green surface, joining and branching at right angles. It put me in mind of a circuit board. A dim light of suspicion turned on in my head. 'What's your name, friend? If you have one.'

'*I am Zawba'ah, the caged wind. Who are you, that stumbles blindly into the cyclone's pen?*'

'I'm Jack Hansard.' The silver lines passed seamlessly across right angles from the walls and continued under my feet. I searched for any rhyme or reason in the direction of the pattern. A clue. A way out.

The voice hadn't answered back. I looked up, disconcerted. 'Don't you want to know anything else about me?'

The voice, which had the quality of a breeze about it, replied, '*There is no rush. We shall have an eternity to get to know one another.*'

'Oh. Good.' I began to stroll down the corridor. No need to hurry, if my invisible companion was to be believed. At times like this a slower pace might be exactly what you need in order to keep up with the rapid unravelling of reality. 'Only us here, is it?'

'*Who else do you expect to find?*'

'Oh, I don't know. A coblyn-shaped individual, maybe.'

'*You shall find no friends here.*'

Comforting, in a way. It meant I only had myself to worry about.

After a few hundred metres I reached a crossroads. Left, right, or straight?

'Does direction matter here?' I wondered aloud. All paths looked identical. The walls towered to a height that I certainly couldn't scale, so climbing up for a look wasn't an option.

Looking up – and up again, because the green walls filled the horizon – I saw an oblong of starry night-sky above me. Deep shades of blue and purple fooled the eye. After another glance my brain caught up and recognised a pattern in the twinkling, and suddenly the 'stars' were just tiny LEDs blinking on and off in the firmament. I frowned, deeply unsettled.

I looked again at the crossroads.

'Does it matter which way I go?' I said, this time with purpose. 'Is this an M. C. Escher situation, or what?'

'*It might matter, if you could find the way out. But. You won't.*'

'Look, I get it. I'm inside the flash drive we stole, right? This is probably some astral projection stuff going on, this place isn't really real, blah blah. And you: I'll bet you've been captured on this bloody data stick, right? That Steve and his damn digital curses. What *are* you?'

'*I am the Eternal Whirlwind,*' said the voice, '*and this is the labyrinth that holds me. None who enter shall leave, unless called.*'

'A labyrinth,' I said dully. 'Any minotaurs I should be worried about?'

'*The only demons are the ones you bring with you.*'

I rolled my eyes. 'You better not turn out to be a goblin king, that's all I'm saying.'

The crossroads remained. Three identical paths, stretching to nothing.

Oh, hell. I picked left, and walked.

Not long this time before a path opened up on my right. What was that trick they taught you when you were a kid? I had fuzzy memories of family outings and daunting hedge mazes – a horrid, dark and solitary netherworld for a lost five-year-old. The scent of wet leaves entered my nose. I heard rustling and turned; my coat caught on prickly branches. Thick, shadowy hedges loomed where green circuit walls had previously gleamed.

'Thanks, brain,' I said quietly. I'd remembered the advice, though. Touch the wall with your right hand. Just walk, and follow the wall the whole way round without breaking contact. Eventually, *eventually*, it would lead you to the way out.

Uncertainly, I brushed the damp hedge with my hand.

'You cannot leave without knowing the way. One cannot simply chance upon an exit,' said my new chum. *'I would know.'*

'What are you, some type of jinn?' I asked, more to keep my mind occupied as I started walking. 'Genie in a flash drive? What happened to your lamp?'

The ensuing silence had a surly quality that reminded me of Ang.

'No offence meant, or anything,' I continued. 'There's a reason you've been trapped here, though. Jinn is just what jumps to mind. You could be a demon, I suppose, but I don't know much about them.'

'And what do you know of jinn?'

'Oh, the usual Aladdin stuff. Powerful, wish-granting spirits. Trap 'em in a vessel, call them forth to do a master's bidding, etcetera, etcetera. But obviously only an idiot would actually make a wish from one of them.'

'Why is that?'

'Everyone knows how this story goes,' I replied, happy to be on familiar ground. It was almost nice to have someone to talk to while I followed the oppressive path of the maze. 'You wish for wealth: the jinn causes you to lose a limb to win an insurance payout. You wish for fame: you wind up a celebrity for the way you died. You try to be clever and wish for next week's winning lottery numbers in a specific draw, at a specific time: and you get run over on the way to cash your ticket in. There's always a catch.'

'*You think people only wish for fame and fortune.*'

'And power. That's a biggie.'

'*They also wish for reunion. And release. And freedom.*'

'Ah, 'bring my lover back from the dead' kind of deal? I expect that'll be the actual corpse knocking on the door, then.'

'*You could be a jinni yourself, Jack Hansard.*'

'No thanks,' I said quickly. 'You won't get me trading places, no way.'

It *harumphed*, a sound partway between a huff and a snide laugh.

'You've never seen the way out, then?' I tried peering through a hedge, but the branches were densely packed. You'd need some hefty equipment to cut your way through. 'How long have you been in here?'

'*Time is irrelevant. I have been caged before; I have been free before. Before this, I tore up the sands of a great desert. Eventually, I will be free again, and I will sink many ships on the ocean.*'

'Ah. You ever wonder that maybe people trap you because you do evil things?'

'*Is the wind evil?*' it said mockingly. '*I am powerful. I go where directed. Sometimes, mortals direct me. But they never last for long.*'

'I could use some direction,' I muttered to myself.

I wondered how Steve had designed this infernal trap. How do you plant an abstract prison on a piece of hardware . . . ? Was this actually a computer program? If I squinted, would the maze become a wall of ones and zeros?

Technology and magic were becoming too closely related for my liking. The thought of my peculiar, gloriously uncanny world evolving into mere science fiction-fact bothered me greatly. Like that scrying spell on Steve's phone. It was only a hair's breadth away from planting an actual tracking device on me instead. So uninspired. So *mundane*.

A thought that had been tickling at the back of my mind finally got through. My eyes widened. I stopped and felt through all the pockets of my trench coat.

My hand closed around Steve's phone.

It felt real enough. Barely daring to breathe, I pulled it out and turned it on.

'*What is that?*' said the jinn. '*You brought magic with you? Still, you cannot alter the fabric of this place. I have tried.*'

'I don't think I need to,' I said, inspecting the occult interface. I tapped the symbol shaped like a compass. 'You said I just need to know the way, right?'

'*Yes. But you would not know, unless you were called.*'

'Or, y'know, unless I had something to guide me.'

I took the jinn's silence for bafflement. It didn't matter. What mattered was that the bright blue pixels assembled on the screen were pointing *away* from me.

I started walking again, and quickly picked up into a run.

It felt as though the jinn was staring right over my shoulder as I turned corners with purpose, zig-zagging a frenetic path through the maze. The air was damp. I always remembered mazes being damp.

'*Where does it lead you?*'

'Back to myself,' I answered between heavy breaths. 'I'm pretty sure. I think.'

'*How?*'

'Beats me, guv. Magic.'

'*Harumph.*'

Soil slipped away under my feet. There was a sense of the sky opening up overhead. Tendrils of real sunlight crept into the tableau.

'*Take me with you,*' the jinn said into my ear.

'No can do, friend.' I kept my eyes pinned on the phone. 'I'm pretty sure this isn't the right way out for *you*, anyway.'

'*You can call me forth. Free me once you are outside. There will be vast rewards. More than you can imagine. Call the name of Zawba'ah and I will do your bidding. Bring me out . . .'*

The jinn's voice faded, replaced by a brief memory of static crackling. Wet leaf mulch turned to singed plastic in my nose, accompanied by the soundtrack of Ang's gravelly wittering in the next seat.

'. . . din't know it was going t'do that,' she was saying. 'Ye din't have to shout so. And anyway– *watch out!'*

She sprung for the steering wheel – the car jolted sideways – and we narrowly missed a collision.

'Bloody hell!' I yelled, gripping the wheel. An angry car horn trailed into the distance.

'Ye bloody *twpsyn,'* said Ang. I could feel her glaring, until the expression melted a little. 'You all right, *gwas?* Ye looks all . . . muddled.'

'I'm fine. I think we'll pull over for a moment.'

'Aye.'

She watched me carefully as I de-frazzled. It didn't seem like she'd noticed I was gone. Had I not disappeared? Just gone vacant for, what – a second? I shuddered at the thought of my comatose body sitting at the wheel, steering into oncoming traffic.

I wrapped the slightly charred flash drive in a piece of cloth and pondered the fate of the jinn.

That kind of power was probably not something that should be placed into careless hands. Even good men can make evil wishes. On balance, it would probably be better for everyone if the thing found a new home at the bottom of the ocean.

Too bad.

'I don't know about you Ang, but I'm ready to sleep this day off,' I said. 'What do you say to a hotel? My treat, by way of thanks for use of your bluecap, and putting up with all this mess.'

'Afford it, can we? Ye wouldn't let me buy that fancy pie the other day, for lack o' coin.'

'You can have the whole bed to yourself. Extra pillows, the lot.'

I could see she wanted to hang onto her scepticism, but the allure was too strong. 'Them big white fluffy ones? With the mattress ye can drown in? An' a duvet an' everything?' She shook herself. 'Seems like an unnecessary lux'ry,' she sniffed, 'but I'll takes it.'

* * *

It wasn't often that I'd pay up for a night in a hotel. Ang was right, it was an unnecessary luxury – especially when you possess a spacious backseat, and showers can be easily acquired by sneaking into gyms and leisure centres. But on this occasion, I was more than willing.

Only the cheapest rates, you understand, and preferably without breakfast included – my earnings wouldn't stretch *that* far. Besides, it's often easy enough to sidle in and swipe a few croissants from the continental. And what better kind of breakfast is there than a free one?

We rocked up at gone nine in the evening, and ushered Ang past the tired receptionist in her now standard disguise. (That is, a set of kids' clothes, plastic sunglasses, and a wide-brimmed hat. Adults are accustomed to looking over the heads of children, and Ang is perfectly toddler-height.)

I waited until Ang was face-down and snoring in a nest of bedding, before slipping quietly out of the room.

Down in the empty common area, there was only one other patron. A man in a smart suit, sat on an uncomfortable purple sofa in the reception's lounge. I tipped my head to him. 'Seb.'

'Hansard.'

I sat next to him, staring ahead at the wall. A gaudy abstract painting filled most of my field of view.

'You got the artefact off Steve?' he said.

I held out the USB stick wordlessly.

'Very good.' He examined it closely. 'What are these marks?'

'Only cosmetic. The . . . contents . . . are perfectly intact.'

He frowned deeply. 'You didn't try to use it, did you?'

'What do you take me for? I'm not stupid.' I stretched out my legs, leaning back on the sofa. The cushions were hard and unyielding. 'Gotta wonder about the fate of whatever sucker is going to try, though.'

'Indeed.'

That's all he was going to say on that. I knew it was no use pushing Seb. He was a simple mediator, an expert in acquiring things from people to provide to other people. Certainly someone had paid top dollar for him to acquire this captive jinn, and perhaps even more for him to keep quiet about it.

Besides, it was none of my business what happened to my wares after I sold them.

'So what can I get for that?' I asked, inspecting the ceiling.

Seb slipped the flash drive into his suit jacket. 'Top tier warding spell, I should think. Should last a little while, and I'll renew the circles around her, too.'

'Nothing else?' I looked straight at him now, and he avoided my gaze.

'I haven't come across anything yet, Hansard. Protection is still the best I can do. No nasties will be coming near her, I can guarantee you that.'

'Does it . . . does it stop things getting out, as well?' I mangled the question a little, afraid to really ask what was on my mind.

Seb gave a me a puzzled look. 'Out of where?'

Now I looked away and leaned forward over my knees, suddenly intent on the lines in my knuckles. At the creases that become just a little deeper, more apparent with age. 'If Cora were . . . trapped.

Somewhere. Could she get out, with all those wards around her? Even if she knew the way? What good is finding the exit if it turns out the doors are bolted shut?'

Seb regarded me for a long, pensive moment. 'I can't reach her, Jack,' he said. 'You know that.'

'I know.'

He slapped me on the back, the empty gesture of comfort from someone who doesn't know what to say, to someone who wouldn't want to hear it anyway.

Seb stood, straightened his jacket, ready to go.

He paused, taking in my hunched form, my crumpled coat, my unwashed hair. 'You're doing the best you can for her,' he said. 'Don't invent more nightmares for yourself.'

He strode to the doors and, with a final nod as one professional to another, he left the hotel.

I stared moodily at a painting on the wall. I hate abstract art. Cora loved it.

I thought about the jinn as I made my bed on the floor underneath Ang's ceiling of grunts and snorts. I estimated I'd spent most of an hour talking to it and wandering through the digital maze – at least, it *felt* like an hour. But based on Ang's reaction, I was only gone (if, in fact, I was gone at all) for less than an instant.

The dark thought had already crossed my mind that I could have tried to use the jinn instead of handing it over. I could have made a wish. Maybe I could have wished Cora home.

It was treacherous thinking, that. We all know the story. I could have wished her back, but it wouldn't have been her. I could have wished her whole, but she would have lost something else. I could have wished for the power to save her, but wound up using it the wrong way.

Wishes are dangerous like that.

That's the thing with impossible solutions. They have a way of biting you in the arse. I should know – I make a living out of selling them to other people. I like to dabble in the impossible. There's a thrill in holding miracles in the palm of your hand.

Cora did more than just dabble. Merely holding miracles would never be enough for her. She needed to *be* one.

I'd find the right miracle, one day. The one that would bring her back. Until then, the road stretched long and far, and there was always another sale to be made.

Business, as usual.

Episode 2: Dinogad's Coat

When I was just a *plentyn* – a wee child – my first job in the mine was trapper-watchin'. That's watchin' the trappers, them kids who held the doors open for the minecarts. Powerful dangerous job, it was. For the trappers, that is, not me. As a coblyn, I knows the dark ways of a mine better than any human could.

What?

You was expecting the tall bloke, was ye?

Classic bait 'n' switch, as me Partner would say. That's Partner with a capital P, on account of it being official now. Hansard gave me equal rights to his business, such as it is, and I intends to keep it equal. Even if he won't let me have a go at the drivin'. (Dunno what he's so het up about; I only asked to turn the wheel that once. We survived, din't we?)

Anyway, trappers. Scared little buggers, all of 'em. Just old enough to hold a candle and pull a lever or tug a cord. The doors open, the air rushes past, letting the whole mine breathe, and a hurrier comes through with his tub. Or her tub. I remember back as when women were as common as their husbands in the deep dark, hauling coal and lugging clay.

'*Ang!* Are you even listening to me?'

That be Hansard, packing up the sales table under this here derelict aqueduct. We'd picked it as a good spot to attract the 'seedy types' that Hansard pegs as his regular customers, but between rain and the squalid surrounds, we've seen hardly anyone. It's been a slow day of trade, and we're famished. Hansard's spoutin' some gaff at me as usual, about the art of the sale or somesuch.

'Am listenin', *gwas*,' I says. I ain't. Am too busy staring across the street. There's a ruined old grocer's shop with broken windows and vulgar graffiti on its shutters. And in front of it, two children. ''ere, *gwas*. What're them kiddies up to, y'reckon?'

He gives 'em a look. Boy and a girl. The lad's real young, maybe seven or eight, but the girl's got the look of age about her that comes with being too young for how old ye feel. I seen that look before. Bet she's scarce seen a decade, but by her eyes you'd be forgiven for thinking she was nearing her second.

'What about them?' Hansard says. *Twpsyn.*

'*Look* at 'em. Skin and bone wi' carrier bags, is what they are.'

He squints at them. He can see as well as I. They're done up in big puffy coats, but their faces are gaunt and sallow. They carry plastic bags what look to be holding blankets, and maybe an old teddy stuffed in there as well. Also, they're starin' right back at us.

'Looks like they be in need of a kind hand?' says I, patience embodied.

'Don't think I have any of those. A cursed hand, now, maybe I could do you a deal on.' He brandishes a near-skeletal appendage from our stock, a clawed shape of curled fingers robed in parched flesh.

'Stop tryn'a call that shrivelled monkey foot a cursed hand. No one's buyin' it. Lit'rally,' I says.

'It's a *paw*, actually. And I'll have you know that cursed items sell *very* well.' He waves the dirty thing at me, then puts it back in its box. 'Anyway, we're not hanging around.'

'Thought we was campin' here tonight, *gwas*?'

'No-o.' His eyes flick to the kiddies, and then to some mess of cardboard and other flotsam tucked by the wall under our blackened arch. 'I think we'll be on our way. Don't wish to intrude.'

I stares at the pile of rubbish while Hansard packs the rest of his own rubbish into the car boot. There's a grubby pillow and some empty sweet wrappers, laid on what some might fancifully call a bed of newspaper and boxes.

I looks back at the kiddies, and it seems like they're waitin' on us.

The boot snaps shut. Hansard dusts his hands.

'Right, all done. No thanks to you, I might add. Shall we be off?'

'I know you din't just say that,' I says.

'What?'

'I think ye meant to say, "Why don't we buy dinner for them unfortunates across the road?" Come t'think of it, I reckon that is what you said.'

'You're not serious.'

I cross my arms. 'I know you ain't leavin' them kiddies to fend for themselves on the streets tonight. I know you ain't, because although you ain't honest, you also ain't bad. 'Tis getting rotten cold an' all.'

He pinches the bridge of his nose. I've struck a nerve, sure enough.

'Ang, my moral inclination is neither here nor there on this matter,' he says, with hands flapping. 'The fact, the actual *fact* of the situation is that we barely made twenty quid today, so at present I'm doubtful we have enough funds to cover our own dinner–'

I shakes my head and turn to step off the pavement.

'–let alone the endless stream of pastries you consume, and I thought we'd agreed we were going to . . . *What are you doing?*'

I was striding across the road, is what I was doing. The lass eyes me right up while the little lad shrinks behind her. Of course, I ain't all that tall by human standards, so when I reach them she's actually eyein' me right *down*.

'Hello,' I says, from about a yard away. 'What're you kiddies doin' out so late? Do ye need help finding a way home?'

'Fuck off.'

Hansard sniggers behind me.

Pentwp. For a man so cunning, he can be half blind when he wills it. Then again, maybe he just ain't familiar with that kind of expression on a face so young.

But me, I seen eyes like hers before.

I takes a step forwards. 'No need fer that language. We ain't gunna hurt yer, and we ain't gunna take you anywhere ye don't want t'go. My life on it. And his, though I can't say it counts for as much. All I'm offerin' is a hot meal and mebbe a warm place to sleep if you wants it.'

Hansard snorts and mutters, 'With what money?' but it ain't important so I let 'im fuss.

'My name's Ang,' I says, stretching up my hand to the girl.

She takes a hard look at it. Worn hands, mine are. Real working hands, with cracked nails and dirt so deep in the creases that it ain't never washing out. Slender, too, on account of being a not-quite-three-foot coblyn.

'Why're you so small?' she says at last.

I shrug. 'It's how I am. Why're you so tall?'

This passes muster. Children are often smarter than adults. They can see the world in an uncomplicated way.

She grasps my hand. 'I'm Sable,' she says. 'This is Buck.'

'Ye brother?' They don't look related. She has straight, dark hair and a light brown tone to her skin; he is pale and freckled, with a fuzzy mop of reddish hair on top. Them's surface looks, though. What counts is deeper.

'He might as well be,' is what she replies. 'Who's he, then?' She thrusts her chin at Hansard.

'That's me business partner, name o' Jack.' I smile a mite wickedly. 'Ye can call him Uncle J.'

There's a huff from behind and Hansard finally joins us. 'A burger and a drink. That's it, right?' he says.

Sable sticks out her chin. 'Only if we don't owe you nothing for it.'

Hansard is good at Empty Face – that expression which pretends there's nothing going on behind the eyes – but I was watchin', and I saw the flicker there. What a thing, it said, for a child to have to make a deal out of the right to receive food.

'It's free,' he says gruffly.

I grins to myself. 'In the car, then,' I says. 'There's plenty of room in the back.'

The lass is suspicious as we opens the door. 'What're these?'

Hansard replies. 'Crystal balls, very delicate. Please don't touch them. They make an awful noise when they're disturbed.'

'Are they to see the future?' She peers closer, eyes squinting. 'Or to speak to ghosts?'

'The latter. But they have nothing interesting to say, I assure you. It's mostly old folks asking for one more cup of tea.'

Sable gives him a look, and it's an impressive one. 'That's ridiculous,' she says, and climbs in.

The boy shuffles after her. Hansard reaches for their bags.

'*No!*' the lad shrieks. They both snatch their bags close. *'No no no!'* Buck wriggles backward and stares at us with plain fear.

The lass spits. 'Don't touch our stuff.'

'Now, now,' I says as soothingly as I can. 'We won't. We ain't here to take from ye. Yer possessions be safe in our corner. Me Partner were just bein' considerate to yer comfort. Keep it all with ye in your seats. But put the seatbelts on, mind.'

Hansard shares a brief nod with me as we climb into our own seats. I hear the click of seatbelts behind. It were a new addition, Hansard's insistence on proper car safety. When I first met him he were as lackadaisical as I with wearing a belt, but ever since our journey through the Nether some months ago (for which I were gratefully unconscious) he's been adamant. 'Seventeen hundred people die every year in car accidents,' he told me. Seems a strange thing to be suddenly fixed on, but we all got our quirks.

I keeps an eye on the kiddies as Hansard swings the car out from under the aqueduct arch. Little Buck is near quivering in his seat and jumps at every pop and rumble from the engine. Sable sits tall and straight in hers, though I catch her startling at a bright flash of lights by the window. For all the tough talk, there's still a flightiness about her.

'What's this place?' she says as Hansard pulls into a drive-through line.

'The best I can afford,' he replies.

'What food is it?'

'Nothing special. Burger and a drink, like I said.'

'One wi' a toy in,' I says.

Hansard has the nerve to argue. 'They don't need a bloody–'

'Language.' I can see it in his face, he wants to cuss me out too, and I can barcly hide my smile. I keeps it stern, though. 'Them's children back there. Yer the grownup. Act it.'

'Buck doesn't eat meat,' Sable pipes up primly.

Hansard gives me a withering glare. 'Doesn't he, now?'

'He won't eat the burger.'

'Then he can eat the bun instead.'

I nudges him hard in the ribs – which takes some effort, 'cuz of having to lean all the way over the gearstick. 'Get the boy some potatoes at least, or some greenery. 'Ave they got leeks on the menu?'

Hansard sighs. 'He can have a salad, then.'

'I would like salad,' Bucks says meekly from the back.

We pull up and Hansard shouts our order into the metal pole. We pay in carefully counted coins and grubby notes.

'Have a great night,' intones the server as she passes our meals over.

Sable perks right up at the smell of food. She leans forward eagerly. 'Can we have it now?'

'Wait til we're parked. I prefer not to eat and drive,' says Hansard. He squints at road signs. 'Is there a train station round here? Usually good places for an overnight.'

She sniffs. 'You can park by our arch, I suppose. No one will care.'

'Someone might have stolen our bed,' Buck whispers.

I sees it, the crack in Hansard's face. I'll save him the embarrassment of offering another good deed.

'Ye can kip wi' us tonight, if ye likes,' I says. 'Them's comfy seats, an' we has plenty o' blankets.'

Buck looks like he wants to say yes. Sable considers it for moment, maybe. 'No,' she says after a pause. 'We can look after ourselves.'

'Suit yourself,' Hansard says, though under his breath.

He's taken us back to the aqueduct, where the arches are now deep in dusk shadow. He parks right up where our pitch was – and next to where their cardboard mess is – and flips on the inside light. The kiddies blink in the yellow glow, but their eyes widen as Hansard passes over the little parcels of food. 'And here's the toy,' he mutters.

I'm already at mine. A burger ain't half as good as an oggie (that's a pasty filled with lamb, leeks, and potatoes, for them as is unfortunate enough to have never heard of it) but it'll do on a bare stomach after selling nefarious goods on the streets all day.

Sable's a nibbler. She takes tiny bites with her front teeth and gnaws through her food like a rodent. Buck shoves handfuls of lettuce into his mouth and crunches noisily. He finally seems at peace. With a bit of delight, I sneak glances as he fiddles the plastic toy out of its packet.

It's a garish thing, some monstrous imagined character all in yellow with rosy red cheeks. It has a tail, and a button that makes it wag clunkily with each press. Buck sits there pressing it, fascinated.

Sable leans over, staring intently. 'Is it an animal?'

Buck shrugs. 'It's my friend. I'm calling him Rocky.'

'That's a stupid name.'

'Is not.'

'Is too.'

'Is not.' Buck cradles it. 'Ignore her, Rocky. I'll keep you safe.'

Sable's little mouth opens like she's about to bite him with a put-down. But she don't. She catches my eye and bites at me, instead. 'What are you looking at, goblin?'

My hairs bristle all over, pinpricks of fury raised on my skin.

'Not goblin, child,' I says, holding my calm. '*Coblyn.*'

Her eyes blaze like she wants a fight. 'What's the difference.' There ain't no question mark there.

I leans over at them between the seats. 'Ye wouldn't know if I were a goblin, child,' I says, 'because if I were, *I would've already eaten ye, bones an' all.*'

Buck chokes on his leaves, losing half his dinner to the footwell. 'Don't eat us,' he squeaks.

'She won't,' Sable declares, though I knows she flinched. 'She's just trying to scare us.'

I settles back a bit. 'Not scarin'. *Warning.* If ye ever see a goblin, child, *run.*'

Buck nods furiously and hugs Rocky close for comfort. I gets the sense that Sable lowers her hackles a bit, too. 'What are you doing with this guy?' She jerks her head at Hansard. 'You're a weird pair.'

'There's plenty weirder out there, kid,' Hansard says around a mouthful of food.

'We're business partners,' I explains. 'We sells strange an' unusual merchandise, the like o' which would awe an' befuddle ye.' I shield me mouth with a hand so Hansard won't hear. 'But between you an' me, most've it's garbage potions 'n' lucky charms that've gone off.'

Buck hasn't got the joke, but Sable lifts an eyebrow. I shift over and make a seat for meself on top of the handbrake, so I can turn round properly and look at them square on. My feet dangle into their footwell. 'Anyway, that's the *what*. As fer the *why*, well. Some of my kin disappeared from home – kidnapped, so's we think. Hansard here is meant t'be helpin' me trace 'em, when he ain't too busy countin' money.'

'We've made progress!' he insists.

'Aye, aye. It's just painful slow, *gwas*.'

Buck whispers from his corner. 'Do you know who kidnapped them?'

I'm about t'say when I note he's clutching his carrier bag again. Real tight, as though he's afraid of losin' it. Something like coarse fur pokes out the top – but he snatches it away as soon as I leans in to look.

'You can't have it,' he says, almost fierce.

'Just lookin', that's all,' I assures. 'What're you carrying that's so precious to ye?'

Sable's slyly pushing her own bag out of my reach with her foot, like she think I don't notice. There's dark brown fur in that one, shiny and soft.

I moves a bit too quick – startles 'em both – but all I'm doing is reaching back for my lantern. I holds it out to them, and her blue light falls soft on their little faces.

'That's pretty,' Buck says uncertainly.

'This is me bluecap.' I undoes the catch and let her out. If you knows how to look, you'll see the phoenix egg she holds in her centre, safe and sound. But to passing eyes it just gives her flame a more solid countenance. 'Bluecap is a guardian spirit. Mine own Mam, is this.'

I hears Hansard chuckle and see Buck's reaction is more fearful than I intended.

'It's a ghost?' he stammers.

This is a hard one. Some ideas don't translate well. 'Not like ye might understand such. This were my mother's essence, that what guides. We coblyn come from the earth and return to it, but leave behind a spark o' what we were. We looks to the past t'guide us, and our spirit selves remain to guard the future.'

Buck's concentrating hard trying to wrap his head round it. I smile and cradle the bluecap in my hands, then usher it in his direction. She drifts against his cheek, and by his wide eyes I know he feels the echo of a mother's touch.

'Mam used t'tell me all sorts o' stories,' I continue. 'Ancient legends from the old country. An' then I'd tell them to the kiddies in the mine. That's where I lived, see. In a deep coal mine where coblynau and humans worked together.'

'That sounds horrid,' Sable butts in.

'Fer some, lass. Especially the kiddies. This were back when the big 'uns still sent their children down, see. Kids younger even than you, Buck.' I point my thumb at my chest. 'Coblyn children, we're born fer it. We got the eyes and the skin for the dark. But not a wee human *dwtty*. Oftentimes they were put to work as trappers.'

'What's a trapper?' asks Buck. A note of dread trembles on his voice again.

'Not like it sounds,' I'm quick to reassure. 'Trappers opened an' closed the trapdoors in the mine tunnels. Ye had to sit still, though, as a trapper. Sometimes for hours and hours. An' they had to stay awake. Terrible things befell them that slept. Them trapdoors was heavy and could crush the bones of a *dwtty* – a little 'un, that is.'

I pause as a few memories threaten to overspill into sadness. Buck and Sable lean forward, prompting me to clear my throat and continue. 'So's they had to keep awake, this little *plentyn* all alone, weepin' in the dark as their candle sputters out. So I'd come by an' keep them company, an' I'd tell the old stories and sing the old songs to 'em.'

They're rapt on my words. Hansard's still looking straight ahead out the window, but his head is tilted so I knows even he's listening intently too. I pulls up the words from my memory and start to sing:

'*Peis dinogat e vreith vreith*
O grwyn balaot ban wreith
Chwit chwit chwidogeith . . .'

Buck's eyes are drifting while I sing. He yawns and snuggles into his seat as the song ends.

'What does that mean?' Sable asks.

'It's a daft old rhyme in the Old Tongue,' I says quietly, mindful of Buck beginning to doze. 'Mam sung it as a lullaby to me. It goes, "Dinogad's coat is spotted and speckled, from the skin of a pine marten it was made . . ." I always thought ye'd be a *ffwl* to make a coat out of pine martens. Ye'd need a lot of 'em, 'cuz they're so small. Fine coat for a coblyn, maybe, but this story is about some human hunter bloke. Won't catch no coblyn hunting wild boar up a mountain, not on your life.'

I stops suddenly, having only just accounted for her face. It's gone awful pale, and right rigid. She looks as though she might throw up.

'Ye all right, child?' I says with a shadow of worry. Even Hansard's picked up on the tone in my voice.

'What's wrong, kid?' he asks. 'Ang's voice isn't that bad.'

She's about to shake Buck awake but I grabs her hand. 'Hey now,' I says as gently as I can. 'What's spooked ye? 'Tis just a silly tale.'

'About a nasty hunter.' She bares her teeth around the words, like a scared animal. Scared animals are often the most dangerous.

I keeps my voice level but firm. 'Enough o' that, now. Ye knows we ain't gunna hurt ye. We've fed ye an' offered you a bed. It's up to you if ye'll take the hand offered, but I ain't gunna force you either way. Look at 'im.' I nods at Buck, who's gone right to sleep. All scrunched up with his plastic bag in one hand and Rocky in the other. 'That one needs carin' for. You too, though I knows you'll say otherwise. What are ye runnin' away from, child? Because sure as my bluecap lights the night, ye are runnin' from *something*.'

She goes still. Watchful. Them long lashes blink at me slowly. I gets the feel she's testing me, seeing who'll look away first.

Hansard saves me from sighing.

'Where are your parents?' he asks.

He ain't fazed by her silence – he's used to prattling on in the face of disinterested customers, so he keeps nagging. 'Do you have any family? Is anyone looking for you? Friends? Relatives? Where did you live before? Is there anyone you can stay with, instead of out on the bloody– I mean, on the darned street?'

He turns round fully now, catches Sable's attention proper. 'Look, we can take you wherever you need to go. I'm not above giving you a ride. Just one, mind. I'm not in the habit of picking up hitch-hikers.' He throws me a sardonic glance, which I tactfully ignores. 'Just tell us where to take you.'

She shrugs. 'Can you take us to Siberia?'

'If it's on a map, then yes,' I says.

Hansard's shaking his head frantically. 'Uh, *no*. Siberia is a *long* way away.'

'So what? You spend yer life drivin'. What's one more long journey?'

'I can't drive *across the sea*, Ang.'

'. . . Oh.'

Sable doesn't look too put out. Her expression's looking into the distance. 'So we'll need a boat,' she murmurs to herself. She snaps back to Hansard. 'Have you got it on a map? Can I see?'

I'm digging the big road atlas out from under my seat, but Hansard's tutting and shaking his head again. 'Ours only does the UK, Ang,' he says, as if I should know this already. 'I'm sorry, but I don't have a world map to hand right now!'

She ignores him, already scanning the map with interest; even beckons my bluecap over to get better light on it. 'What do all these funny symbols mean?'

'Ah, I've been learning these,' I says. 'Some ye've got to guess hard at, like these little triangles which be campsites. But I likes the proper picture ones best. See, this one's a fish. Apparently it marks a place where people keep fish, but not fer eatin', just for lookin' at. Same wi' this one, the elephant. Least, Hansard tells me it's an elephant. I ain't seen one in person, just in pictures. But it marks where they keep all sorts of animals for lookin' at, in a thing called a zoo.'

She recoils a bit. 'Do they keep animals in cages there?'

I hesitates. I don't rightly know the answer.

'Big cages,' says Hansard, and for a moment I think he's been completely oblivious to her disposition. 'But they're mostly to keep the people *out*.'

She settles again, tracing the maze of lines with her finger. She stops at every symbol it encounters and asks me the meaning, even if the name of the place gives it away. It strikes me then that she doesn't know her letters, and she ain't reading the map so much as observing it.

'And this one?'

I have to squint to see what's she's pointing at. With some imagination, it's a deer head with antlers. I reads her the words next to it. 'Deer park. It's like a big lot o' land o' fields an' woods for 'em to live in. Protected, like.'

Something in her lights up. She glances at Buck. 'Just for deer?'

'And other animals what happens to be there, I assumes.'

'Protected?'

'Aye. No huntin'.' I'm watching her face, careful like. There's a glow in her cheeks that ain't my bluecap. I know Hansard's been cottoning on, too, though he's much slower.

He clears his throat. 'Humans won't go near it much. Maybe just to watch, sometimes. But they'll keep a distance.' He ducks his head, trying to catch her gaze. 'We can take you there, if you want.'

'Can we . . . ?' she breathes, eyes still glued to the map. Then she's all decisive. 'Yes. Take us there.'

I glance at Hansard and he nods. 'In the morning,' he agrees. 'Best you get some shut-eye now.'

She's all tense still; you can see the excitement jumping in her bones. She seems the type to live like a taut bowstring, always on the edge of either snapping or letting loose something fierce. As she accepts our proposal the bowstring slackens and, finally, for the first time we sees her relax as I rustles out a blanket for her. She curls up, head down on the seat resting against Buck's leg, and closes her eyes.

We turns the lights off and sit in silence for a fair while.

Only when there's evidence of gentle snoring does Hansard incline his head to me. 'What's your take on them?'

'That they be wayward children in needs of help,' I says, disinclined to give much detail.

'Don't be obtuse with me. I know you think there's something . . . uncanny . . . about them, too. Do you think they're really children?'

'Aye,' I says, too fast. 'Oh, don't look at me so. Look at the *dwtty* boy, there. Ye can't claim he be anything less than innocence.'

'And what about the girl?'

'She's a sharp one,' I yields, 'but I doubts she means harm, if that's what's worryin' ye.'

'So you don't think she's dangerous?'

'Din't say that, *gwas*. Jus' that she probably don't *intend* to be.' I shoots him a quick glare for good measure. 'Ye best not be thinkin' of leavin' 'em. D'you really think they'd hurt ye?'

'No,' he says softly, 'but I do prefer to know what species my passengers are. Saves on complications later.' He chews his cheek for a minute, thinking in that dawdling way of his. 'You said they were running from something.'

'Aye. Would bet me bluecap on it.'

'What made you think so?' He glances meaningfully at the map. 'I get the impression they're a long way from home.'

'I seen hunted eyes like hers before. Them kiddies in the dark–' I stops.

He's gotten good at telling when not to push me, I'll give him that. He lets the silence tick by again. Then he speaks in this far away voice, like he's remembering some story from his Mam.

'I visited this museum, once. I think it was with school, learning about the Victorians or something like that. Anyway, they took us into this fake coal mine. You could tell it was fake. If you knocked on the walls they sounded hollow. Lots of electric lights everywhere. And these really ghastly plastic mannequins with pickaxes and lanterns. One of them was a child in a harness, pulling a minecart. I remember thinking, what an awful job, being a cart-puller–'

'A hurrier,' I cuts in.

'Right. Being one of them *and* having to live in Victorian times. With no fish and chips, or anything, and–'

My brow crinkles. 'When's this? We had fish 'n' chips when I were a lass.'

'What?'

'The big'uns brought a great big battered fish down fer us, once. Just had a big tunnel collapse, see, an' they all got out alive.'

'Thanks to you?'

'We knocked like the devil, *gwas*.'

'Right.' I sees him trying to pick up the train of his thoughts. I appreciates the effort, even though he don't quite grasp the gravity. 'So what I'm getting at is, I suppose you've seen some . . . some awful things in your time.'

I speaks with the weight of cold experience. ''Tis true. There was worse than hurrying minecarts, *gwas*. And not just the dark to make a *dwtty* cry. There were starvin' an' there were losin' family to the cruel fates of the mine – and to the fates above it too, what wi' sickness an' poverty in their stars. But worst, *gwas*, worst was when I saw kiddies huddled in the dark as if it were better than home. Better than *being* in their home. Them's were the ones that were always runnin', even if they was sitting right still. Runnin' from the back of a hand and a mouth full o' hard words.'

'I get the feeling these ones would prefer to go home.'

'Aye. Ye might be right on that.'

Hansard shunts his seat back a bit and wraps his coat about him. 'We'll do what we can for them, Ang. Best sleep, now.'

'Aye.'

He huffs and squirms a bit, trying to get comfy. He'd usually be in the back. Me, I'm right comfortable in my regular seat. I stows my flat cap away and bids the bluecap dim her light. When I glance up at Hansard I see he's staring at the ceiling with his thinking face on.

There's a soft whimper from the back, and quiet rustling as the two children shift positions. They dream fitfully.

I close my eyes to memories of hunted eyes and scared animals.

* * *

It's angry voices what wake me.

The night is black outside the car. No fizzing electric lamps by this abandoned aqueduct. So it shows up right nice, the white bar of light that's flashing to and fro over the ground. Held by a shadow cursing nastily, and answered with equal venom by another dark spectre. There's malicious growls too, like of dogs chafing at the bit for blood.

I jumps – only slightly – when Hansard puts his hand out to me.

Noticed I'm awake, he did. Looks like he ain't slept, but right now that's for the better, as he turns an eye back on the goings on outside. 'Let's hope they pass,' he says, so quiet I nearly misses it.

I strain my ears to make out what the voices are saying.

'–swore we'd fucking find them!'

'Shut your gob and let me work. How're they supposed to hear anything with you yakking on?'

'They should be fucking *smelling* for them, you piss-stain.'

'Give 'em a fucking minute and they'll pick up a scent, all right?'

'Hurry it up.'

'What do you want me to do? Get down on the floor and sniff with them? *You* fucking–'

They ain't even trying to hide their voices. Damn near shouting at the top of their lungs at each other. It's a miracle the kiddies are sleeping through it.

I hears rustling behind me.

Ah.

I turns to whisper, 'Easy now, ye'll be safe wi–'

'It's them,' Sable hisses over me. Buck's frightened expression says it all.

'Be calm, be calm,' I repeats as urgently and gently as I dare. They're tensed right up, on the very verge of flight. Hansard's still fixed on the window. Doesn't seem we've been noticed yet.

'I didn't see a car pull up,' he mutters. 'They've walked here. So they won't be able to catch us up. You kids better get strapped in.'

'What?' Sable snaps. She hasn't taken in the words. Her eyes are too busy darting around for an escape route.

The torch lights flash across the window.

'*Oi, look at this . . .*'

Buck squeals. Sable pounces over him to open the door and they both tumble out into the night.

'Wait!' I cries. I scrabble at my door handle and throw it open.

'You get them!' Hansard shouts. 'I'll distract these oafs.'

The men are shouting, the dogs baying. I spares a prayer for Hansard as his voice cuts in behind me ('Good evening, gentlemen . . .') then I'm leaping into the dark on the trail of the kiddies.

My legs is short but I can run fast – you gots to be able to run when a mine tunnel is collapsing on ye – and I can trace them ahead of me by the crackling of their carrier bags. Still, I'm more've a sprinter and my legs begin to fail as they cover more distance. Lucky then, that they stops so suddenly that I barrels into the back of their legs.

Sable's shaking Buck by the shoulders. 'What do you mean you've left it?' she's screaming. *'How could you be so careless?'*

Buck can barely talk for sobbing. 'I didn't m-mean to . . . there wasn't . . . there wasn't . . . time . . .'

'Hush child, hush. What've ye lost?' I says, and I pulls him low and gathers him into a *cwtch*. A true Welsh hug. He needs it and buries his head against me shoulders like a babe.

'My coat,' he bawls. 'I left it behind.'

'We have to go back for it,' Sable says with a grim frown.

I looks at her with surprise. I thought she would run no matter what. 'It'll be safe,' I assures. 'Hansard'll think of something. He usually does.' As I says it, the sound of the growling dogs comes back to my mind. There's no talking your way around dogs like with people. 'We should prob'ly go back and check on him, though.'

I think about telling Sable that she shouldn't have run – but what would it prove, now? It would've been easier if she hadn't, but there's no accounting for survival instinct.

I address her bluntly. 'Can ye tell me first, please, the nature of them that hunts you? What manner o' beasts are they? What magicks or suchlike might we be encounterin'?'

'They are just men,' she spits. 'Evil, evil men, with evil dogs that bite and shake you in their mouth.'

'They put us in cages,' Buck whispers.

'I see.' My suspicions be confirmed, right enough. 'Then here be our plan. Back to the car wi' both of ye, soft and quiet like. We see what state me Partner's in – hopefully still fit to drive. You kiddies get straight into the car – don't argue. I'll see about freeing up Hansard so's he can join ye. He'll take you far away from here. Trust on it.'

Sable pauses. 'And what about you?'

'I be distractin' men and dogs away, mebbe. I'll look after meself, girl, don't you worry on that. Hurry now. No tellin' what extra mischief that *twpsyn's* got himself into. Has a knack fer it, he does.'

We creeps back to the aqueduct. The dogs don't be barking no more, but there's pained snorts and snuffles what sound animal-like. Buck's ears be pricking, eyes wide with true terror. I motions him next to Sable – though no need, as he sticks to her like gum anyways. *Ready?* my eyes ask. Sable nods. Clutches her bag tight in one hand and Buck's shoulder in the other.

I peels away and hurry up to the car first. The men are obscured from view on the other side of it. I goes underneath, crawling on my belly. My eyes are good in the dark an' don't need the glare of torchlight to see the right mess my Partner has got himself in.

Hansard is backed up against the wall, holding somethin' out in his hand like a weapon. One of the men is doubled over retching; the other is covering his face with an arm and slowly advancing. The dogs, I sees three of them, all squirming in a heap pawing at their noses as if overcome with madness. A whiff of something vile hits my nose, and I realise what Hansard's got in his hand.

'Ye mad bastard,' I mutters, aghast.

He's only gone and opened the Triple Distilled Odious Miasma, the utter *ffwl*. We'd agreed *never* to touch that stuff again after what happened last time. Nearly a month before the stink was out of the car. I was tasting it in my pasties for weeks.

I dunno how Hansard is still standing. Maybe he'd managed to lob the stink at them from afar somehow, but he obviously missed one of them. The last man standing is being cautious, but he'll soon work out that Hansard won't dare open the bottle again at point blank range.

The shadows show me this man is a broad one, muscles like a blacksmith and face as ugly as an *unlucky* blacksmith. I reckons I could jump on his back, bite his ear off or something. As I crawls to the edge under the car, my hand knocks into something smooth and round.

I stares in befuddlement for a moment, then realise they must have fallen out when the kiddies made their run for it. There's five or six within arm's reach.

Slowly, I smiles a big, wide grin.

I grab the first crystal ball and huff on it. 'Wakey wakey,' I says. 'I hears there's some nice chappies who'd like to talk wi' ye. They wants to hear all about yer life and accomplishments and such.' I gives the silent glass a tap. 'Come on now. I hear there's tea and biccies, too.'

'*Biscuits?*' says a faint voice from within.

'Yep. Them hob-nobbly ones wi' the chocolate on.'

'Did someone say hobnobs?' pipes up a second voice to my left.

'The finest,' I says gleefully, and I starts rolling out every one I can find. It spreads like a tremor as they each wake up, the voices getting louder and louder as they roll closer toward Hansard and the men. The man that ain't gagging has a stupefied look on his face as the disembodied crowd pours out their demands.

'*Where are the hobnobs?*'

'*Who woke me up?*'

'*I would love a cup of tea.*'

'*Someone fetch a nurse . . .*'

'*Is that my Billie, there?*'

'. . . *can't find my pyjamas* . . .'

'*Can I have a biscuit, please?*'

The big man swipes madly at the air around him. I can't help but cackle when I understands – he don't know where the voices are coming from, and he can't see the crystal balls in the dark! He thinks he's being attacked by tea and biscuit ghosts!

Hansard's already slipped away.

'Ey, *gwas!*' I pops out from hiding. 'Not bad, right?' Then I wrinkles my nose with disgust. 'You stink.'

'Hazards of the job,' he replies, out of breath. 'Did you find the kids? We need to go!'

I points to where I left them, but in looking up I see Sable's face peering at me from inside the car window. I nods to her. 'They're good. Let's go.'

We piles in and Hansard peels the car away with a squeal of frantic tires. No need, I thinks, watching the mess we've left behind us. Them dogs might've lost their noses forever, and them evil men will be thinking twice about setting after their quarry again, that's for sure!

Yellow streetlamps strobe across our laps until we hit the edge of town and rural country roads swallow us in the night.

Buck cuddles up to Sable in the back. She strokes his hair, the first real affection I've seen from her. Her face is still hard though, like she ain't yet willing to believe they're out of trouble.

I holds the roadmap under my bluecap's light and give Hansard directions on where to go.

It's a few hours' drive, and dawn is peeking over the fields when we eventually pull into a lay-by on a deserted country road.

'We're here,' Hansard says, then checks his mirror and sees them both asleep.

Birds are waking up in the hedges outside. We sits quiet like, until Hansard breaks the silence. 'Bit on the nose this, isn't it?'

'What d'ye mean?' I says.

'What with this being a deer park, and the kid's name being Buck. Are you thinking what I'm thinking?'

'I gots some idea. Ye seen what's in them bags o' theirs?'

'Yes. Brings to mind selkies.'

'What's them?'

'A type of shapeshifter. Live in the ocean. They look like seals, usually. Until they take their skin off. Then they're, you know, human.' He looks out at the pink-blue sky, visible only to our right. The view is blocked by the towering hedgerow on my side of the car.

Hansard picks up his train of thought again. 'I doubt if these kids came from the sea, though. They must have parents somewhere. Who named them?'

'The men did.' The girl's voice shuts us both up. We had no notion she were awake. Her sharp little eyes pierce us both in the rear-view mirror. '"Fetch the sable," is what they'd say when they wanted me out of my cage.'

Hansard cocks his head. 'Where are you from, really?'

She shrugs. 'Mountains. Trees. Snow. It was high and cold.' She pauses. 'I don't know where Buck comes from. Our cages just happened to be next to each other.'

'How'd you end up in a cage?'

'Vicious trap,' she hisses. 'And then it was a horrid iron collar around my neck so I couldn't escape.'

'I notice ye ain't wearin' such a collar now,' I says.

Her smile is a bit nasty, but probably deserved I thinks. 'That was their mistake. They took the iron off so that they could force us to remove our coats. They thought I wouldn't bite them with human teeth. They were wrong.'

Hansard nods, putting thoughts together. 'Black Market poachers, I should think. I saw a selkie coat for sale, once. Always wondered what happened to its owner . . .'

I nudges him to be quiet as I see Buck blinking awake.

'Are we here?' he mumbles sleepily.

'Aye, lad,' I says. 'Are ye ready to take a look?'

He sits up eagerly and gathers his bag in his arms.

We steps out into the dawn. Hansard is holding up the map book and turning it every which way. 'I'm pretty sure it's just the other side of this hedge, if we can find an opening.'

'Over here!' We turns to see Buck scrambling through a small gap in the branches. Sable follows swift behind, and me as well, leaving Hansard muttering to hisself behind.

'. . . prickly bugger, this . . .'

We emerge to a wide, rolling land. Gentle sloping hills with trees scattered here and there, and what looks to be some forest in the distance. It's an open space with open sky above it, such as might be trusted to open up the soul. I takes a big breath in of morning air. There are many sights ye don't see inside a mine, and this is one of them.

Hansard makes it through. 'Looks like a bit of a ditch there, but I'm sure you kids can scramble over it. What do you think . . . ?' His voice trails off.

My eyes land on the same thing as his. Where Sable had once stood, now a soft little creature with rounded ears and thick brown fur is looking at us from the ground. It stands upright on its hind paws, whiskers quivering, as it stares at us with shiny coal-speck eyes.

'What is that, a stoat?' Hansard murmurs.

'Looks more like a pine marten t'me, *gwas* . . .'

Buck is rummaging hurriedly in his carrier bag. He pulls out the coarse reddish-brown hide I'd spied earlier – in better light I can see there are white spots on it too. He also pulls out the plastic toy, Rocky, and places it carefully on the grass at his feet.

He looks at us briefly, a little nervous smile playing on his lips. 'Um. Thank you. I'm glad there are people like you. Sable would say so, too.'

Before we can say anything more, he throws the bristly fur over his head. It wraps around him as if it's alive, fitting to his shape, and then not his shape as it fills out, stretches and distorts, and in a split-second which leaves me feeling like my eyes have hiccupped, there's a skinny fallow deer standing in Buck's place.

Hansard and I are suddenly mute. The young buck bows his head to us, and then very delicately picks up Rocky in his mouth and trots away.

The little marten flicks its tail and twists fluidly onto all-fours. It gives us one last look with a twitch of its nose, and then scampers after the deer.

We watch them disappear into the distance.

Hansard clears his throat. 'Well. That sure was something.'

'We did right by 'em, *gwas.*'

'I'm sure we did. Once again, though, I can't help but observe how we've come away with nothing to show for our efforts. You might even say that we're poorer for it.'

'Them crystal balls were never gunna sell, *gwas.*' I smirks at him, knowing my next remark is sure to get under his skin. 'Besides, ye be all the richer fer havin' saved two lost souls today.'

He grunts at me and walks back to the car without a word.

'Yer a good man, Hansard,' I calls after him. 'Despite yer best efforts!'

The car door slams, but I knows he takes it well. Needs reminding sometimes, he does. I smiles to meself and take the pleasure of an extra moment to enjoy the unfolded landscape. It's a big world for sure. And many people in it all trying to find their way, for better and for worse.

Just as well then, I thinks as I climbs back into my seat next to Hansard, that I be lucky enough to have a friend to be finding my way along with.

As we pull out onto quiet country roads under a clear open sky, I sings softly to myself.

> 'Dinogad's coat were speckled, speckled,
> From the skin of a pine marten it were made . . .'

Episode 3: Knockers

Dawn's watery grey light filtered in through the moth-holes of my windscreen blanket. The blankets pinned to the side windows were more intact, but the light was persistent in its exploitation of every tiny gap that allowed it passage into my car and beyond my eyelids.

I threw an arm over my face, but it was no use. Not even the comforting dark could shield me from the hellish sound that had dogged me all night and followed me into the grim light of day.

It was the sound that nightmares are made of: a dull rattle of machine guns in fog; the rumble of thunder over a restless ocean; the snorting and grunting of bulls readying to charge.

It was Ang, snoring.

With huge reluctance, I opened my eyes. I couldn't see Ang from my bed on the backseat. Not long after her 'moving in' to my car I'd taken to pinning a blanket to the ceiling at night to separate front seats from back, for some small semblance of privacy between us. Often, I wished it were a thick granite wall instead.

As my mind sharpened into full consciousness, I became aware of a strange weight on my chest. I craned my neck and came almost nose-to-nose with a rat.

It had a large, greasy parcel strapped to its back.

'You could at least knock,' I told it. I shifted the creature off me and thumped the back of Ang's seat with my foot. 'Wake up, you bloody bulldozer.'

'Whuh?'

'There's a rat here. Think it's for you.'

She was sharp as a tack within seconds. 'Why didn't ye say?' She whipped down the privacy blanket and glared at me. The effect was somewhat ruined by the fact that she still had her nightcap on. It was a remarkably clean thing, given the grubbiness of Ang's other supposedly white clothing. The hint of frill at its edges, along with her curly grey hair poking out from underneath, made her look like a little old Victorian grandmother.

I jostled the rat off my chest and Ang welcomed it into her lap. The parcel contained exactly what I expected: a thick Cornish pasty, gently oozing gravy at one corner where it had possibly been nibbled in transit. Ang placed it lovingly to one side. The amount of tenderness she showed toward pastry worried me, sometimes.

She smoothed out the paper it had been wrapped in and stared at it intently. Coblyns, I've learned – and knockers, for that matter – won't waste anything if they can help it, and if a thing can be put to more than one use, then all the better. How the rodent postal system worked was an utter mystery to me, but it somehow reliably delivered Ang her Cornish pasties wrapped in letters from her not-exactly-a-friend every few weeks.

Her mouth moved very slightly while she read over the words. Meanwhile, I peeled back the rest of the blankets and rolled open a window. The rumbling of lorry engines and stale smell of exhaust fumes filled the car. We'd spent the night in a run-down truck stop off the A14. It was a ragtag assortment of portacabins with toilets, showers, and a greasy spoon café outside.

'How's Goron?' I asked, reaching past Ang for my shaving kit.

Her eyes snapped up. 'What's t'be saying it's from him?'

'He always sends you food.'

She looked like she wanted to argue – but Ang wasn't quite so good at arguing with the truth as me. 'Good pasties, they is,' she deflected. She broke off a corner of the crust and fed it to the rat. It twitched it whiskers in thanks, then darted out of the open window.

'I'm sure.' My stomach gurgled as the thought of hot bacon and eggs crossed my mind. 'So, how is the old knocker? What's in the letter?'

'Dunno, *gwas*.' Her brow furrowed as her eyes cast back down. 'Trouble.'

'What makes you say that?'

'He's askin' us for help.'

I scrutinised my razor. 'What kind? We're not really in the business of helping people.'

'He don't say.'

'Well, unless he's after a batch of faulty curses, I doubt we can be much use.'

Ang didn't argue immediately, which put me on alert. She looked like she was carefully composing something in her head. I remembered that, despite their apparently friendly correspondence, Ang was brought up by her fellow coblynau to believe knockers were nasty, dirty, horrid creatures (despite being practically cousins, if not entirely the same species) and so perhaps it was with some reluctance that she was contemplating an offer of assistance.

Eventually, she seemed to settle on a permissible line of reasoning.

'Knockers will have wares to trade, *gwas*,' she said. 'Our stock is lacking right now. Ye'd like some magic tinware, aye?'

I pretended to give it thought. As if I wasn't already dead set on leveraging Ang's friendship with Goron to fiddle the knockers out of as much enchanted metal as I possibly could.

'It's true,' I said. 'We could use a fresh acquisition to spice up our display, and there's a slight possibility your knocker friend will own some interesting trinkets. Might not be worth the risk, is my concern.'

Ang's hands went to her hips, winding up to deliver a reprisal. I jumped back in before she could start. 'Tell you what, Ang. We've been official business partners for a couple of months now, but it strikes me that you've not yet had a go at actually steering the business, as such. So, this one's yours, eh? Your very first trade operation. Proper contribution to the biz. If you think this is good business, then I'm in.'

She looked stunned for a moment, but recovered immediately with a sour comment. 'Oh? So them bluecaps I first traded you all that time ago don't be worth anythin' now? Not enough of a *contribution?*'

'We weren't partners back then,' I reminded her. 'And besides, *you* traded *my* bluecaps to that bloody knocker!'

'Knew he'd take care of 'em,' she grumbled. 'All right. I says this be good business, *gwas.* Let's see what nasty knockers has to offer. And if it be good, then you are to stop bringin' up the thing about the bluecaps.'

I grinned. 'Deal done.'

'Good.'

I stepped out for some housekeeping. My coat was crumpled and in need of a good shake from where it had acted as my blanket overnight. It was warm and comfortingly heavy, weighed down by Black Market goods stowed deep in many pockets. There was always a mild risk, however, of rolling the wrong way in the night and accidentally getting pricked by a spindle of everlasting sleep, or inadvertently crushing the vial of hot air, or, god forbid, releasing the swarm of incandescent screeching beetles from their cocoon. These I considered to be admissible hazards of the job.

After giving the coat a good (and careful) flap outside the car, I availed myself of the stop's wash facilities, and followed my nose to the café for breakfast. When I climbed back into the front seat, it was with a sausage sandwich dripping with onions and ketchup.

'So. Where are we headed?' I asked around a satisfying mouthful.

Ang held up her oily letter. She was already halfway through the pasty, I noted. 'Looks like it says . . . Menantol. But the 'e' has a little hat o'er it.'

I peered at where her grubby finger pointed to the words written in a surprisingly neat hand. It read: *Find us at Mên-an-Tol, that what be the Crick Stone in men's tongue. It be right holey. Ye can't miss it.*

'A holy place? Like a church?' I said, puzzled. Didn't sound quite right, although my knowledge of knockers was admittedly limited. 'Good of him to not give directions or anything. Right. Get the map.'

I made the reasonable assumption that we were looking for a place in Cornwall – the native region of knockers, after all – but it took a long time of squinting at the map grid by grid to eventually locate Mên-an-Tol, written in very tiny text, positioned in what might be an empty field. It was also a full day's drive away.

'I might be losing faith in this venture,' I said.

'It's only a bit o' drivin'. We'll find it.'

'Tell that to the petrol tank,' I said, but started the engine anyway. Unlike Ang, I'd had the good fortune of doing business with knockers in the past. They showed up occasionally at Markets, brandishing shiny and ornate sculptures with magic woven into the very atoms of the metal.

They'd been miners once, just like Ang's people. But when humans closed the mines, the knockers found themselves a new type of work. Upskilled, I suppose. Adapted, like everyone seems to be doing these days.

'I hope it is a church,' Ang said, as we pulled onto the busy A-road. 'I like them stone ones we see in the country sometimes. The one near our mine in Ironbridge were made o' metal.'

I paused before replying. Sometimes it was worth waiting to see if Ang's more curious reminiscences could be translated into a meaningful image. Like the time she brought up 'them great gushing privies wi' the chains' and I realised she was talking about flushing toilets. But on this occasion, I drew a blank.

'A metal church?'

'Aye. Made o' corrugated iron. It were a pretty thing, though. I liked the plinky music an' the singin'. Though they could have cheered up a bit, in my opinion.'

I chalked this one up to cultural differences. I hadn't figured out quite how old Ang was – and I got the sense I wasn't allowed to ask – but I was fairly sure it was more than a century or so. I'd once tried to work Queen Victoria into a conversation, only to learn that coblynau didn't give any passing thought to the reigning monarch of the time. If it wasn't underground or covered in pastry, then it didn't hold much interest.

We settled into a patter of conversation as I navigated off the main road and wound a rural, convoluted B-road route down to the very south east tip of the country. I avoided motorways as a matter of course. These days there are cameras everywhere, snapping license plates, checking insurance, and overall making my life tricky.

Ang grew more intent on the map as the hours wore on. We knew we'd hit Devon when the roads morphed into narrow country lanes with ten-foot-high hedgerows and hairpin bends, and then they opened out again as we crossed into Cornwall and sailed over green and rolling moorlands. Occasionally we glimpsed the sparkle of ocean as we zig-zagged further and further south along the coastline.

It was late in the afternoon when we finally entered the area of the map where we hoped to find Mên-an-Tol.

If only we knew what, exactly, we were looking for.

'I swear, we've driven up and down this same road five times, Ang. I'm fed up,' I said wearily. Although the scenery we were passing through was picturesque, it was also bland in the way that endless green fields and bracken tend to be when you've been staring at them for several hours.

'There's meant t'be a right turn, that's all I'm sayin', she said, jabbing a finger at the map book.

'Well, there bloody isn't one!'

'Why don't we ask at that house, *gwas?*'

'What house?'

'That one we've passed five times.'

'Ugh.'

My eyes ached and my legs were cramping from the long drive. The sausage sandwich seemed like a lifetime ago. So it was in an incredibly grumpy mood that I swung into the layby opposite the solitary farmhouse on this empty country road, and stamped out of the car.

''Ere, *gwas*,' said Ang's voice behind me, before I'd taken another step. 'Look at this sign.'

I trudged over to find her reading a very small signpost, tacked onto a metal gate at the end of the layby. *Footpath to Mên-an-Tol.*

I stared in disbelief at the path. 'We have to *walk?*'

Ang snickered. 'Ye be good at runnin', *gwas*. A little walk ain't beyond yer measure.'

'No, but I'd rather hoped to have more assets about me when we negotiate our deal.' I retrieved my fold-up table (a nifty thing with folding compartments) and strapped it on my back, and slung a bag of wares at Ang to carry. 'Let's go do business.'

It was a half-mile walk in fading light, with nothing much but fields on the horizon all around us. This did at least mean that Mên-an-Tol was, eventually, easy to spot.

'Oh, I see.' I stared at it. 'He really did mean *holey.*'

Set in the middle of a meadow, three standing stones – two uprights, and one circular with a hole in the middle – created a peculiar formation in the landscape. They were too small to be called monoliths, but nevertheless exuded the air of one.

'Granite,' Ang said with an air of authority.

'I don't see how that helps us.'

A familiar fizzing sensation – like of many ants crawling over my brain – told me we were in an uncanny space. A place where the real meets the unreal.

I walked around the central donut-shaped stone and peered at Ang through the hole. There was a faint distortion in the image, like the subtle wavering of heated air; the shimmer of reality thinned out and caught in a breeze.

'This is a bridge,' I announced. 'The knockers must be hidden on the other side.'

'Aye. Knew you'd spot it eventually, *gwas.*'

The arrangement didn't much surprise me. A bridge is any place where reality – the universe, the ether, quantum particles or whatever – is stretched and easily warped. If you know how, you can cross a bridge to see what's on the other side. I'd met Ang this way. Her clan of coblynau had created a neat little pocket dimension for themselves across a bridge, and effectively shut it off from the rest of the world.

'On the count of three?' I suggested. 'One, two, thr–'

I unfocused. This was the equivalent of mentally unravelling my physical edges, bit by bit. I applied a soft focus to my being, and slipped into the spaces where reality warps.

'–ree.'

Momentarily giddy, I could see tendrils of fog curling out of the hole in the stone. Ang poked her head through while I adjusted.

'Can't see nuthin' yet, *gwas.* D'ye want to– *Ack!*' She disappeared through the hole.

'Ang!'

I dove after her in what I believed would have been an extremely graceful and acrobatic manoeuvre if it weren't for the table strapped to my back which *cracked* into the edges of the stone. I struggled to disentangle myself while falling backwards and backwards and backwards into fog . . . until finally I came free and flumped awkwardly onto the ground.

Several narrow, pointed faces looked down at me. I was relieved to find their expressions curious rather than angry.

'*Dynnargh dhis.* Awright there, big 'un?'

The speaker wore a brimmed hat with an oversized flashlight mounted on the front. His simple shirt and trousers were much like Ang's usual costume minus the waistcoat, and with the addition of a brown neckerchief.

'Branok, me,' he introduced himself as I lurched to my feet. He was a bit taller than Ang, the top of his hat nearly reaching my hip. He promptly ignored me in favour of her. 'Wasson, maid. Haven't seen you round before. One of our Cousin Jacks, are yer?'

Ang blinked owlishly at him, her face a rictus of suspicion. 'My name's Ang. 'E's the one called Jack.'

I extended a hand downward. 'Jack Hansard. Mystic pioneer and tradesman of occult goods.'

Branok shook it politely. 'Nah. Cousin Jacks is what we calls knockers that left way backalong. All right, big 'un.'

'I ain't no knocker,' Ang said. 'Coblyn, me.'

Branok turned back to her with a wide grin. 'Cor. Yer Goron's maid then, aren't ye? 'E'll be made up you've come, no mistake.'

'I ain't his nobody!' she replied hotly. 'Where is the lyin' knocker? I'll knock his head fer sayin' such things!'

'Ah, right. Weel. 'E be along dreckly, I s'pect.'

'Directly?' I repeated, trying to wade through both the thick Cornish accent and idiosyncrasies of dialect.

There was a brief exchange in Cornish between Branok and his friends with much nodding and shaking of heads. Rather than try to fathom what they were arguing about, I took stock of our surroundings. We were in a small, wooded glen; a stark contrast to the barren moorland we'd criss-crossed to find Mên-an-Tol.

It was a near perfect circle of grass and wildflowers bathed in a beaming shaft of yellow sunlight. A dense thicket of trees enclosed it like a wall. Foxgloves, snowdrops, and bluebells were all in flower, completely out of season with each other. And despite being late in the day (on the outside, at least) the sun shone bright and warm, catching on droplets of fine dew which hung from every leaf and stem. The flowers sparkled.

I couldn't help thinking it was all beautiful in a very exaggerated way. Even the air was faintly twinkling, and I could feel my brain being tickled towards a calm and happy state. So, naturally, I was extremely uneasy about it.

'Say,' I tapped Branok on the shoulder, 'there aren't any . . . fairies here, are there?'

He laughed. ''Eck, no. Wouldn't catch us gaddin' about with fairies. This were a piskie den once, though.'

I started. 'Piskies? Tell me they aren't still here!'

'Y'awright, no piskies left. Little hellers, ain't they? They comes back sometimes, but we sees 'em off.'

I pointed to a set of metal and stone structures which were the only eyesore in this otherwise perfect place. Some of Branok's crew had lost interest in us and drifted over to them, and were now busily pulling out tools and leather aprons. 'These are your forges, I presume?'

'Thassit!' Branok replied.

Ang crossed her arms. 'Goron told me you knockers were livin' in yer old mine. What's to mine here, apart from pixie dust?'

Branok nodded happily. 'Zactly!'

It took both of us an extra beat to realise this was Branok's total response, and that he had apparently taken Ang seriously.

'I suppose there's a lot of residual magic here . . .' I prompted, 'from the piskies?'

'Right on! Loads've it. Keep trippin' over the stuff. It goes right well with the tin.' He pointed to one knocker who had been at work all this time in the background – face obscured by thick goggles and hands encased in mitten-like welding gloves. 'Tha's me daughter, Merouda. *'Ee, Merouda! Cummas 'zon, showum y'werks!'*

'Dreckly, Tas!' she called back.

'Na, na, na. Now, I says!'

The knocker at the forge appeared to sigh and removed her protective gear. She pushed the goggles up to rest on top of her frizzy brown hair. *'Ya, ya . . .'*

She crossed the magical glen with a purposeful stride, stomping delicate petals into the ground with steel-toed boots. When she reached us she flicked an inquisitive glance up at me and across at Ang. Perhaps she'd been too busy to notice our arrival.

'Wasson, Tas?' she said to Branok.

'Showum what yer workin' on, girl.'

Merouda gave a shrug and produced a tin sculpture from the front pocket of her leather apron. It was oversized in her hands but fit nicely in mine when she passed it up.

'It's a very nice . . . toy?' I held the thing closer to inspect. It was a little tin figure – unpainted, still rough on the edges – a caricature of a monkey holding two symbols clapped together. I knew better than to assume this was the whole of it, though. Anything made by a knocker would be a lot more than it seemed. I thumbed a key-shaped protrusion. 'Clockwork?'

'Thassit, sir,' she said. 'Clockwork curses.'

'My Merouda's hands be right good at workin' the fiddly parts,' said Branok, chest puffed with pride.

'*Na, Tas*. The parts is easy. Gettin'um wound up's the tricky bit.'

She held out her palm to retrieve the tin monkey and began turning the key. It made a smooth clicking sound with each turn, pulling the cymbals apart. When she let go, the sound became a constant ticking from within the metal.

I instinctively took a step back. 'It's not about to blow up, I hope?'

Merouda held up five fingers, and silently lowered each one in a count down. Five, four, three, two . . .

The monkey clapped.

The ensuing sonic boom rattled my head long before it hit the floor.

When we'd all picked ourselves back up, I gave my ears a thump and mouthed a question at Merouda.

'*Ya!*' she shouted back happily. '*Ver' re-usable! Wind up and go. Whee! At least forty times I've tried thiss'un.*'

I saw the other knockers around the forge also rising from the ground. The way they shot peeved glances in our direction attested to Merouda's claim.

Branok aggressively wiggled a finger in his ear. 'O' course, the magic dies out eventually. But Merouda's working on makin' 'em long-lastin'.'

A stream of Welsh curse words told me Ang was recovering, but not happily. '*What was that*, ye great stinkin' knocker?'

Merouda's smile split into an even wider grin. 'Knocker be right! This's me knockin' curse, so's it is. A great bleddy big knock!'

'It certainly was loud,' I agreed. The tinnitus would go away eventually, I hoped. 'Very impressive, madam.'

'Had enough o' this, I have,' Ang said. 'Where's Goron at? He best be here soon!'

'He be along dreckly.' Branok grinned.

'You keep saying that,' I said carefully, 'but I don't think you actually mean he's on his way.'

''Ee, no. Goron's busy elsewhere.'

Ang's whole demeanour turned decidedly chilly. 'Where?' she said.

'Off'n the business he wrote you about, right?' replied Branok. 'Diddenwanna wait, 'e said. Else the hag'd get away.'

'What hag is this?' Ang demanded.

Branok's smile twitched nervously. 'I dunno if I follow it, right. But when Goron came home from the last Market where he met you, he reckoned some woman were responsible fer the disappearin' of our fellows. That she'd lured 'em away on some nefarious purpose. So he's been watchin' fer word on her ever since and, well, we thinks she's been back again.'

I listened to this with a sinking stomach. We knew the woman he was referring to. We knew her as Quiet Eyes, a thief with the gift of dodging recognition. I'd tried before to memorise her facial features, but the information simply melted out of my brain. Except for the feeling I got from her eyes. Her eyes were always terribly, unnervingly calm.

Otherwise, she might as well be invisible.

She was also exceedingly dangerous. When we'd last encountered her, she'd used us, betrayed us, and shot a man dead. The whole thing had ended with two demi-gods battling it out in a pillar of lightning and fire.

Ang sucked in a breath between her teeth. 'Goron, ye daft *ffwl*. What's he thinking, goin' after her alone?'

'He was sure it's the same woman?' I asked.

'Seemed so,' said Branok. 'We'd heard this lady were in our lands huntin' bluecaps an' the like. It were all over the towns, when our Merouda came back from her trading.'

That surprised me. 'You go into the towns?'

'What, out in the open?' Ang chimed in.

Merouda treated her to a raised eyebrow. 'Don't you?' She grinned again, showing teeth more pointed than Ang's. 'We needs to do business. We sits an' waits in shadows fer them that come as needs us, an' we trades what they needs fer what we wants. Last I went, we traded our tin woven with piskie magic fer other metals and engineering parts.'

The knocker plucked a bundle of silver wire from her apron. 'Always in need of solder we are, and batteries, too. Humans may've left our mines, but we be keepin' 'em shored up and well in use.'

The forges behind her puffed out a column of viscous smoke, as if to prove the point. It left a dark stain on the artificially cerulean sky.

'An' your customers be wantin' toys such as this?' Ang said, scowling at the tin monkey.

There were sharp edges to the way Merouda smiled. 'I makes meaner curses, too.'

'I don't doubt it,' I cut in, and sent Ang a warning glance. I knew the charmed trinkets of knockers to be vicious little things: arcane booby-traps scored in metal. If a knocker hands you a piece of jewellery, it's probably best to pass it on to your worst enemy instead. 'So Merouda, what *exactly* was the word on the street about this woman?'

She shrugged. '*Zactly?* That she's from up country, lookin' fer fairy folk round our parts. One incomer said he'd seen her with little cages full o' dancing lights, what sounded much like bluecaps. Saw her in the Big City, he said.'

My mind tripped up over this. 'Which city? Surely not London?'

Merouda cackled. '*Na*, ya great bleddy *tuss!* I means Truro.'

'That best be a place an' not another made up word,' Ang hissed under her breath.

'We passed it on the way here,' I said loudly. 'Probably, what, an hour's journey by car? Did Goron go all that way by himself?'

'Ain't nothin' fer a knocker what has the knowin' of the leys,' Merouda said.

I couldn't step back fast enough. 'Hey now. Ley lines? I'm not messing with those.'

'Whassat, *gwas?*' asked Ang.

I grimaced, staring at our glittering surroundings. 'Fairy pathways. They criss-cross the country where the damn things used to live. Like scars they've left on our reality. It's as dangerous as trying to travel through the Nether.'

''Tis only a skip to Truro,' Merouda said in a sing-song tone.

'Aye, and Goron knows it well,' Branok added. 'Well acquainted with the ol' fairy relics, we are.'

I rattled the car keys in my pocket and cleared my throat. 'Nevertheless. We'll drive.'

Ang was already halfway to the donut-shaped entrance stone. 'What're ye waiting for, *gwas?* The ol' fool's probably in trouble already!'

She was overtaken by a beaming Branok and a cackling Merouda, who both hopped through the hole ahead of her. As Ang stopped short, Merouda's head poked back into the glen. The goggles fell lopsided over her face, but didn't obscure the smirk in her expression. 'Need a guide, don't yer?' she crowed. 'C'mon now. Me an' 'Tas will see you right!'

She promptly disappeared again, and Ang and I shared a look.

We'd learned to read each other's glances – an important skill, when you need to be able to silently distinguish between 'Run' and 'Unleash the incandescent shrieking beetles'.

This one said simply: 'Oh dear.'

Episode 4: The Fairy Hunter

When I said 'we', I hadn't intended for Branok and Merouda to join us.

As it was, Ang sat next to me in irate silence while in the back father and daughter jabbered loudly and enthusiastically in a mix of old and modern Cornish. Knockers, I was quickly realising, did not have the same sense of restraint as their coblynau cousins.

'Whassis?' Branok yelled at a road sign.

'Lookithat!' Merouda cried at a brightly lit house.

'Go, go, go!' they chorused at traffic lights.

Despite multiple admonishments, they'd both abandoned their seat belts and spent most of the journey stood up with faces pressed against the windows. I could only be grateful that it was dark and there weren't many other cars on the road.

In their roundabout way of getting to the point, the knockers had eventually given us the full name of Goron's destination: a bed and breakfast on the edge of town. Dusk had long since fallen during the time we'd spent at Mên-an-Tol, and now the Cornish moors passed by unseen as we hurled along the winding roads towards the outskirts of Truro.

When Ang declared our arrival, squinting with her nose up against the map, we pulled onto a wide and neatly kept driveway. In the glare of my headlights the name 'Three Stones Retreat' swung on a genteelly styled sign with a scrolled font. Ang and I shared a sceptical glance. It didn't look like the kind of place Quiet Eyes would hole up in.

The reception building was a sprawling old farmhouse, with what might be converted barns lining the courtyard. Warm light spilled from the gaps in their curtains. It had an air of tranquillity about it.

'This doesn't feel right,' I murmured, killing the engine.

'Nothin' about that *ast* were right, though,' Ang added quietly.

''Ere, lookit that wheel o'er there!' Merouda screeched.

''Ee, it's off a pit head, that is!' shouted Branok. 'That'd be a right useful spare fer back home!'

I lunged into the back seat and grabbed them both by their collars. 'You listen to me,' I said, pulling against their wriggling, 'there's to be no stealing here, got that? We need to have our wits about us!'

Merouda cocked her head, looking at me slyly. 'Then ye needs more wits than yer have, merchant man.'

I glanced down. She held the clockwork monkey in one hand. The other was poised over the key.

I relaxed my grip. 'Hey now. It was just a warning, all right?'

'*Ya*. A warning,' she replied sweetly, tucking the toy away.

'What's the plan, *gwas?*' said Ang. 'Want me to grab the crowbar?'

'No . . .' I hesitated at the suggestion. The crowbar, though my usual weapon of choice, wasn't easy to hide and would project perhaps too aggressive an intent. But Ang had a point. Iron was always handy to have nearby.

'I'll take a horseshoe,' I decided. 'Pass one up, would you?'

Ang located one from under her seat and handed it to me. It was a reassuring weight inside my coat. As protective charms go, it was a very solid one.

She pocketed a handful of iron nails for herself and turned to look at me, expectantly.

I surveyed my three diminutive yet grizzled companions. 'Perhaps you three should stay here. As back-up. I'll . . . I think I'll just knock.'

A trio of penetrating gazes followed me up the gravel drive. The path to the front door was marked by a neat row of shrubs and petite solar lanterns. Ornate plaster moulding framed a brass bell. I pressed it.

There was no answer, to which I wasn't surprised. Who'd expect travellers at this hour? But I saw a curtain twitch high above, so I pressed again.

At length, there were muffled footsteps, and the grand wooden door opened just a crack. A tired middle-aged man in a fluffy pink dressing gown was partially revealed.

'It's an emergency!' I blurted out before he could say anything. 'I'm here for . . . There's a . . . Let's see, shall we say . . . There is a lady of *great importance* staying at your fine accommodations. Very private individual, I'm sure you'll understand, and I wouldn't know what name she's given you. But I must speak with her urgently. If you please, Sir.' I imposed an inflection on the *sir* to convey a meaning as close to 'my lord' as feasibly possible.

This kind of confidence trick only has a few seconds in which to work. The mix of urgency, brashness, and flattery should pummel the recipient into assuming you have a right to be wherever you are, and thus overlook your shortcomings (in my case, the scruffy hair, rumpled trench coat, and general untrustworthy demeanour).

In this instance I fear that our man was still waking up, and so his sleep-addled brain took several crucial extra moments to digest the situation.

He squinted at my shirt, which I realised held a smear of mud from where I'd fallen into the knockers' home. 'D'you know what time it is?'

Bugger. I wasn't in the mood to try genuine persuasion.

'I'm terribly sorry,' I lied, 'but this can't wait. Do you know the woman I'm talking about? I'm certain she's here and she must be given this . . . this incredibly important news.'

He grunted at me. 'Write it on a note. I'll gi'it her in the mornin'.'

I glanced behind me, hoping for inspiration. To my fortune, Branok and Merouda were in full view. They both stood with faces pressed up against the windows of my car, staring right at us. I thought I saw Ang jumping up and down behind them.

'*The children!*' I said desperately, waving an arm at them. 'You wouldn't turn them away, would you?'

His eyes widened – possibly because his brain had registered that one of the 'children' had a beard – but I snapped his attention back onto me with a sorrowful, imploring tone. 'Please, sir. The children have lost everything. Parents, home, the lot. The lady will want to see them. Discretely, you understand. Just point us at her room.'

'Oh, dearovem! The poor little tackers,' he muttered. He nodded across the courtyard to one door in the barn row. An impish stone ornament stood guard outside. 'Give her my condolences.'

I waited until he'd certainly shut the door.

Crossing the distance to the barn, I held up a hand for the others to stay inside the car. I wanted my full wits about me, and no distractions.

If I were to face Quiet Eyes again . . . it would be like balancing on the edge of a knife. A serrated one, at that. Just like her appearance, her words were illusory and her motives impenetrable. I'd been a victim to her mind games before – hell, I'd been stupid enough to think that I'd won one, for a while – but now I was wiser, and I knew the violence she was capable of.

My palms were sweating as I approached. More pretty solar lights and a tinkly wind chime fixed to the doorframe jarred with my inner tension. I hadn't been expecting a confrontation in a holiday cottage.

Was I really just going to knock on this door and face her again?

Should I feel guilty about this nervous burbling of excitement in my chest?

I wonder if she's been thinking about me, the fish that slipped the net?

'Hey, *gwas*–'

I jumped.

'–why haven't ye knocked yet?'

I hoped my face wasn't red. 'Preparing. You don't need to be out here, you know.'

'Aye. But no luck getting' these two t'sit still.'

These two were busy inspecting the garden ornament. 'Looks like you, *Tas*,' Merouda snickered.

I ran a hand through my hair. 'Oh, cripes. Fine. In that case, here's the plan–'

As if on cue, my words were cut in half by the sound of a lock clicking. The door swung open and light spilled over our faces.

Looming in the glow, a vision of tweed and tightly wound curls frowned down at us.

'*What*,' she said, 'is the meaning of this?'

As a group, we were stunned. There's nothing quite like the tone of a school ma'am to whip the nervous system into fight-or-flight mode.

This woman – who, by her extremely palpable presence, was obviously not Quiet Eyes – looked each of us up and down with a thunderous frown. I risked a return appraisal and noted the fuzzy slippers peeking out from under her skirt, and the dishevelled state of her tweed jacket which suggested it had been thrown on last-minute to cover her blouse.

She clapped – startling us all again – and suddenly *beamed* down at Ang.

'More fairies!' she exclaimed. 'How *delightful!*'

'Who're ye callin' a–'

I gave Ang a quick kick. 'Ah, good evening my . . . dear? Would it mean anything to you if I say we are looking for an acquaintance of ours?'

'I am not your dear,' she said pointedly. 'But I am entertaining some wonderful company tonight.'

She stepped aside. A familiar face perked up from its position in a pillowed, paisley armchair.

'Wasson, shag?' said Goron happily. He was holding a cup of tea.

Ang barged past me, swinging her arms furiously. '*What* did you jus' say?'

'I means hallo, my bewty!' Goron jumped down from the chair. His navy overalls, covered in mud and glossy oil stains, left a black mark on the cushions.

He swept up his orange hard hat, which had been resting on the arm of the chair, and doffed it theatrically at Ang. 'A right good sight, you are, lass. Knew you'd come, I did.'

'We was in the area,' Ang said sharply. 'Wouldna bothered otherwise.'

My gaze slid sideways. Tempting though it was to contradict Ang – and despite how entertaining it was to watch her embarrassment deepen – my attention was fixed on our tweed-clad host.

She'd stepped back to watch this reunion with a simpering expression that was entirely at odds with her otherwise haughty bearing. Her clothes, though a little creased, were in no way shabby. A quality herringbone weave, lacking in frayed edges or scuffs, but with a certain faded quality to suggest the material had been well-used for a long time. A gold brooch with a sapphire was pinned at her collar. My salesman's nose told me it was probably as genuine as the air of privilege about her.

I was hardly unaccustomed to individuals pretending to be more than they seem (and sometimes pretending to be less than they are) but there's something about a gentrified heritage which is difficult to fake and easy to spot. It might be the intrinsic self-assuredness that comes with owning several hundred acres of land, or the unshakeable confidence of knowing there are few people in the world who can order you about. And possibly it was in the way this woman suddenly grasped my hand and emphatically shook it while I stood nonplussed in the doorway.

'Name's Bernice!' she shouted jovially into my ear. 'Call me Bernie! Come in, please do. Oh, I am *so* glad to have such special visitors.'

We shuffled in, awkwardly. A fake fireplace flickered merrily at one end of the cosy room. The rest of it was taken up with a pair of armchairs and numerous end tables, leaving very little space for three knockers, a coblyn, myself and . . . Bernie.

'Whassis then?' said Branok, as he and Merouda clustered at the fireplace They tapped the glass front, making appreciative remarks about mechanisms. Ang was still giving Goron a heated dressing down, though he seemed quite happy about it. Bernice, meanwhile, picked up a large leatherbound journal and began eagerly scribbling away with a pencil. The scene was so bizarrely familial that I nearly forgot why we were there in the first place.

'Excuse me,' I said faintly, 'but is Goron your guest?'

Bernice dropped the journal and clapped her hands to her face. 'Oh, goodness, excuse *me!* Where are my manners? Would you like some tea?'

'No,' I said, over the top of the loud 'Yes!' from the knockers.

'I'll be right back with the teapot!' She bustled off into the next room.

I turned helplessly to Goron. 'Who is she? Why are you having a tea party?'

Goron grinned. 'Just some old bird, in't she? Harmless. But makes a good brew.'

'And what about the bluecaps she was supposedly carrying? Isn't that why you called us all the way down here?'

'Ah.' He revealed a shade of humility, looking down at his empty teacup. 'Made a mistake, we did. Thought she was thievin' 'em, because of the rumours in town. But it ain't quite like that.'

I snuck a peak at Bernie's journal, where she'd left it open on the low coffee table. A quick impression of landscape sketches and dated entries made it seem like a holiday diary.

'Did somebody say bluecaps?' Bernice re-entered with a large pink china teapot and a tray of floral cups. Merouda and Branok rushed over as she set it down on the coffee table and poured. With eager grins, they snatched up the hot cups with both hands and then made loud, appreciative noises as they downed the beverage – to Bernie's apparent delight.

'We heard you were interested in bluecaps?' I asked her, over the cacophony of slurping.

'My good man, you might say I'm something of an *enthusiast*,' she replied, sidling past the knockers.

'A bluecap enthusiast?'

She chortled, though I didn't see what was funny. 'No, dear boy. I'm something of a fae aficionado. That is to say, I study faeries.'

I could *hear* the unnecessary 'ae' she put into the word. It's the archaic (and, frankly, poncy) way of spelling 'fairies' – or, more accurately, 'those savage little winged bastards that don't deserve to be in pleasant children's stories'.

'I certainly hoped to discover some bluecaps on my travels here. They are such an elusive sprite.' Bernie beamed around the room at her assorted company. 'But I must say that I never *dreamed* that a gentleman like Goron would actually *knock* on my door!'

'I tried the windows but it were locked,' Goron supplied.

'And such lovely company he's been, too. Such fun stories! Did you know Goron's people still live in abandoned mines all throughout Cornwall? I suppose you all come from the same place, don't you? You have such a wonderful culture.' This she said to Ang, before turning back to me as though I were her student. 'They used to dig out the tin, right alongside our boys. But now they mine piskey dust! Isn't that *marvellous?*'

Bernice was hard to keep up with. She overflowed with enthusiasm like a burst water main. And it, along with her overly quaint surroundings, told me another thing: she was a tourist.

She'd come here, *here*, to a comfortable holiday B&B with a rustic farmhouse aesthetic, to find knockers and bluecaps and other 'fae' creatures. Except, the way she'd said the word proved she didn't know what it meant. Knockers were not fairies. Nor were bluecaps. And generally speaking, actual fairies were not things you wanted to find, under any circumstances.

I could just imagine her out on the moors in her tweed suit, looking under rocks with a butterfly net in one hand and a cup of tea gently stewing on a tussock in the background.

'Fancy that,' I said, when Bernie's gushing finally subsided. I swung a glance at Goron, reclining again in the armchair. 'Sounds like you two are best friends. Practically told her your life story, eh, Goron?'

He shuffled backwards into the cushions. 'Old news though, innit? Most folks knows about knockers. Don't you worry lass, I ain't mentioned your kin at all,' he added to Ang.

Bernie picked up her journal and ushered me closer to take a look. She licked a finger and turned a few pages, revealing neat, curly handwriting and a rough portrait sketch.

'That's Goron, is it?' I asked, nodding to the pointed face drawn underneath a domed hard hat.

'Yes, indeed! It's so rare that the fauna is willing to sit still for a portrait. I wish I had brought my paints.' She looked up wistfully, and I followed her gaze to a brown satchel hanging from a hook. 'You'd think photography would be the answer, wouldn't you? But I can never get the darned thing to focus properly.'

'Well, of course not–' I stopped myself, looking back at the journal. Bernie's other sketches were a mix of detailed landscapes – a specific arrangement of standing stones or a cave set into a craggy peak – and half formed shadows of vague, animal-like shapes.

Tourist, I reminded myself.

Who would try to capture the likeness of a fairy – or any uncanny creature, for that matter – on camera? You'd need more than just a lens to bring them into focus. A special type of mind, for instance. One that had gotten used to hunting for the frayed edge of the real, to seeing past the blurred false impression: to unfocusing your eyes to see what's really there. At least, that's how Cora had once described it to me. And we'd both practiced to become pros.

A camera will just give you a blur, no matter how still your subject sits. This is why Nessie remains a hoax despite presiding over her loch for a hundred years, and why Bigfoot will forever be a fuzzy man in a gorilla suit to all but the most trained eye.

'You've been at this a long time, have you?' I said, flicking through the pages. I was also ignoring the antics behind me, as it seemed that Branok and Merouda had decided to start jumping up and down on the other armchair while Ang tried to scold them like children. Meanwhile, Goron was egging them on with alternating admonishments ('Take them boots off!') and encouragement ('Try them silky pillows if ye wanna real bounce!').

Bernie didn't seem to take any notice. 'Oh, I've been hunting for fairies since I was a girl,' she said. 'I always believed, you see, and Mother knew many things which she passed on to me. These earlier sketches are hers. When I was nine, my father went to live with the fairies, you see. Such an explorer! They invited him, don't you know.'

'Ye-es.' I stared at the early drawings by Bernice's mother. They flaunted petite human-like figures with butterfly wings and flower dresses. Petals in their hair and leaves for skirts. 'And he never came back, I expect.'

'Oh, no, of course not. You can't return from Fairyland. But it's such an honour that they asked him to go! How could he refuse? I'm very proud. I hope that I might follow him one day.' She clasped her hands to her chest. 'I've made such progress. Let me show you something. Won't be a tick.'

She disappeared again into the other room, amid sounds of rummaging. I stared at the book, apparently her life's work and possibly greatest sentimental item, and marvelled that she'd left it alone in the hands of an unkempt stranger, three knockers, and a coblyn.

'Trusting, isn't she?' I murmured to no one in particular.

Ang had finally subdued the other knockers by pouring them all another cup of tea, and now stood with her back against the wall, arms crossed in a temper. She caught my eye and stomped over. I angled the journal down for her to see.

'Them's fairies, are they, *gwas?*' She clambered onto a footstool and pointed to the smiling, frolicking creatures on the page.

'No,' I said quietly.

'What are they, then?'

'A fiction.' I flipped to a later page. Bernie's sketches were rougher, capturing only the barest essence of beasts: the outline of a lurking shadow, a sense of tooth, a smidge of claw. There were a variety of shapes, none of them – I hoped – fairylike. One with pointed ears and folded cap might be another knocker spotted years ago. A hastily scribbled figure with a flash of fins was likely some kind of merfolk. Another, bird-like shape could be any of a whole host of uncanny avian creatures, though Bernie's annotation labelled it simply as a 'talking corvid' – more likely a trickster having some fun with her.

I closed the book with a frown. 'Let's just say I suspect Bernie's dear old dad left the family for other reasons, and her mother was either too soft or too daft to tell her the truth about it.'

'Ah,' said Ang, 'ye thinks he ran off wi' a Loose Woman.'

'I think that would make him a Loose Man, actually.'

A crash from the other room interrupted us, followed by a shrill, '*Oh, goodness gracious!*'

Ang scratched her nose. 'Think we should go help, *gwas?*'

I tugged uncomfortably at my coat. 'I think that's her bedroom, Ang. I'm sure whatever it is, she's fine–'

'*Help! Please!*'

'–but on the other hand, maybe we should take a look.'

The knockers were already peering round the door. ''Ere, what's the racket fer?' said Branok, before he was promptly lifted off his feet and yanked into the room.

'*Tas!*' Merouda shrieked, diving in after him.

Goron darted back from the door. He held an arm out to Ang. 'Careful now! It's bleddy *piskies!*'

'You're joking!' I exclaimed. 'How'd they get in?'

'Looks like she had 'em in cages.'

'You mean she'd *caught* them? Why would *anyone* . . . never mind.'

As my hand touched the doorknob, an ear-splitting *crush* ripped the air and threw us onto the ground. I waited for my vision to stop wobbling.

'Everyone okay?' I said dizzily.

Goron lifted his head and grunted. 'That'll be Merouda's new toy, I s'pect.'

'I hates that monkey,' Ang groaned.

Once upright (or at least bent over), we crept to the door and prodded it open.

It was indeed a bedroom, though you could barely tell under all the frills.

Bernie was out cold on the floor, having apparently been dropped from a height. I knew this, because her torn tweed jacket was still pinned to the ceiling by cutlery.

And then the piskies came into view, catching the eye like stains on a carpet.

They were the colour of tea stains, too. Each only a few inches tall, some clasped their bald heads in their spindly hands, still reeling from the cymbal crash. Their skin crackled like antique paper as they moved, flitting in jarring stop-motion sequence through the air, looking for all the world like a poorly rendered sepia animation on top of the room.

Branok was still dusting himself off, while Merouda swatted at nearby piskies with a frilly pillow.

'Be off, yer nasty bleeders,' she shouted.

One piskey caught her pillow with its clawed foot and swung her across the room. She crashed into the nightstand in a heap.

'*Narsty knockers!*' the piskey screeched. 'It knocks on rocks and *eats dirty fat cocks!*'

Branok growled. 'What did you jus' say about my Merouda?'

The other piskies shook off their dizziness and began to scream at him.

'*Sluts!* They dig like

                 mutts they smell like

rotten nuts!

           They *fuck* like rats and

                       lie their *bastard* brats

on *shit-smeared mats!*'

The school-yard cursing was almost funny. Except with every rhyme a piskey divebombed our necks, looking to sink pincer sharp teeth into the skin. Each savage little fiend was only as tall as my index finger, but their bites packed a punch.

'Where the hell have all these come from?' I yelled, swatting madly around my face. They swarmed in and out of view so it was hard to count how many we faced, but I guessed it was in the region of twenty.

A piskey stopped and hovered at my eye-level. Milk-white pupils narrowed at me.

It hissed. 'Bitch woman caught us in an iron trap. But we throw friends on ferrous teeth, slap slap *crack!*'

I followed its pointing finger to where a large birdcage with spindly iron bars lay battered open on the floor. Bits of bloodied piskey were caught in its door hinges.

I slipped one hand inside my trench coat. 'Okay. So you killed some of your own to get free. Time to leave now, right?'

'Oh no,' it rasped. 'Won't leave yet. Not til we've repaid our debt. We'll snag you all *in a filthy net.*'

The last words came with a rip of fabric and the clatter of curtain rails torn off the walls.

'Argh,' I said, muffled under the heavy frills of Bernice's pink curtains.

The cloth pulled tight against my face, smothering me. I could hear the piskies' shrieking titters and feel their hard tugs on the fabric. Behind that were the sounds of other struggle all around the room. My hand was still lodged inside my coat, clamped on the iron horseshoe which would save our hides if only it weren't for these *bloody curtains* pinning me like a corpse in a comedically rolled up rug.

I strained to get my mouth moving. I probably had enough breath to shout one last thing. *'The Fairy Queen will be very angry if you hurt us!'*

The titters stopped. For a moment just the buzzing of their wings filled my ears.

Then fabric loosened and slipped off my head. I was glad to hear the frantic gasps of my friends also inhaling air.

Pale eyes glared again at mine. 'What do you know of the Fairy Queen? Why should she care if we split you open at the *seams?*'

Quick. Think of every sinister fairy tale, rhyme, and song that skulks in your childhood hindbrain. Somewhere in there is the Evil Queen: the vestigial remains of our species memory for something everyone once knew to be true. Stray to the land of the fairies, and the Queen will snatch you away. She's a lingering, malicious dream on the edge of the stories we tell to our children.

And beyond that, I knew absolutely nothing about her.

'We're here to do her bidding,' I proclaimed. I was still restrained from the neck down with piskies clinging onto me, but now I had their attention. From the corner of my eye, I saw Ang stealthily untangling herself from the deadly drapes.

I quickly jerked my head at Bernice, sprawled on the carpet. 'This lady is very important. We need her to . . . to continue spreading the lie of fairies to humans everywhere. She believes they're harmless. She will pave a way for you to move through the world more freely! The Queen wants her kept safe, in fact, for your own benefit.'

The piskies erupted into a high-pitched squealing chatter, which could just as easily have been laughter.

'It thinks Queenie cares for piskies!' they shrieked. 'It doesn't know its game is *very risky.*'

I drew on every ounce of confidence I owned – and I don't just mean the bottled stuff in the boot of my car. 'How *dare* you speak so poorly of Her Majesty! She'll drag you back to fairyland if you continue!'

The piskey in my face spat with laughter. 'Doesn't know, doesn't know,' it cackled. 'The Fairy Queen walks among you. Better watch out or she'll snatch *you.* Hail Queen Mab! And boy, she's mad!'

The piskies shrieked again and chimed in with more rhymes. 'Long has she escaped her cell!'

'Betwixt the realms she now doth dwell!'

'She'll take you as her tithe to Hell!'

'An' I'll be there t'greet ye.' Ang rose up; a grubby, out of place heroine on top of the floral bedsheets, a horseshoe outstretched between both

hands and a wicked glint in her eyes. 'And ye best afear it, *'cuz I'll smack ye well!'*

She swiped through the throng of piskies with the horseshoe. They scattered, squealing and clamouring. Ang's next swing caught three of them: they dropped from the air with a sickening, sizzling sound.

The lead piskey screamed, 'Catch it! Bind it! Stop it!' They released their hold on me completely and descended on Ang in a swarm. She countered by throwing out a fistful of iron nails. Suddenly the piskies had lost a third of their numbers.

I shrugged myself free and brandished my own horseshoe. 'We can do this the hard way,' I shouted, 'or the very hard way!'

Their enraged buzzing filled the air as the piskies turned as one toward me again. Their heads tracked the movement of the iron. I sensed they were calculating how best to knock it out of my hand.

A metallic *snap* punctuated the buzz. Goron put away a pocket-sized pair of bolt cutters and held up a spiky section of the iron birdcage. He passed a prong each to Branok and Merouda and announced, 'Looks like a whole lotta piskey dust in this room, lads.'

'Could enchant a whole *engine* wi' this much fuel,' Mcrouda said darkly.

I sidled to the window and pushed it open.

The lead piskey hissed at us, long and low. 'Nasty, nasty knockers. She'll come for you too. Queenie will get you one day, if piskies don't *gut you first* as prey.'

The swarm rushed past me – a quick sting of teeth on my cheek – and out the window into the night.

Goron admired Ang, still in her fighting stance. 'Cor. That were right good, lass.'

'Stop it or I'll knock yer eyes out,' she replied, jumping down form the bed.

Merouda kicked Bernie's prone body. 'She dead or what?'

'She's breathing,' I said. I kneeled next to her for a closer inspection. 'I don't see any blood. I think she'll be okay. Help me get her onto the bed, would you?'

I imagined, from the little I knew of her, that Bernie would be genuinely delighted to know she was manhandled into bed by three knockers and a coblyn dragging her by the armpits and ankles (and one human self-consciously trying not to touch anything inappropriate).

We cleaned up the room, sort of. The knockers fastidiously collected the remains of the dead piskies – I didn't want to know what they'd be doing with them. I stopped by Bernie's journal on the way out and flipped to the latest page.

Taking great care, I wrote in capital letters, USE STRONGER IRON, and underlined it three times. She didn't seem like the type to be put off by an incident like this. You could only hope she'd learn from her mistakes.

I waited in the car awhile with the knockers, until Ang slipped silently into the passenger seat. 'She's wakin' up,' she said. 'Looked a bit confuddled first, but then sharp as a pick in no time.'

Goron nodded. 'She'll be right. Our lot'll keep an eye on her fer a bit now as well. It were a good cup o' tea.'

I wondered, on the drive back to Mên-an-Tol, whether I should feel sorry for Bernice. She was chasing a dream she knew very little about, and on false pretences, no less. She wanted to go and live with the fairies, for goodness' sake. She had no idea what she was asking for there.

Neither did I, if I was being honest. Fairies, in my circles, turned up mostly as warnings.

Don't look for them. Pray you never find them. And if they find you? Run as fast as you possibly can.

Piskies were as close as I'd ever come to real fairies. They'd shown up on the Black Market only a few years ago, some idiot flaunting them in a cage at the annual gathering of traders. What a mess that had been. He'd probably been a bit like Bernie.

He ended up nothing like Bernie, what with being fed through a mincing machine. It'd belonged to a merchant of mythical meats, who wouldn't stop screaming for days afterwards. Piskies were banned from Markets now.

I shuddered those thoughts away. We'd had a narrow escape tonight. Iron was good protection, but you can't carry a horseshoe in your pocket everywhere. 'Ain't you glad I picked one up too,' Ang said to me afterwards, with a wily grin.

'You're a good partner,' I told her. 'Best back-up I could have.'

We pulled up at the dirt track leading to Mên-an-Tol, and I parked the car. The walk seemed inviting now. I could use it to clear my head.

'You go on ahead. I'll catch up,' I said to the others.

Ang's eyes glinted in the moonlight as she cast me a look over her shoulder.

'I'm fine,' I said. 'Just fancy a stroll.'

She shrugged and trotted off with the knockers.

I stopped to breathe in the cool night air. What a waste of time it had all been. All that effort, and we had nothing to show for it.

I knew this was not, strictly speaking, true. We now had the hospitality of Goron's knockers at our disposal, and I was certain to acquire some good business there. I'd been itching for a heftier sort of trade recently. Pawning off mouldy charms and feeble tonics on street corners was beginning to wear thin. Normally, I'd be overjoyed at the chance to fill my pockets with genuinely magical merchandise.

So why was that excitement eluding me?

I let my feet drag as I started down the track to Mên-an-Tol. A cloud shrouded the moon for several moments, plunging my path into deeper darkness. *How fine it is, to walk in shadows*, I thought. How exhilarating, to not quite know if your feet will meet the ground.

Then the clouds drifted apart, and mundane moonlight illuminated the tedious reality of a muddy track on a barren moor.

I wished it had been Quiet Eyes.

Disappointment, that's what this melancholy was. I was disappointed that it wasn't Quiet Eyes we'd found lodging in a Cornish country bed and breakfast – as if I'd really thought we'd find her in such a place. As if we really *wanted* to find her, at all.

But I think, perhaps, I really did.

I tried to shake off the thought, but it was already there, worming a cold little trail through my brain. How *exciting* it had all been. To dance with death and power and intrigue, to linger on the edge of answers before having them snatched away, to play a game with invisible players and feel the coyness in a smile that you never actually see.

How thrilling it is, to walk in shadows.

Mên-an-Tol loomed low ahead. It was a disconcerting set of shapes in the darkness, where gloom merged with stone and stretched their silhouettes into aliens in the moonlight.

As I drew near, one tall shadow detached from the rest.

'Ah,' I said. 'I'm going to go ahead and guess you're not part of a welcome party.'

I couldn't make out any features, but the figure's height told me it wasn't a knocker. So, the more likely alternative was: trouble.

'Hello, Jack.'

The voice froze me. It contained a soft slur in the enunciation, an underlying hum of amusement, and a coy smile which I had never truly seen but knew very well.

'You needn't be afraid,' Quiet Eyes said, before I could choke out the witty greeting that had stalled on my tongue.

I shook myself sensible. 'I'm not.'

A chuckle.

'I have something you want, right?' I said, vying to beat her to her own words. 'That's why you're here, isn't it?'

Another, softer laugh. 'No, Jack. You do not have anything that I want.'

'But the e–' I clamped down on my tongue. She must know about the phoenix egg we'd stolen from her. She *must*. What other reason could she possibly have for seeking me out? I was sure she could read the thoughts as they ran across my face.

'Oh, Jack. I don't care for such trivial things. Baines and Grayle have their prize, and you have yours.'

I spluttered. 'I wouldn't call a phoenix egg *trivial*.'

'No longer of consequence.' She waved a hand, as if waving my consternation out of existence. 'It is, what would you say? Old news.'

'You don't even care that we took it from you? Aren't you here for revenge, payback, *anything?*'

Her expression seemed to twist. 'Do you want revenge from me, Jack?'

I swallowed. My stomach was coiling itself into knots. Something was about to happen. 'Why are you here, then?'

She took a step forward into moonlight. I felt like the play of light and shadow perhaps gave me a better sense, for the first time, of her true shape. As if I could trust a mere reflection more than the solid reality: the way the light gleamed an outline of hair, the way darkness moulded a shape out of voided space. I drew contours in my mind like an ethereal dot-to-dot. Still, all I came up with was generically 'woman', and even that left me questioning how and why I'd drawn such a conclusion, and was everything I thought maybe based on her voice alone, and was my only true recollection of her still only a smile and a faintly Parisian accent, if either of those were true at all?

The shapes shrank away, leaving behind the same vagueness of unfamiliarity as the rest of her features.

Then words tripped off her tongue which I knew would be the ruin of me.

'I have a job for you, Jack.'

The moon dipped behind a cloud, concealing my complete lack of shame. 'What's the job?' I said.

'Piskey dust,' she replied softly. 'I need you to acquire it for me.'

'You don't fancy asking them yourself?' I nodded at the dark shapes of Mên-an-Tol. 'Or, forgive me for being candid, but I suspect there's good reason you wouldn't want to approach the relatives of creatures whom you have, shall we say, kidnapped.'

'We shall not say.' She sounded distinctly amused. 'You take me for a kidnapper, Jack?'

'The evidence is stacking up.'

'Such an unkind accusation.' Did her eyelashes flutter? Was there a pout on her lips?

I saw you shoot one of your own men in cold blood, I thought. *Just to prove a point.*

At a more sensible time, I might have tried to calm my thudding nerves and talk myself an escape route. But I was already soaring on adrenaline and ready to push my luck as far as it would go.

I gave a nonchalant shrug and gestured to Mên-an-Tol's entrance stone. 'After you, then. I don't see why you can't fetch the fancy dust yourself. I also – I have to say – don't see anything in it for me. I'm sure the knockers will give you a really *warm* welcome.'

Something subtle changed in her demeanour; like in the way an adder coils before a strike.

'Is the location of your missing coblyns price enough?' she said, voice suddenly clipped of any accent. 'Do not try to play with me, Jack. You only waste both our time.'

Damn. That *was* a tasty prize. 'So why do you need *me*–'

'Your answer is 'Yes,' Jack,' she interrupted. 'We both know it is 'Yes.'

You will take this job. Stop pretending to entertain the notion that you won't.'

My eyes veered back to the stones, as if drawn by a magnet. What would have happened if Ang or one of the knockers had poked their head out at that moment? Would I have bottled it? (Would they have bottled Quiet Eyes?)

But no one saved me from this conversation, or from the deal I was about to make. It was a good deal, after all – right? I'd be a fool not to take it.

It was only piskey dust.

'It's a deal,' I said.

Episode 5: Merry Maidens

After our brush with Bernice and the piskies, it was only natural that Ang and I set ourselves up for a brief stay of business in our new Cornish surrounds.

With it being the literal arse-end of the country on the most south-western tip of England, it had been a while since I'd last stomped Cornwall's rugged moors and trekked its craggy coastline. Apparently, it would be a while before I'd get to do so again – because our lodgings turned out to be underground.

'Ye'll be right comfy,' Goron assured us, as we hiked across a wet field to his home. We'd set out from Mên-an-Tol almost as soon as we'd arrived there. Goron explained the hidden glen was only a nearby workshop, convenient for its abundance in left-over piskey dust.

'Didden wanna say in me letter, in case it were thieved,' he said, bringing us to an old stone ruin. He pointed down a deep, square hole in the ground. 'This be where we really live. In the Ding Dong mines.'

I looked into the darkness of the shaft, while fighting to keep a straight face. ' . . . I'm sorry. What is it called?'

'Ding Dong,' Goron replied.

'Right. Right. Ding Dong as in . . . ?'

'As in Ding Dong Mines, innit?' He threw a doubtful glance at Ang. 'Is he hard o' hearing or jus' stupid?'

'Sounds very traditional,' I said quickly. 'Very, hah, profound.'

Ding Dong mines. What a gift. If you threw a little green cap on each knocker and wiped the genetically-ingrained scowl from their faces then you'd have a right merry band of dwarves fit for a fairy tale. All they were missing was a lost princess and a tune. *Hi ho, hi ho . . .*

Goron summoned a lift for us – a hidden knocker contraption that rose from the depths with a wobbly creaking that made my stomach lurch. We crowded onto the wooden platform. I hugged my fold-up table to my chest with one arm and clung onto the little railing with the other as we descended into the earth.

The insides of the Ding Dong mines were much less quaint than their name. Ang's lantern flared with a welcome glow from the bluecap, illuminating the hewn dirt passing by. The smell of damp mud and rock engulfed us, and the encroaching darkness gave me horrible flashbacks to my brief sojourn in Ang's underground home.

Thankfully, the trip to descend the mineshaft was blessedly short. Stepping out at the bottom, I was pleasantly surprised to find I could stand nearly upright in the tunnel. The knockers had had the run of this mine system for so long that they'd continued hollowing out the main chambers until they were really quite roomy (for knockers, that is, which meant I still had to stoop through most of them).

An abundance of candlelight also made the atmosphere less oppressive, and I found myself wondering how the knockers had kept such a large supply of candles over the years. They burned merrily in neat little alcoves all along the passageway. I absent-mindedly picked one off its rock-hewn shelf and stared in bemusement: it was a plastic, battery-powered tealight, the kind with a static 'flame' and synthetic flicker, to the delight of children and middle-aged women everywhere.

'Fireproof, innit,' said Goron, somewhere around my knees. 'Open flames be a narsty risk in a mine.'

'You trade for the batteries, do you?'

His teeth flashed white in the dark. 'Trades fer many things, we do.'

I set the plastic tealight down and ducked under a low-hanging beam to follow him. 'About that. We hoped to install a temporary commercial station within your grand accommodations, if you and your companions are amenable?'

'He means we want t'sell ye stuff,' Ang said. 'Gots space fer a table, aye?'

'Fer you, my bewty, you can have the whole stope.'

As he said this, we crossed the threshold into a massive chamber. The high, curved ceiling meant I could finally stand straight and stretch out my back. There was more than enough room to swing a cat – or several cats tied together – if you were so inclined.

I couldn't see far into the gloom of this space, but my eye was drawn to several clusters of blueish glimmers: bluecap lanterns, moving with their owners in the dark. They gave an impression of pockets of activity as small groups of knockers went about their work.

Ang threw back her head to survey the rock ceiling. 'What were ye taking out o' here, then?' she asked.

'Tin,' Goron replied proudly. '*Kernow's* finest.' He tramped away into the shadows at the edges of the room. 'C'mon lads, get the lights up!'

'*Kernow* be knocker-speak fer Cornwall,' Ang whispered to me. 'I been pickin' up some o' their nonsense from his letters.'

Suddenly, there was starlight.

Ang gasped. I admit to nearly dropping my table.

On all sides, around and above, little lights twinkled, as though a net of stars had been hung over every surface. Goron reappeared, grinning. 'Pretty, right?'

As my eyes readjusted, I began to make out odd shapes encasing the lights. Here, a string of foam flowers. There, a translucent set of shells. One set blinked on and off like Christmas lights. Next to it glowed a string of bearded cartoon faces of the jolly red man himself. There, another set in the shape of sliced fruit. And yet another was a line of sharks, suspended as if swimming futilely upwards to the surface. There was every variant, in fact, of tacky fairy lights that one might find in any pound shop, knotted together and nailed to the walls at all heights. The clacking of cheap plastic could be heard when knockers brushed past them.

The knockers themselves also occupied much of this cavern – or stope, as Ang corrected me – pressed into the corners and peering down from high ledges. They were quiet, but not hostilely so. Several sipped from steaming mugs.

They were curious, probably, about the outsiders, but overall exuded an air of indifference that said: 'All right, bud. Don't be any trouble, and we'll let you leave on your own terms. Don't be that rude guest who has to be booted out without possession of his trousers or, indeed, his legs. Capiche?'

I took it all in cheerfully. 'Very cosy. Feels like home, eh, Ang?'

'Not like any mine o' mine,' she murmured, still gazing at the lights.

Goron nudged her. 'There's many more sights I can show yer down here, an' all over *Kernow*.'

'Actually,' I butted in, 'there's something that we rather want to show *you*.'

Privacy was at a premium in the mine, but Goron led us to a moderately secluded corner. As if following a secret signal, the other knockers shifted and a soft buzz of chatter filled the air.

'Go on then,' said Goron.

I nodded to Ang and she withdrew the bluecap from her lantern. It curled around her fist and then slithered up her arm, leaving behind the amber phoenix egg in her palm. It was about the size of a duck egg, so looked quite oversized in her small hands.

I kept my voice low. 'We want to know what you make of this.'

Goron tapped his chin. 'S'arock, right?'

'Look closer, *twpsyn*.' Ang said. 'Smells it.'

He did, and made a face.

'Myrrh,' I supplied. 'It's a sap from some tree. But we're more interested in . . . in what it . . . contains . . .'

'Why don't yer crack it open, then?' he asked. 'I gots a hammer, here.'

'No!' Ang and I exclaimed in unison.

I cleared my throat with a fretful little laugh. 'Uh, look. Goron. This is a very delicate matter. We think there's something powerful inside this egg. And we think we probably don't want to let it out. Ever. But – and here's the crucial thing – we want to find out why someone else *would*. You see our problem?'

Goron gave me a thoughtful stare. 'This t'do with our thief of bluecaps and knockers?'

'Yes,' I replied.

'She wants it, do she?'

I tried to tug my thoughts away from the clandestine talk I'd had with Quiet Eyes. 'Well . . . we don't know for sure . . .'

'Her bosses wanted it,' Ang cut in. 'An' we stole it, so we reckons she'll be after us at some point. Best we knows what we carryin'.' She cupped the egg with both hands, like an offering. 'We saw that you and yours have the knowin' o' piskey magics, so we thinks mebbe ye've got some tricks we don't. Can ye help us, or no?'

Goron nodded solemnly. 'No promises, right? But I'll try me best. Does yer know what it is, exactly?'

I watched Ang carefully. There was only the slightest hesitation, but she didn't fail me. 'No,' she said.

'Right then,' said Goron. He looked at me. 'Only yer called it an egg jus' a moment ago.'

'Did I?' I smiled brightly. 'It's certainly egg-shaped, don't you think?'

He glanced at Ang. 'And you ain't gunna tell me how you came by it, neither?'

This time, she visibly grimaced. 'If you don't know, then no one can ask ye, see?'

'An' I s'pose I won't be spreadin' rumours of it fer unfriendly ears to hear? Don't look so surprised, merchant man. This ain't my first dance wi' lies.' Goron held his hand out to Ang for the egg. 'I wish you trusted me more, lass. But I'm helpin' yer, either way.'

'This's an act o' *great* trust,' Ang said quietly. She held his gaze as she dropped the egg into his palm. 'Trustin' you wi' the only clue I have to find mine kin, knocker.'

He bowed his head, though I'm certain I saw the edge of a smile. 'Then I be guardin' it wi' mine own life, coblyn.'

* * *

I left them to it for a while. Goron was keen to show Ang some of his 'instruments' (best not to let the mind wander too much on that) and I was content to explore more of my surroundings.

I found a suitable nook in the middle of the stope where the ground was mostly flat, and unfolded my table in front of the backdrop of fairy lights. This would do nicely.

As I began pulling wares out of a sack, I tried to distract myself by watching the comings and goings of the knockers. They paid me little mind in return. Everyone seemed busy, hurrying to or from some other corner of the mine, and even those at rest gave the impression that it was only for five minutes – *Just a quick tea break, guv.*

I felt lethargic by comparison. Wasting time by adjusting and read-justing the position of the ceremonial daggers next to the ritualistic tea caddy. Counting away seconds by counting out cursed rosary beads and sprigs of dried wolfsbane.

Later, Ang would grill me over why I hadn't been intent on watching Goron get to work on the phoenix egg straight away. 'Looked like you two needed some privacy,' I'd joke, and swiftly sidle away from her prying gaze.

The truth was, I was no longer at all certain of the significance of our phoenix egg. My assumptions had been knocked on their arse after witnessing Quiet Eyes' complete indifference to the subject . . .

I'd been so *sure* she was coming after us to steal it back. But she spoke as if it was of no consequence, as if Baines and Grayle didn't care a jot that a legendary object of untold power was in our possession.

Do they even know? I wondered. What if she simply never told them?

Had we put all our mythical eggs, so to speak, in one basket?

Of course, I could have talked all this out with Ang. But it wasn't the right time to tell her about the deal with Quiet Eyes. I'd need to ease her into the idea. If she needed to know, at all.

Still, a twinge of doubt coiled through my thoughts.

So it was an act of self-preservation, in this strange underground starlight, that I made my hands busy in a futile attempt to drown out the unease rippling through my mind.

* * *

'May I have your attention, please!' my voice rang out through the tunnels of the Ding Dong mines. The sales patter was familiar and reassuring. 'Roll up, roll up, and other such old-fashioned nonsense! Prepare to be amazed and bedazzled! Such delights as you've never seen! All for sale, for a limited time only!'

In the dim light of the cavern, only a vague sound of shuffling greeted my call. A few knockers looked up, but otherwise returned to what they were doing.

Ang watched me deflate and nudged my knee. 'Lemme try, *gwas*. I speaks their language, like.'

'I didn't think you knew Cornish?'

She tutted. 'Not like that, *twpsyn.*'

She clambered on top of our table and stuck her thumbs into her belt. Striking a cavalier pose among the potion bottles, she cleared her throat. 'We gots pies, lads!'

Suddenly, scrabbling and chattering filled the stope.

'That's cheating,' I said.

She grinned at me. 'Learned it from you, I did.'

'And I'm very proud. *A free pie to our first five purchases!*'

I had to shout over the top of the growing hubbub. There's nothing that gets the attention of a knocker faster than a bit of pastry. I plucked a curio from the table and held it aloft.

'Our newest acquisition, the Melancholic Tonic! Need a dose of solemnity for a special occasion? Do you want to create a poetically brooding persona? It's all the rage!'

'What's in it?' asked the nearest patron-in-potentia. A dozen pairs of eyes swivelled my way.

I turned up the melodrama in my voice. 'A truly woeful combination. The base is mixed from the tears of a career clown; a deeply profound body is provided by the mulched works of Schopenhauer fed into a blender; and then of course, it's rounded off with the most vital of seasonings: the petals of a forget me not crushed into the leaves of a chamaebatia plant.'

The knocker scratched his nose. 'Sounds like a recipe fer misery, if y'ask me.'

'Yes, that's– Never mind. How about . . . this!' I dropped the tonic and pushed forward an ornate brass compass nestled in a velvet box. 'This delightful device will point the way to your heart's desire! Always know the direction of your deepest ambitions! Never be stumped by existential paralysis again!'

He prodded it, unimpressed. 'Does it point North, too?'

' . . . Yes.'

I knew Ang was muffling a snigger, but she hid it behind her neckerchief and started playing one of the Tibetan singing bowls for the amusement of the crowd. It produced a clear, high note, like the continuous ringing of a bell, and the knockers listened with eyes wide in rapt fascination.

My knocker, on the other hand, still stared moodily at the compass. He chewed what looked to be an old breadcrust while he made up his mind. 'I'll 'ave it, then,' he finally said. 'What's yer price?'

I nearly sagged with relief. 'How about a small measure of piskey dust? Just a pinch, and it's all yours!'

'Yer what?' The knocker's face screwed up in amusement.

'Piskey dust,' I repeated. A blooming silence alerted me to the fact that Ang's bowl had stopped singing, and the knockers had all turned their attention on me. I blinked in the face of a dozen cold stares. 'Come now, it's like actual dust to you people, isn't it?

''avin' a laugh, you are!' the knocker scoffed.

I patted my pockets. 'I *do* have a specimen of bottled laughter around here somewhere, but that's besides the point. I'm here to trade. Valuables for valuables!'

The knocker stepped up onto a rock to reach eye-level with my table, so he could sneer at it properly. 'Nothin' here as valuable as piskey dust.'

'That can't be true,' I persisted. 'You'd trade me a . . . a metal charm infused with the stuff, wouldn't you? All I'm asking for is the raw ingredient. Less work for you, surely!'

The knocker left in a huff. The remaining crowd became decidedly more leery as well. They prodded a few of my trinkets with disdain and began to disperse, despite Ang's efforts to re-engross them in the singing bowl.

She gave up and threw down the brass vessel with its wooden baton. Jostling aside a stack of printed curses, she sat on the table with her legs swinging off the edge. 'What di' we do wrong, *gwas?*' she said, frowning at the retreating backs of our unwilling customers.

'Beats me,' I replied, scratching my head.

I spotted Branok, who'd been hanging on at the back of the pack, puffing on his pipe while our misfortunes unfolded. Now he sidled up to the table, cleaning his pipe on his waistcoat. 'Wouldn'a be askin' fer piskey dust, if I were you.'

'Why not? Seems like a reasonable proposition to me,' I said.

'Ain't, though.'

'I don't see what's so—'

'Listen mate, you'll start offendin' if yer carry on so,' Branok insisted. 'S'like askin' a farrier to gi' you all his iron.'

'But the thing is, you see, I'm not asking for all of it, am I? Just a . . . sizeable measure.'

He knocked his pipe on the edge of my table, spilling spent tobacco onto the floor. 'What fer? We gots other magicks to trade.'

Ang intervened with a welcome note of support. 'Me partner has a nose for novelties, see. Piskey dust be useless to him, but he wants it 'cuz no one else has it. We're not out to steal your own trade,' she added shrewdly. 'I don't know the workin's of it, neither. But t'have some o' your fine dust in our stock, well . . . we'd be a right talking point everywhere we go.'

'How's that help us, then?' asked Branok.

Ang answered with cunning confidence. 'People would come from all over and ask where we found such treasure. We could proudly say to them, 'twas knockers what give it us. What a decent an' upright folk, I'd say, such as worth doing plenty o' business with. Surely worth travellin' miles to find those same knockers and pay good money to yeself.'

I wanted to applaud. I couldn't have hoped for a better load of fallacious flattery from Ang. Branok, if not entirely convinced, certainly seemed to be listening. It's true that money talks, and it *always* has something interesting to say.

Branok's eyes fell back to his pipe. 'Maybe them folks could also come to learn the name of Merouda in relation to the great works of knockers. What a fine thing that would be, eh?'

'She'd be at the forefront o' my mind, that's fer sure,' Ang said.

'Good t'hear. Now, I ain't offering you nuthin' of ours, understand?' Branok spoke to the table with an idle tone, as if merely recounting a mildly interesting anecdote. 'But if you were to happen upon some abandoned piskey dust . . . I s'pose none could blame yer for helping yeselves to a portion. Provided you left plenty behind for knockers still, aye?'

I leaned in hungrily. 'Mistakes do happen. Supplies left unguarded, that kind of thing.'

'Oh, I wouldn't call this lot unguarded.' Branok lifted the pipe to his mouth, chewing thoughtfully. 'Yer might even say it's *so* well guarded that it's not being of any use to knockers right now.'

'I see. Branok, are we talking about piskey dust which is not, in fact, in your current possession?'

'Thassit.'

I sighed. 'All right. What do we need to do?'

'We stealin' again?' Ang said.

Branok arched an eyebrow in her direction. 'Surely I ain't doing business with thieves. This ain't theft, anyhow. Can't steal a thing from someone it don't belong to in the first place.'

'I quite agree,' I chipped in.

'What about them piskies it belonged to in the first place?' said Ang.

Branok waved the question away. 'Gone, in't they. Ain't too many piskies left round these parts since all the iron went up. Some still live in the hills, as far away from people as they can get. But most left, and they left their piskey glens behind, full o' that precious dust of theirs. You've seen one, at Mên-an-Tol. We just moved in after they left. There's more like it all round here.'

'Aha. And I expect *other* things may have moved into those,' I said.

'Right.'

'I imagine we can assist with a neighbourhood relocation project. Any knowledge of the current . . . tenants?'

Branok smiled without any humour. 'A Green Man, it be.'

Oh dear. But still, I reflected, this might be the best offer we'd get. What was the alternative? Steal from the knockers' own supply?

That would probably be easier, pointed out my somewhat treacherous common sense. But I suspected that wasn't a line I'd be able to convince Ang to cross.

I clapped my hands together. 'Green Man, eh? I can surmise why you haven't raided this piskey glen yourself. But I'm sure we'll manage. It's a deal, Branok.'

'No deal here,' he said. 'I'm just givin' you a location. Up to you what yer do wi' it.'

'And we're very grateful,' I said.

IIe strolled away, leaving behind a detailed map scrawled on my totally authentic copy of the Shroud of Turin.

After we'd packed up our makeshift stall, Ang and I spread out the fabric and scrutinised Branok's directions under the glow of the knockers' twinkling fairy lights and Ang's bluecap. My heart sank as I deciphered his written notes.

'Ley lines,' I said heavily. 'He reckons you can only get to it by ley lines.'

'They bad news, *gwas?*' said Ang. She was perched on a slight outcrop of stone opposite me, looking down on the map. The bluecap, free from its lantern, appeared to rest on her shoulder.

'Very bad news.' I passed her a packet of crisps. The knockers had been kind enough to feed us during our stay, and we'd learned they'd modernised somewhat from a solely pastry-based diet. On this particular evening, the enticing smell of burgers and chips was wafting over to us from one corner of the mine. Apparently Merouda and a group of other young knockers had hit up a fast food joint earlier, though what they traded for the meal I have no idea. Magic cutlery, perhaps?

I shook the smell out of my nose. 'We'll need a lift. Because there's no way I'm stepping into a ley line by myself.'

'Don't want to travel unprepared, like?' Ang said, crunching through the packet.

'Exactly.'

'Not like when you stepped onto that ghost ship, right?'

'Not at all like– What?'

'That time you nearly drowned us both travelling to another dimension.' She pointed a crisp at me. 'Or like that time you got us trapped journeyin' through the Nether. You ain't one fer travelling blindly, eh *gwas?*'

'This is different. I already *know* that ley lines are bad.'

'So if ye didn't know, ye wouldn't care?'

'They say ignorance is bliss.'

'Is stupidity, more like.'

'Eat your crisps.'

As I contemplated tomorrow's perils, I allowed myself to enjoy the cosy ambience of the stope. High above, two knockers had climbed the walls to replace batteries in several strings of lights. Away to our right, a small cooking-fire held court to a handful of older knockers sipping cups of beer.

We'll need to take some alcohol, I added to my internal checklist. *Good stuff, too. Won't get away with cheap grog. A bit of chocolate wouldn't go amiss, either.*

'Full moon tomorrow, isn't it?' I said aloud.

'Aye,' said Ang.

'That's good timing. We'll need to meet with the Maidens.' Under my breath, I added, 'Let's hope they've forgiven me for last time.'

Ang wiped the salt from her hands and jumped down from the rock. The bluecap followed, clinging to her arm before slipping back into the lantern. 'What's that, *gwas?*'

'Nothing, just thinking aloud.' I rustled around the carrier bag of food from the knockers and found a cold chicken sandwich and a packet of pork scratchings. Practically a feast. 'Eat up, then we'll get some kip. Busy day tomorrow before we embark on our noble quest.'

'What's noble about pinching fairy dust off've some leafy squatter?'

'You heard me agree to leave some for the knockers, didn't you? Any endeavour where we're not keeping the entire haul to ourselves sounds pretty noble to me, Ang. Magnanimous, even.'

Ang lowered her voice. 'Seems t'me we could do the job, then come back sayin' we failed. Too fierce a monster it be, not worth trying for.'

'Now *that* is a good idea.' I looked at her with genuine surprise. 'Is it possible that I've rubbed off on you?'

'I takes me business duties seriously.' She rearranged the pile of stock bags around her, nestling down into a comfortable nook between the hexed corn dollies and the sack of sacrificial poppets. 'It's you an' me, right? That's what partners means. So long as you're all in on findin' my kin, then I'm all in on yer nefarious business. No secrets between us, eh? Jus' the rest o' the world.'

'I'm lucky to have a friend like you, Ang.'

She grinned. 'Too right.'

Soon her rattling snores – in no way gentle or melodic – nevertheless leant a soothing familiarity to the character of the mine. Though the knockers had wound down in parts, there was still a low buzz of activity, a general coming-and-going of groups around the sleeping bodies, some that roused to go off to work and others that were just now bedding down. The knockers around the fire had been joined by a few more, and now they poked at a stew in an iron pot. The daytime drone of conversation had merely dulled to a hum, and still carried ripples of laughter and occasional arguments within it.

They were the sounds of family, and kinship – of mutual dependence, and trust.

I tried to listen to all of it for a while, and then none of it. Ang had lived in a place like this. Knockers were more predisposed to travel than coblynau, but still, they always returned home. Loyalty to family, first.

The ambiguous image of Quiet Eyes encroached on my train of thought, unwelcome but inevitable.

No secrets, Ang? You should know me better than that.

That's what I tried to tell myself, anyway, as the sneaky stain of guilt leached into my plans.

I really ought to tell Ang about the deal with Quiet Eyes. She'd understand. Eventually. If I explained that we were just doing it for the info, and that we'd play her at her own game, together. I just had to tell her everything. It was the sensible, honest thing to do.

So it was probably a foregone conclusion that I didn't.

* * *

After a full day of preparation, we arrived at the home of the Maidens as the sun dipped below the horizon of the Cornish moors. Into a wide field we carted along a crate of wine bottles, and a duffel bag full of glass jars to hold our hopefully massive haul of piskey dust. The lone feature in this field, standing proud with elongated dusk shadows, was an ancient stone circle.

'Shall I jus' dump it down by these big rocks, *gwas?*'

'In the middle of them, perhaps.'

I winced as she dropped her crate, unconcerned for the tinkling of close-packed glass.

'Why are they all in a circle, *gwas?*' Ang rapped on one of the standing stones which were nearly twice her height, poking upright out of the earth. Her interest became a frown. 'There's somethin' uncanny to 'em, ain't there?'

'We shouldn't have too long to wait,' I said. 'Let's pop open a bottle. Ah, and maybe don't lean on those.'

She pulled away from a stone which she'd had an ear to, as if listening for something inside the rock. 'Ver' strange.'

'Music?'

'Aye. How'd ye know?'

'You'll see.'

The stones glowed in the fading golden light. The circle was set in a wide area of open ground, and the fields around it exuded a sense of warmth despite the lengthening shadows on their crests and furrows. Like the knockers, I felt the land here was never truly asleep.

This was Old Country, after all. Ancient memories ran deep within the folds of ageless earth.

I cocked my head, picking up the first bass notes of a tune.

'You hear them drums, *gwas?*'

'Yes.'

'Jus' checkin'.' Ang shifted uneasily. 'S'it coming from the stones, or beneath our feet?'

'Both, I should expect.'

The drum beat, distant and muffled at first, grew into a distinct and lively rhythm thrumming against the soles of our shoes. The trill of pipes suddenly became discernible, followed by the ringing of bells and a toe-tapping kind of melody.

I hastily pulled bottles out of their boxes, uncorked several in advance – and then poured a healthy libation of red wine into the ground.

That got their attention. Voices, now. Excitement: chatter, singing, laughter.

The standing stones were hard to focus on; they swam in front of my eyes. I glanced at one and swore it hopped sideways. Another kept sliding away from my gaze, impossible to pin down. Yet another kept dancing into my periphery, like it didn't want to let go.

'Am gettin' dizzy, *gwas.*'

'They'll slow down when they notice us.'

In fact, our voices cut through a sudden silence in the hubbub. The stones stood still and attentive. I cleared my throat.

'Evening, ladies. How are we all?'

Silence.

And then:

'It's *him!*'

'*Get the bastard!*'

A haze of figures materialised on the edge of the circle and lunged inwards.

'Wait, wait!' I cried, holding out wine bottles and a box of chocolates. 'I'm here to make amends!'

They stopped short of us, whipping up a frenzied wind instead. It whirled around the edge of the circle like a miniature storm, twisting monstrous shapes out of grass tips and leaves. The ground rumbled beneath our feet.

'Can't we talk about this?' I shouted into the vortex. 'Take a look at our gifts, at least!'

The wind parted, and three solid figures strode out of it. Three women, with dark hair and bright eyes, wearing simple dresses fastened by round brooches.

I nodded a greeting to them, as if we weren't in the middle of a magical squall. 'Eseld. Wenna. Jenifry. Lovely to see you again. May I say you look particularly striking, Wenna–'

'Keep your snake-words,' she replied sharply. Her yellow dress fluttered in the wind. 'Why do you interrupt our merriment on this night?'

I kept my voice light and buoyant. 'Oh, you know, I was in the neighbourhood. Thought it would be polite to check in. Catch up, sort of thing . . .'

'Get to the point, Hansard. You prattle so.'

'Well, you know I can't help talking nonsense when I'm around you, Wenna.' I held out the open bottle of wine. 'Can I tempt you to a drink? For old times' sake? I remember how much you liked that merlot we tried . . .'

Her glare softened just slightly as she took in the label. 'And did you bring back my bracelet, as well?'

'Aha.' I tugged at my collar. 'I hoped you might've forgotten.'

Beside me, Ang pulled her flat cap over her face and buried an exasperated sigh.

Jenifry, the tallest of her sisters, stormed forward. 'How *dare* you! What nerve you have! You beastly, *selfish* man! You–'

'I know, it was awful!' I exclaimed, holding the chocolates up like a shield. 'I did a terrible thing in stealing from you. But I never meant to actually hurt you. Honest to god, I didn't mean it to turn out that way. Things just . . . got complicated.'

'Always do, dun't they,' Ang muttered.

'I made a mistake,' I said. 'And I'm truly sorry.'

I caught Ang's incredulous expression, but hoped the real note of sincerity in my voice might overrule it as Wenna regarded me fiercely. The squall danced around us, filled with voices eternally uplifted in song and laughter, while she and her sisters appraised my poor apology.

'You broke my heart,' Wenna said at last.

I cleared my throat. 'In fairness, you were going to turn me to stone.'

'I offered you eternal life–!'

'As a big piece of rock.'

I gestured at the other occupants of the stone circle. Nineteen standing stones: ageless dancers locked in this moonlit pocket of endless existence. The drums of their music reverberated beneath our feet.

'I'm doing things more formally, this time,' I said. I tapped the crate of wine with my foot and pulled more bags of snacks from my coat. 'A proper offering, in exchange for your assistance.' I rolled an additional proposition over in my mind. 'And – before you say no – a promise of reparations for past wrongs.'

Wenna's eyes narrowed. 'Unless you can lift the curse that binds us here, I am doubtful of your ability to compensate.'

There was a muffled snort from Ang.

'Would it interest you to know that we shall be visiting a Green Man?' I rocked on my heels. 'They grow a very curious fruit, so I hear.'

Eseld – only a silently hostile presence until now – piped up. 'One for each of us?' she said. For a moment her visage flickered, revealing what was truly underneath. Deep, greedy hunger laced her voice. '*Bring three.*'

'We shall!' I chirped, pushing Ang behind me. ('But *gwas*, did ye see what–!') 'We need your assistance to reach our destination, however. It's known as Trethevy Quoit, in the here and now.'

Wenna closed the distance between us, woollen dress whipping at her heels, yet her raven hair barely disturbed by the wind. I think, perhaps, I am a sucker for women with sharp eyes. Wenna's were the kind that could cut through you like silver shards of glass.

'You want to access the Leys.' A dark smile tugged at her mouth. 'You regretted it. Last time.'

'I trust you fine ladies to carry us safely.'

Her eyes read mine. I hoped my own air of certainty would convince her that this was not, in fact, an unrealistic expectation.

'Leave the wine,' she said.

Wenna and her sisters retreated into the squall, swallowed up by wind and music. The vortex we were at the centre of began to rise and expand.

'Ever travelled by Ley, Ang?' I trilled.

'Never had call fer it, *gwas*,' she shouted over the growing maelstrom.

'I think you'll be fine with it!' I shut my eyes tightly. 'But I hate how it feels like being squee–eeeeee–eeeeeeeeeeeeeeee–'

The really awful thing about Ley Lines is the fact that they are an entirely liminal space. Not merely a boundary between real and unreal; not just some interplanar space . . .

. . . where time means nothing because every moment is connected to every other moment and every atom is in some way connected to every other atom, so in reality you are not really so much covering distance as you are simply aligning your own atoms with those of where you want to be . . .

. . . where, for what you'd want to call moments but only because moments have no meaning, you feel as though you can know everything and *be* everything, and if you let your mind dwell for any length of non-time on this then you'll start to slip-slip-slip away from yourself, stretching and *thinning* until all that's left of you is just mindless atoms which happen to be connected to everything else in the entire universe and then . . .

'–eeeeeeeeeeeeeeeeeeeeeeeeeeeeeeeeeeeeeeeeezed. *Oof!*'

'All right, *gwas*?'

My eyes creaked open.

'Wifflepish,' I slurred, and shook my head. My legs slumped, apparently jellied. 'Urgh. That's god*awful*. Did we make it?'

'Depends,' said Ang. 'Branok said it were a big door o' stones, right?'

'That's right.'

'Well, there's a door. But it's inside a hill, like.'

I followed her gaze to a large mound of green earth, topped with a flat slab of stone. The word 'barrow' sprung to mind. A place where dead things rested. My neck prickled with goosebumps.

An entrance was cut into the side of the mound, though it was blocked by another slab, standing upright. The only way in was through a small rectangular opening in its bottom right corner, receding into darkness. We would have to crawl.

It also prickled with the familiar sensation of wavering reality. This place was a bridge, just like Mên-an-Tol.

'Looks like the only way is in,' I said.

'Aye.' Ang pulled the lantern from her belt and held it up to the dark. 'After you.'

Episode 6: Green Man

The earth holds echoes of itself.

The way land rises and falls. The flow of water as it cuts channels across landscapes. Every grain of sand holds a memory of being a mountain; raindrops remember the depths of ancient oceans. Primeval memory bounces across the lengths of existence like a really dull broken record from an old prog-rock album entitled 'Geology'.

People leave echoes, too.

We have a habit of stamping our presence into the very fabric of reality, what with our inconveniently active imaginations, dreams, and belief systems. And while an individual might not leave much of a mark on the surface of reality's metaphorical armchair, an entire culture can certainly leave behind a rather large arse impression on the leather upholstery.

Sometimes, you can find the place where the upholstery dips. With a little push, you can find yourself in the literal arse-end of nowhere – an echo of a time and place that once was, but isn't any more.

'An' what *time* are we actually in, *twpsyn?*' Ang impatiently tapped the rock wall around us. 'Don't care much fer the reasoning of it. Jus' want to know the reason *we're* here.'

'Where's your sense of curiosity?' I grumbled. 'Here I am, trying to illuminate the marvels of the universe–'

'Illuminate this, would ye?' She held the lantern up, throwing our silhouettes into blue relief on the walls of the cramped chamber. We were in the bowels of Trethevy Quoit.

The construction itself was quite bare. The walls and ceiling of the tomb were mere slabs of granite, apparently balanced on top of each other. They seemed to be held together by nothing more than gravity and maybe the pressure of the earthen mound bearing down on all sides.

But from between those slabs hung long braids of fabric: strips of reddish wool that had been plaited together and wrapped across the rock like man-made vines. Peering closer, I saw some braids were rotting away. They had been here a long time. This place was probably ancient even when it was still in use.

'We're in an echo,' I stated, 'of some time probably four or five thousand years ago. Back when humans were still finding their feet in the world.'

'Before they took it over, ye mean.'

'If you like.'

My foot kicked into a ceramic pot on the floor. It held a selection of berries and three sprigs of mistletoe. I calmed my itchy fingers. How tempting to grab a souvenir.

Neolithic fashion accessory for you, madam? How pretty these braids would look in your hair – probably enchanted, would bet my life on it. Or how about a piece of mistletoe that has crossed millennia? The perfect ingredient for a rare witch's brew

I shook the idea from my head. No time to daydream a sales pitch right now.

Ang poked at one of the fabric braids, which crumbled under her touch. 'What's all this old rope lyin' around for? And what about that waste of food on the floor? Careless, 'tis.'

'I imagine it's an offering, of some sort.'

'What for?'

'Some god, I expect. Or ancestral spirits. Or the earth itself. Who knows, with humans.' I admired the chamber for a moment. It was cramped, and hardly pretty, but there was something impressive about the lengths humans would go to in the name of veneration. The slabs of rock must have weighed several tons to place, presumably cut from a local hillside and dragged by hand to this open field.

People had lived here, *believed* here so strongly that they'd left behind this very depression in the armchair of existence.

'*Dwp,* it is,' Ang said.

'*Dwp?*'

'Daft, *gwas.* Like you.'

I gave her a sidelong look. 'Didn't miners used to leave scraps of food out for coblyns?'

'Aye. To show their gratitude, like.'

'As an offering, you mean.'

The flickering bluecap revealed her scrunched expression. 'Ah. We-ell . . .'

'Not so daft now, is it?'

She grunted reluctant agreement. 'We goin' in properly or not, then? Branok said t'were over a bridge.'

Branok's instructions had been complicated, and our jump into this echo was only the first part. The Maidens had been a helpful shortcut. They lived in a similar kind of reality-depression, though theirs was probably a special case, what with having an extra dose of magic to help things along.

Wenna and the others – all the eternal dancers – existed within their own echoes of themselves. The perfect answer to immortality, or so Wenna had wanted me to believe, when I first met her.

To the Maidens, all they'd helped us do was jump sideways in time. Now we were here, we had to enter the piskey glen hidden in the tomb.

I hefted our bag of glass jars onto one shoulder. 'All right, let's get this over with.'

'Got a plan?'

'I thought you knew me.'

'Right, *gwas.*'

I heard her voice trail off behind me in a tinny sort of way as I began to unfocus. '*. . . problem is, I still never knows if that means ye do* actually *have a plan or not . . .*'

I felt the chamber expanding. The people who built it had done so with a purpose that moulded it. Or rather, with such purpose that moulded reality around it. Whoever left those offerings here were leaving it for something on the *other side . . .*

Humans have been building portals for thousands of years. What is a tomb, if not a portal the dead? Ancient Egyptians even built fake doors in theirs for the soul to fly out of to reach the afterlife. And what is a church, if not a teleporter for prayers to your chosen deity? And as for physical offerings to make contact across the threshold? Christians have some weird ideas about wine and crackers, I'll say that much.

These thoughts corkscrewed in my head as I unfocused, and as the world around me melted away into something sharper all these ideas convalesced into a single question: What was *this* place built as a portal to . . . ?

The wall opened into a dark hole in front of me: the bridge.

I stepped over it.

The darkness lifted. Stone morphed into leaves. Packed, damp earth shifted and bloomed into a tangle of damp foliage.

This piskey glen was crowded with plant life. It was dim. The sunlight – or whatever light was overhead – barely filtered through the mass of creaking boughs that stretched skyward, each caught in a race to out-strangle the other for precious resources. Vines snaked over every available limb; ivy choked out the ground and swamped the shapes of smaller trees. Everything was green, yet struggling to survive.

I tasted humidity in the air. I wondered if this was how it felt to be in a rainforest.

Ang stepped forward and tripped on a tangle of stems. '*Cach.* Ain't anyone been looking after this place?'

'Quiet,' I said. 'We don't want to . . . wake anything.'

'Let's jus' get this piskey dust an' go.'

'Right. Any ideas where it might be?'

She shot me a scowl of what was briefly disbelief, which quickly dissolved into shrewd scorn. 'After all them notes, didn't ye even think to ask Branok?'

'Did you?'

She huffed and glared pointedly elsewhere. 'This don't look pretty enough fer piskies, does it? Thought they made a place more . . . *unreal.*' She kicked a nearby root. 'This place is real 'n' ugly.'

The ground trembled under our feet.

'And *alive,*' I breathed. I trod gently through the ivy, brushing creepers and low branches away from my face. 'Let's aim for the middle of the glen. Over there: I think I can see more light in that direction.'

Ang followed me cautiously. The rustle of our movements seemed vulgar in the otherwise stillness of the glen. No birds twittered in its trees, no crickets chirped in the undergrowth.

Something crunched underfoot. I lifted my leg carefully and found the dried-up husk of a rodent – squirrel, maybe – tangled up in weeds.

'Choked to death?' I said under my breath. The bones crumbled as I nudged them.

Ang swept a mass of green tendrils aside and pointed. 'Looks like somethin' sparkly, *gwas.*'

'That's a good sign.' *I think.*

There was a definitely glittery quality to the ground cover ahead. It reminded me of the synthetic dew drops on the fairy pastures of Mên-an-Tol.

The vegetation thinned out as we came closer, revealing something of a clearing. Branches still stretched and twisted high overhead, blocking out everything but a dappled light from entering the shady green dell.

The lack of sunlight didn't really matter, as the twinkling piskey dust made it a vision of inverted starlight instead. And there were *tons* of it. Heaped upon the ivy like thick snow; you'd be wading if you walked through it. Which you definitely shouldn't.

'*Don't!*' I yanked Ang back just in time. 'Are you crazy? Don't let it touch you. Unless you fancy turning into a frog or a tea kettle, or some other nonsense. This is proper old fairy magic. Bloody unpredictable – also bloody *and* unpredictable.'

'Gotcha, *gwas.*'

We stood silently for a moment, scrutinising the area for any sign of movement, any whisper of sound to indicate we'd been detected. When none were forthcoming, I dug into the duffel bag for our supplies.

I fished out two pairs of rubber gloves and passed one to Ang. 'Wear these.'

Next, a set of kilner jars and two cast iron ladles, courtesy of the knockers' fine smithing. The jars were specially enchanted, Branok had told me. *With the essence of iron,* or somesuch, so they wouldn't be transformed by the touch of the piskey dust. Good thing too, because I wouldn't have thought of it. I'd have used any old jar and ended up in real trouble.

'Now we reap our rewards.' I said. 'But very, very carefully.'

'Talkin' to someone who's used to shifting soil without collapsin' a tunnel, *twpsyn.*'

Nevertheless, I winced while watching her awkwardly manhandle a too-large jar under one arm and precariously scoop up piskey dust with the other. I gritted my teeth and set to work, hoping that my colleague wouldn't inadvertently turn into something gruesome next to me.

'Where's the green fella, then?' she asked.

I paused my own efforts to concentrate on a reply. The dust had an oddly slippery texture. It wouldn't sit in the ladle as you'd expect a powder should, but sloshed slightly – or *glooped*, perhaps – over the sides, to make our job even more precarious. 'Hopefully, we won't find out. If we're quick and quiet, it may never know we were here.'

'What kind o' beast is it?'

'It's more like a parasite.' I couldn't help glancing at the strangling ivy. 'I expect it put its mark on this place after the piskies left. And judging by those trinkets in the tomb, that was a very long time ago.'

'What do ye mean?'

I stared grimly at the piskey dust. 'I mean that humans will worship bloody anything. Let's get moving now, be quick, remember.'

The Green Man is terrifying for its pervasiveness.

Stone carved faces depicting it adorn the walls of churches all over the world. Its green visage stares out from ancient Roman mosaics. Even a great multitude of pubs are named after the leafy bastard. The Green Man is so ubiquitous that you'll find him in private gardens on cheerful little plaques and hanging from living room windows like a member of the family.

Of course, that's the point. To appear like it belongs there.

The Green Man hides in plain sight, and it feeds on faith.

That's why you'll find it in places where belief unfolds like a flower. In the place where prayers are uttered. In the festivals of spring and winter, when cycles of life and death are so conspicuous. At the local bar, where the only thing holding you together is the belief that this pint will make the pain just a little more bearable. There you'll find the Green Man, unfolding his tendrils, blending in with the stonework, and feeding on the convictions of the people within.

As I steadied my ladle again, a glint of crimson caught my eye and I looked up. Suspended in the middle of the clearing was a ripe, red fruit about the size of a football, hanging like a gigantic uvula from the cluttered branches overhead. It pulsed with a soft glow, and my penchant for metaphor switched its likeness to a quietly beating heart.

It was also the only fruit I'd seen in this otherwise verdant dell. So, logically, there was only one thing it must be.

Ang's hand clutched my coat as I rose. I pointed, directing her questioning gaze to the ripe appendage.

She grimaced. 'Looks disgustin'.'

'We need it for the Maidens. Otherwise we haven't got a ride home.'

She secured the lid of the jar, now filled with the peculiar shine of piskey dust. 'What's your deal wi' them, *gwas*? Ye in the habit of courting big lumps o' stone?'

'I'll tell you some other time,' I said. 'But what's important is they'll do anything to make their tedious eternity feel more *alive*. They exist in an endless party just to make infinity seem a little less monotonous.'

'That's what the booze were for?' she said, stretching out the ladle again.

'Easier to tolerate mind-numbing boredom while drunk, I suppose.'

Ang jerked round suddenly, staring into the dark overgrowth.

'What's wrong?' I said.

'D'you hear that?'

'What?'

She turned back with a frown, eyes darting suspiciously from branch to branch. 'Like a slitherin' sound. Best not be snakes here.'

'I doubt it, if that squirrel was anything to judge by. Come on, let's finish this and get out of here.'

I filled my two jars as hastily as I dared. In retrospect, I realised I had never agreed exactly how much piskey dust Quiet Eyes should receive, only that I'd come away having promised a 'sizeable amount'. If just a pinch was enough to severely ruin your day, then surely several pints of the stuff was a potentially devastating quantity.

No time to dwell, I reminded myself. I'm not in the habit of pondering the purpose of my wares after they are sold. Why start now?

We stripped off our rubber gloves and left them on the ground. The four full kilner jars nestled snugly back inside the duffel bag, cushioned by an old blanket. I removed the crowbar which we'd hidden underneath and hoisted the bag, expecting it to pull me down – but the piskey dust seemed to weigh nothing. Less than nothing, if that were possible.

I set it down again at the foot of a spindly tree and plotted my route across to the hanging fruit.

'You really gonna climb that tree, *gwas?*'

'Are you offering to do it instead?' I rolled up my sleeves and buttoned everything up. Not the time to have my wares spilling out of my pockets, but I'd be damned if I'd risk losing the coat by leaving it behind.

'Nuh-uh.' Ang crossed her arms. 'What's so special about this ugly fruit, anyhow?'

The tree looked reasonably sturdy, and extended towards the middle of the clearing. I felt I could make it. 'It's a story I heard on the Black Market. That Green Men grow fruits full of . . . what they call Ambrosia. Food of the gods, supposedly. The ultimate party food, and just the thing, in fact, to spice up a dull immortality for spirits attached to big lumps of rock.'

I hefted the crowbar in one hand. Even if it was only for psychological comfort, I wanted to have some iron about my person for this endeavour.

Ang watched stoically as I clambered up and out onto an overhanging branch, gripping the bark with my knees. Below me, the carpet of piskey dust leant a deceptively pretty factor of peril to my climb.

The clearing was only a few metres wide, so I figured I could reach the hanging fruit with ease. But it's funny how distance changes when your life (or at least, your human shape) is on the line.

Tucking the crowbar under one arm, I wriggled my way to the end of the branch. It dipped precariously as I lay full-length wrapped around its thinnest section. The pulsing fruit was only an arm's length away.

I could reach it with the crowbar, I was sure. I glanced down at Ang. 'Be ready to catch!'

Her eyes widened. 'Wait, *gwas–!*'

Thwack!

The fruit hit her in the stomach and bowled her backwards.

'Just like cricket,' I said, as the branch supporting me snapped.

For a long second I was the equivalent of a cartoon character paddling on thin air. Only when it turned into several continuous seconds did I realise that my coat, hooked on the end of the branch, was the only thing keeping me from falling the last three feet into the well of piskey dust.

'Ang! Help!'

She staggered upright, rubbing her chest. 'Help yeself, ye bloody great *coc oen*.'

'Ang, this isn't the time! Unless you really want to be the one scraping me up as a pile of goo afterwards!'

'Deserves it, ye do–' Rumbling in the trees cut her off. We both went still. The sound travelled along the branch holding me. I felt it as a tremor in my shoulders and prayed for my life that it didn't judder my coat off its perch.

The sound died away.

'What were that?' Ang said quietly.

'Don't talk!' I hissed. 'We don't want to catch his attention.'

'Whose–'

'Shh!'

'But *gwas–*'

'No.'

'*Behind you!*' she cried.

I twisted myself – stupidly – to look, dislodging my coat as I did.

And then I had all the breath knocked out of me, as a woody vine caught me round my stomach and *squeezed.* Then it yanked me backward.

I landed hard in ferns and stinging nettles, and caught sight of many twisting tendrils of ivy creeping toward my face.

Desperately huffing for air, I swung wildly with the crowbar – which, *oh no . . .*

My hands came up empty: I must have dropped it when I was grabbed. It was lost to the pool piskey dust now.

Meanwhile, I was being swallowed by a bush.

Ferns crowded on top of me while more creepers wrapped around my torso and pinned my arms. Serrated fronds dragged across my skin. They were tough like limbs rather than leaves. I struggled, but like with a rat caught by a python, it only made them squeeze harder.

The sound of fast-approaching Welsh curses persuaded me to freeze and keep still for five seconds longer. A stem was just tickling its way up my left nostril when Ang crashed into view, wielding her iron ladle like a sword. A few wide swings threw the ferns aside: immediately the vines loosened their grip, shrinking away under the taste of the iron.

Ang jumped on my chest. She pulled me up by the lapels and roared:

'*We gotta go!*'

'Hang on,' I puffed. My ribs felt bruised. 'Steady now. You just watch for any more cocky vegetation while I get my breath, okay?'

'We got bigger problems, *gwas.*'

Over her shoulder, I got a glimpse of the Bigger Problem.

The pool of piskey dust roiled and surged upwards. It mounted into a liquid peak as though it was a volcano readying to erupt.

'Shit,' I squeaked. 'Let's run.'

'Way ahead o' ye!'

Ang was already bounding into the undergrowth, hacking a ferocious path with her ladle in one hand. In the other she dragged the duffel bag, into which she'd unceremoniously stuffed the Ambrosia fruit.

Iron is a fantastic repellent to certain old magics. Something about the way the metal has been wrought, an ancient magic of its own that's all tied up in human belief and superstition. Back when everyone used to hang iron horseshoes on their doors, it wasn't just to honour tradition. It was common sense. It turned away the things you didn't want to come inside.

So what happens when you drop a long piece of iron – like a crowbar – into the middle of a pool of piskey dust?

Like a tidal wave, it frothed up behind us as we ran. It spilled over roots and gushed through ferns with a rushing, tinkling noise, a cross between glass and sand and certain doom.

'Up a tree! Up a tree!' I yelled.

I caught Ang by the back of her shirt and swung her up onto a mass of clinging ivy. I scrambled up it and hooked my arm around the lowest branch. A second later the flood of piskey dust came whistling by. It lapped at the tree and a good splash hit my right foot.

Suddenly I was no longer wearing a shoe, but a large orange pumpkin. 'Gah!'

Ang grabbed me from her perch on the branch, half-strangling me with her grip on my collar. 'All right, *gwas*? Did it get ye?' She peered down and muttered a Welsh obscenity. 'Yer half vegetable!'

I pulled away, gasping, and found a better handhold on the tree. 'Got lucky.' My foot felt distinctly slimy inside the pulpy shell. I tried to bash it against the trunk, to no avail. 'Bloody thing's heavy.'

Piskey dust continued to stream by about three feet below us, though it looked to be slowing down. Ang's sharp eyes followed its path into the shadowy undergrowth. 'Why ain't it changed the trees, *gwas*?'

'I think it has, actually.'

Now that the level of dust was settling, the glen's lower vegetation gradually resurfaced. Luscious green leaves unfolded like yawning blossoms and sparkled with dew-drop diamonds on their smooth, rounded edges. It was no longer a carpet of tangled weeds that poked through the twinkling layer of piskey dust. Instead, fresh, bright blades of grass and rainbow-coloured wildflowers swayed in a breeze that I definitely couldn't feel, but which looked very inviting from the humid atmosphere up in our gnarled and still rugged tree-top sanctuary.

I tightened my grasp; thorns and rough bark bit into my fingers. The ground below looked unnaturally soft. It beckoned to be touched.

We looked back to the middle of the glen. The clearing had widened, where the throttling vines had turned to dainty curtains of wisteria and honeysuckle. My crowbar lay in the middle of a silky green earth, which looked like spongy moss heaving and rolling across the ground as though mighty lungs lay beneath. It was no optical illusion.

The crowbar dipped as the ground breathed.

It slid toward the centre of the glen where a gaping orifice was blowing hot, clammy air into our jungle prison. After pitching up and down a few more times, the crowbar fell in.

It was followed by a guttural, gasping sound from deep within the earth.

'What be that hellish thing, *gwas?*'

I gulped. 'I think . . . it may be the Green Man waking up.'

'Bad, is it?'

'I should expect so.'

Ang tutted. 'What ain't, these days.' She rolled up her sleeves and passed me the duffel bag. I slung it over my shoulder, while she yanked a section of vine away from the tree trunk. I followed her determined gaze. She was eyeing up the path to the next tree.

'Don't,' I said dully.

'Gunna stay here, are ye?' She tugged on the vine, which frankly looked quite brittle. Might stand a coblyn's weight, perhaps. She doffed her cap. 'Give me regards to the green bloke, then.' And pushed off.

I groaned. Ang stuck the landing and waved as she swung the vine back to me. She bent to fiddle with her lantern. I looked between the ground below – now trembling, causing the layer of piskey dust to jump in the air – and back at the spluttering orifice, out of which a thick, green mass was now emerging like a serpentine tongue.

I shut my eyes. 'I don't want to turn into a vegetable.'

I wrapped the vines tightly around my forearms and launched off the tree.

They snapped mid-swing.

'*Argh!*'

My face smacked into bark and ivy. My right foot felt suddenly light, on account of the pumpkin smashing upon impact. But I was still held aloft – by what?

Ang's sniggering penetrated my leaf-filled ears. 'Quickly, *twpsyn.* Up, up! Bluecap can't hold ye fer long.'

I found some handholds and Ang's bluecap detached from my coat where it had apparently caught me mid-flight. 'You could have warned me that was your plan!' I said.

'Tables turn, eh, *gwas?*' Ang said smugly. She pointed across the next gap. 'Reckons we can jump it, I do.'

'Only if it stays still.'

The ground-tremors intensified. Trees toppled behind us. Our target swayed to and fro as if tossed by a storm. Ang's bluecap hovered in a jittery way over our heads, as though it was nervously preparing to catch us. As we finally lined up our jump, the ground buckled violently and our own tree uprooted.

'*Hold on!*' I shouted, though it was a completely unnecessary instruction.

We crashed slowly downwards. Sparkling meadow rippled below. Just a few feet away it merged back into unwelcoming nettles – which were rearing up, standing on their roots like legs, and crawling away across the woodland floor.

We landed among these fleeing nettles, relatively gently despite the stings, and took off in the direction of the threshold to Trethevy Quoit.

The whole glen was crawled with movement. What had been an initial recoil from the piskey dust now swung back and in on itself, with craggy plants prowling round the newly formed piskey meadow and clawing at its edges. The giant green tongue in the clearing lapped at the sky, tickling what remained of the leafy canopy. Was it tasting the air, trying to trace the whereabouts of its former meal?

New, sinewy plants were sprouting all around us, a furious bid to reclaim territory – or perhaps a sign of the Green Man's growing wakefulness. Creepers fell into our faces, vines raced us along our path. The stone tomb loomed large out of the undergrowth and we plunged wholly into darkness.

* * *

I tumbled into pressing silence. Ang landed beside me with a soft thump.

'Yes!' I kissed the cold floor and felt for the rock walls wrapped in their fabric braids. My eyes struggled with the tomb's dark. 'We made it, Ang!'

Her bluecap flared behind me, accompanied by familiar grumbling: the usual threats on my life and oaths to never trust me again.

'It wasn't that bad,' I said. 'Admittedly, I regret losing a shoe. But much better than losing a whole foot.' I sat down and leaned against the reassuringly cold stone, glad to catch my breath. Fumbling in the duffel bag, I pulled out a jar of piskey dust and marvelled at it. Its silvery light twinkled off the walls in kaleidoscope colours.

'Never thought I'd ever be holding a batch of this stuff for myself.' I said. 'Reckon I've only seen it once on the Black Market, and that was only enough to fill an eggcup. This is a proper big haul. It's the kind of thing Mercer would go for . . .'

From the lack of curse words, I thought Ang had merely calmed down. But I looked up to see her alert, lips drawn thin and eyes intent on the walls.

'Them braids is movin', *gwas*,' she said.

'Surely not. Just a trick of all the lights . . .'

My voiced died in my throat. Vine-like shadows danced over the wall behind her. A dry slithering sound reached my ears. I ducked just as a serpentine root snatched for my neck. '*Shit.*'

Around us, the whole chamber was sprouted green tendrils.

Why had I assumed the Green Man wouldn't follow us across the bridge?

'Run!' I wheezed. Ang was already swinging a wild path to the exit with her ladle.

The rock walls creaked and shifted around us. The invading roots and branches were displacing the weight of the barrow, forcing stones apart and punching through the earth as they escaped their sheltered pocket of existence. The new growth coiled into every available recess, reaching for the promise of life and sunlight.

We crawled out of the tomb, coughing soil from our throats. I threw my coat up over Ang as a huge stalk burst out of the mound, showering us with heavy clods of damp earth. One smacked me in the ear and left it ringing.

The small hill fell to pieces around the stone innards of Trethevy Quoit. It was now entombed in a tangle of trees and budding vines. They strangled the small shrine with layer upon layer of fervent growth.

The Green Man's baritone breathing emanated from inside it.

'Time fer leavin', *gwas*.'

'I don't disagree,' I said weakly. 'Give me that fruit.'

Ang hurriedly dug it out of her sack. The thing throbbed uncomfortably in my hands. This was another Big Haul, if only I could keep it.

I weighed up the odds. I'd like to think I'm above grovelling, but when it's my life on the line I'm decidedly less picky about such things.

'Wenna!' I called into the fog. 'We'd like our ride back now! *Quite urgently please!*'

'Why ain't we just runnin'?' Ang exclaimed. The tomb's capstone heaved, like something was pushing from underneath. 'Let's go!'

I grabbed her shoulder before she tore off. 'Not into the fog! You don't know when you'll end up!'

'Better'n being eaten by a tree, *gwas!*'

I spun round and saw the horrid green tongue burst from the top of the mound, collapsing one of the tomb walls. Soil pattered onto my head.

We backed off. Fog curled around our ankles.

'Go back to sleep, you ugly sod,' I moaned. 'What do you *want?*'

'Mebbe what we stole?' Ang said, jumping from foot to foot.

'We only took a teaspoon compared to what he has left in there!'

'Not the dust, *gwas*. That fruit.'

I opened the bag and looked down at the crimson fruit. It looked more like a mutated melon than a magical treasure – but then, one of the first things you learn in this business is that magic is often ugly. I squeezed its flesh with my fingertips. My nails bit straight into spongey red pulp, and the juice dribbled over my hands onto the ground.

The tongue snapped toward us like it had tasted the flavour on the air.

I sighed, pulled back my arm – 'I sure hope Wenna will still give us a ride.' – and hurled the Ambrosia fruit as far as I could.

A green tendril snatched it mid-flight. It was tossed up onto the giant tongue, which curled around it, crushed it, and then bathed itself in the shining juices.

I glanced longingly at my fingertips, coated in what could be honey if honey were made of gold. The aroma was sickly sweet, and very tempting.

Cora would have tasted it, just to find out.

I knelt down and carefully wiped my hands on the grass. The Green Man seemed to have forgotten us for now. All its fronds and vines spiralled in on the tongue's horrendous lapping motions.

The faint sound of drumbeats and a musical voice reached my ears.

'Do you have what you came for, Jack?' Wenna stepped out of the fog. Incorporeal wind swept her hair into a mane.

I stood, straightening my shoulders. Ang tucked behind me. 'I've got what I needed.'

'And our prize?'

'You might say I have something better.'

'I might. If I were a fool. But I have played your word games before.' The wind around Wenna sighed. 'Why must you make things difficult?

You could have stayed with us. We could have danced together forever.'

'Yeah, it's the 'forever' part that bothers me,' I said. 'I notice the others aren't here.'

'They thought you would have been swallowed.' Her eyes drifted to the tongue of the Green Man. The ghastly appendage was still occupied with slurping juices. She bowed to it and hushed tenderly at the ground. *'Sleep, Old One. Return to the deep earth. Curl your ever-spring under the living soil. We leave you to feast and slumber.'*

With a deep rumble, the tongue slowly sank back into the mound. The Green Man's tendrils shrunk away, retreating through cracks and crevices and soft dirt, until all that was left was the stone chamber poking out of a crumbled pile of earth.

I cleared my throat, a bad attempt at hiding my awe. 'Was this . . . one of yours, then?'

Wenna's smile held a wicked glint. 'When I roamed the earth, we did battle with such things as piskies. This place, we won it from them. We made it ours. A place of life and veneration. And we welcomed the Green God, who gave us many bounties. We drank his divine nectar and knew the taste of power, and of adulation.' This time the sigh came from her lips. 'But now he sleeps. And he bears fruit for us no more. That one you wasted took a thousand years to grow, you know.'

Ang and I stood mutely, staring at the eerie shadow of what we'd called tomb, but Wenna called temple. Perhaps in a show of generosity, or just to sate her own nostalgia, Wenna waved her arm to the sky. A shaft of sunlight fell through the fog on top of the granite capstone. I gasped.

'It sparkles,' Ang said.

'Fey dust.' Wenna's voice contained a sense of earned pride. 'Baked into the stone. No one knows the way of it, now. There were many magics we used to wrought with that powder.'

'Used to, you say?' I said, my ears pricking.

'You know we cannot touch iron any more, Jack. There is no other way to collect it.'

'Yes. So what you're saying is . . . that you would benefit from a new supply?'

Ang wrinkled her nose. 'We worked hard fer that stinkin' dust, *gwas*.'

Wenna's demeanour changed. Her mouth dropped open a little, and the wind fluttered around her in excitement. 'That's why you were here? To collect fey dust?' She laughed joyously. 'You mad fool!'

I pulled a jar from the bag. 'How's this for making amends? A ride home, and we'll say no more about the past, eh?'

As she saw the glittering essence, Wenna's face sallowed. Her eyes became hungry. '*Anything,*' she rasped.

There, it shifted. The glamour of her face fell away and revealed what lay behind. Stretched and blackened skin, cracking like dry leather, pulled taut over sharp cheekbones. Sunken, empty eye sockets, and the desiccated wisps of long-dead hair. The profile of a bog body, intact but not at all whole.

'It's yours,' I said.

The husk-face of Wenna grinned. Her bent hands reached out knuckle-first, locked into claws by decay. '*You are forgiven,*' she croaked.

* * *

Back at the Ding Dong mines, negotiations were in order.

I was huddled with Ang in a corner of the stope we'd been calling home for the past week. It was some time in the afternoon, though the only clue to this was the sudden proliferation of sandwiches among the knockers as they went about their work behind us.

'Half a jar,' I argued with Ang.

'Branok ain't gunna like it *gwas*, that's all I'm sayin'.'

'And I feel we deserve a higher percentage of the profits, if you see what *I'm* saying.' I held the duffel bag between us, concealing the jars of piskey dust from view. 'We're the ones who risked our lives for it!'

'But what's it matter if we have an extra half or not?' Ang said. 'Ain't two jars enough, what wi' how valuable this stuff apparently be? *Twpsyn.* It's worth keepin' nasty knockers on our side, right?'

Goron ambled up behind her. 'Nasty knockers?'

Ang froze for a millisecond, then crossed her arms with a cursory huff. 'Only nasty knockers be eavesdropping.' She turned back to me and said firmly, 'It's good business, *gwas.* Ye knows it. Give Branok the whole jar.'

'This about yer spoils from Trethevy Quoit, eh?' Goron asked. 'Don't look at me like that, lass. The whole mine knows where you've been. No good trying to keep secrets from knockers, eh? We're right up in each other's business.' He leaned in. 'But between you an' me, as knocker to coblyn, none other knocker knows that you're keeping some piskey dust for yeselves. Right? So best keep that hushed, and give Branok his whole jar, in case he has a change o' heart.'

He grinned toothily at me. 'What heroics our guests do us! T'be gathering new piskey dust, free of charge, as a gesture of friendship. Surely we'll be doing good trade together fer many years to come.'

'All right,' I conceded. 'But you better come through on that.'

Ang gave me a friendly wallop on the leg. 'We still gots two whole jars to ourselves, *gwas.* Plenty rich with that, right?'

'Right.'

Except, of course, I was going to have to find a way to explain the disappearance of one when I handed it over to Quiet Eyes.

'Now then. Got news fer you, I do,' Goron said, straightening his hi-vis vest. 'Come see. Your definitely-not-an-egg has some mighty curious qualities to it.'

Oh yes. My shoulders slumped. The phoenix egg. But if Quiet Eyes wasn't interested in it any more, was it even worth still pursuing?

What am I thinking? It's a phoenix egg! Of course I want to know everything about it!

Can't let Mercer have all the glory. If Quiet Eyes didn't want to sell it to the highest bidder, well then – I would!

Goron led us to his work space, where a small forge glowed red with embers and a bench displayed neatly hung tinkerer's tools. The egg was suspended in a weird metal contraption in front of what looked like a magnifying glass made of smoky quartz. When viewed through the crystal, murky shadows curled around the egg's blurred shape.

Goron selected a tiny hammer from the bench and an instrument that looked rather like a tuning fork. He rested its prongs on top of the egg.

'Watch close, like,' he said.

He hit the fork with the hammer. There wasn't the high-pitched *ting* I was expecting. Rather a low, deeply unnerving timbre that slunk into my ears and prickled down my spine.

In the window of quartz, the shadows coiled into an ominous shape.

'Ah, a skull,' I observed. 'I don't suppose there's any chance of that being a good thing?'

'Rarely,' Goron replied.

'Whassit mean, then?' said Ang, craning her neck to see.

Goron lay down his tools. 'Death, usually.' He glanced quickly over his shoulder, but the knockers behind us were busy fixing a pump to drain some other part of the mine. 'Ill-omened it be, fer sure. And then there's this.'

Goron fiddled with the wires that held the egg. The wires glittered, I noticed, like piskey dust.

From a tray underneath the bench, he plucked a handful of thistles which were just beginning to flower. He added them into the construction of wires and egg, and stepped back.

Within a matter of seconds, the thistle withered to a bleached brown husk. Goron prodded the lifeless stem with his hammer. It crumbled into dust.

'That's a little alarming,' I murmured.

'A *little?*' Ang shrieked. Some of the knockers looked up at the outburst. I shushed her to quiet down, but she was having none of it. 'Ye means to tell me we've been carryin' around this thing that can suck the life outta other things? I've had it in me *pockets,* Hansard!'

Goron chuckled. 'Calm, lass, calm. This is just a little trick o' mine, fer ascertaining the true nature o' things. It shan't harm you as it is.' He began disassembling the contraption, and his voice grew solemn. 'But I should get rid of it right quick, if I were you. Because whatever's inside it is mighty dangerous.'

'I suppose we knew that already,' I said. 'Thank you for your services, Goron.'

He was still looking at Ang with a note of concern. 'What's your plan fer it, exactly? Why carry it around?'

Ang faltered. 'We-ell . . .'

'Leverage,' I said simply.

'Thassit,' Ang agreed. 'Against the quiet-eyed *ast.*'

Goron gave me a final appraising stare before handing back the phoenix egg. 'Hope you knows what you're doing, merchant man.'

'I've never been more certain.'

* * *

I was not at all certain about what I was doing.

Not for the first time, while standing under the waning moon some yards away from the eerie shadows of Mên-an-Tol, I questioned the wisdom of my actions. Should I be selling out on a haul of ultra-valuable piskey dust just to make a deal with an enemy?

To be fair, I made deals with my enemies all the time. But usually, they didn't know they were going to become my enemy until after the fact. Enemies-in-waiting, you might say. (Or simply, 'customers'.)

I'd convinced myself that this deal was worth it. The exchange was for the location of Ang's missing friends, after all! I could finally make good on *that* deal, and Ang would be pleased as punch about it. She didn't have to know where the information had come from. Although she'd definitely ask. And she had a habit of following questions to their answers . . .

'Hello, Jack.'

I startled. When did–? But quick, straighten up, roll out the confident smile. Hope the moonlight gives it a dashing glint.

'Good evening,' I said to Quiet Eyes. This time she stood by the path leading away from the stones. 'I hope I can trust you to make good on our arrangement.'

'You don't trust me, Jack?'

'Just how foolish do you think I am?'

Well, *her* teeth certainly glinted in the moonlight. 'You did make a deal with me in the first place, Jack. I do find your naivete quite sweet.' The Parisian accent slipped back into her words, alerting me to its original absence. I wondered if it was put there just for me.

'If you're willing to betray Baines and Grayle, then I think it's worth a risk,' I said, and inwardly kicked myself for admitting it was a risk at all. That's not how these chess-game conversations are won. I twitched open my trench coat, plucked the gleaming jar of piskey dust from its pocket. 'Obviously I'm not just going to give this to you. How do I know you're going to hold up your end of the deal?'

A rustling sound, and something fluttered into my face. I flapped at it, nearly fumbling the jar, and caught a slip of paper floating in the air. An address was printed on it.

'Just like that?' I didn't try to hide the incredulity in my voice. 'And

I suppose this isn't a trap of some kind? We get there and you have some boys waiting to do us in?'

'Oh, Jack. What would be the *point?*' Now, something else glinted in the moonlight. It was sleek, metal, familiar. Her pistol.

I swallowed nervously. 'I should point out that if you shoot me now, I'll most certainly drop this jar, which will break, and you'll lose a good portion of this precious piskey dust.'

She sighed. 'You are so *dense.*' The pistol disappeared back into whatever place it was stowed. 'I would have killed you already Jack. If you weren't so very amusing.' I opened my mouth again but she stopped me with a warning. 'You become less amusing with every foolish question.'

Her hand beckoned for the piskey dust.

I paused – thought of the gun – and quickly handed it over.

Then the unthinkable happened.

She flipped the catch on the lid and took a pinch of piskey dust between finger and thumb.

I jumped backward by instinct – but nothing happened. She admired it, glittering on her fingers like a glove, and I briefly wondered if the dust gave a truer outline to their shape.

I also had to wonder (and with a certain amount of awe) exactly what kind of person – or what kind of *creature* – could handle piskey dust so casually without being instantly turned into soup.

'There are different types of power.' Her voice made me flinch. Though she didn't seem to be really talking to me. 'Some are less subtle than others. Some are less *real* than others.' She fixed me with her cool eyes. 'Who gets to decide who wields the power, Jack?'

I shivered a little in the cold night air. Or perhaps it was with nerves. 'I always thought it was more of a free-for-all, myself.'

'Yes.' She flexed her fingers. 'Except, not everyone is free.'

My heart leapt. Could that be an invitation? A hint to push further, an encouragement to pry? Should I begin to frame a question–

She cut off my train of thought. 'You have your payment. Go find your knockers and your coblyns, Mr Hansard.' Her smile might have been sweet. 'Do not waste your chance.'

I should have left but I hesitated, turning her note over and over in my hands. 'Why would you sell out your employers like this? Aren't you loyal to Baines and Grayle?'

'Oh, *Jack*,' she lilted sympathetically. 'You are so charming, to think of me as loyal.' She broke into a laugh, and for a moment its off-putting pitch reminded me of . . . something. My mind struggled to land on the correct association. I'd heard a laugh like it quite recently. Lots of little, malicious laughs . . .

She subsided. 'Perhaps I should envy you and your small world, Jack. It must be so simple there.' Her fingers sparkled silver as she waved them. 'May you never leave it, for I doubt you'd survive in mine. Oh. That does remind me.' The fingers pulled up to touch her cheek. 'You have a friend. The one in care, in London. The girl with the empty mind . . .'

'Cora?' Shock took her name shuddering from my mouth. Questions tumbled out on top of each other. 'How do you know about her? *What* do you know about her? *Why–*'

'Hush, hush. You think you can cross somebody like me, and keep all your secrets too? Think, Jack, how foolishly you made yourself known to my employers . . . and how little they might care for such a thorn in their side.' Her hand fell gracefully away from her face, leaving a silver trail from left eye to lips. 'Yet you are somewhat transient. A hard thorn to pin down. Whereas some of those connected to you are in a rather more fixed state of being . . .'

My anger rapidly cooled to ice-cold dread. 'Why are you telling me this? What's happened to Cora? *Is she safe?*'

Quiet Eyes covered her mouth as she tittered. 'Such fun. Safe?

Perhaps. But 'safe' is such a relative term, considering the state she put herself in. May I suggest you pay her a visit, Jack? Or perhaps you find your coblyn creatures to be a more pressing errand. Your choice. Do think hard about it, won't you?'

Leaving me speechless, she turned and walked into the night.

* * *

'What's the hurry, *gwas?* We really needs to leave tonight?' Ang watched me anxiously while I threw goods into the car boot with reckless abandon.

'It's important,' I muttered.

She twisted her shirt in her hands. 'Not saying it ain't, *gwas.* Just, I'd like to know what *it* is, see?'

I slammed the boot shut. 'I'll tell you on the way.'

Goron touched Ang's arm. 'What's got his *turmut,* then?'

'Damned if I knows. He ain't usually so skittish . . .'

'Are you ready?' I snapped. 'Get in, or I'll leave without you.'

'I best go wi' him,' she told Goron. 'He looks apt to get into some trouble, if I don't.'

'But you'll return, aye?' he said.

She dawdled on the response. 'Mebbe . . .'

'*Ang,*' I cried impatiently. 'Save the lover's parting for another day, would you?'

The car door closed with a sullen slam as Ang clambered into her seat. She glared moodily out of the window as I pitched the car into reverse, and then forward off the gravel path from Ding Dong mine and out onto the winding road through the Cornish moors. Goron's small shape faded to insignificance behind us.

'Right, *gwas,*' she began. 'I been patient 'til now, 'cuz it's clear somethin's got ye disturbed. But you're startin' to act like a real *pen pidyn,* so I'm gonna ask you nicely just once. *What's this all about?'*

I kept my eyes on the stream of our headlights cutting through the darkness. My eyelids were heavy, but I couldn't risk even a moment's sleep. Ang waited silently for my answer.

I took a deep breath.

'Her name is Cora. And this may be a long story . . .'

Episode 7: Misfits

When I first met Cora, I was on the cusp of true adulthood, studying at university in London.

I'd always wanted to go to London.

Small town jitters, that's what I had while growing up. That disease of youth that makes a thriving market town feel like a slow and sleepy suburb: a place where dreams went to die, or at least to be beaten out of you by the daily humdrum of not very much going on at all.

London was the escape route. The big romantic adventure, where dreams swashbuckled up and down the Thames with the tide. Of course, back then I didn't know that adventure is what you make it, and I hadn't yet heard the call of the open road.

So going to university seemed like my ticket to adventure. All the cool kids were doing it. My grades weren't great, but they were just good enough to scrape me a last-minute place on a Classics course at University College London.

It turned out to be the worst decision of my life.

Or the best, depending on how you look at it.

The problem was academics, and the fact that I wasn't one. By the end of my first year as a university student, a general disinterest in lecture halls and libraries paired with some drastically low exam results had me reconsidering my life choices. At the start of my second, I was already on the verge of dropping out.

The epiphany came on a Thursday, while I was in the Petrie Museum – UCL's stuffy collection of ancient Egyptian dead things – desperately searching for some semblance of pedagogical inspiration. I was looking at a shelf of magic amulets and pondering the mundanity of them (being mere lumps of jet and ivory) when, on glancing up, I saw a girl disappear through the wall.

'What the . . .' was my immediate and unimaginative reaction.

I scanned the room for anyone else who might've noticed the apparition, but I appeared to be alone. It was a good room for disappearing in, crowded with rows of tall glass display cases. Some of them reached to the ceiling with brightly lit innards, while others sat with a more squat profile, mounted on top of neatly labelled wooden drawers. It was on the other side of these lower cases that I'd seen her, purposefully striding toward the wall at the end of the long room.

Slowly, I navigated around the length of the row, and approached the patch of wall.

Apart from some plaster in need of patching up, there was nothing out of the ordinary about it. The cases on either side housed some of the less interesting objects: beads and farming implements.

'Am I mad, or are you a ghost?' I said to the empty air.

It was well known that the Petrie Museum was haunted. Students, (though admittedly well-acquainted with anxiety-induced insomnia and the pitfalls of surviving on a diet of caffeine, energy drinks, and stress) regularly reported paranormal occurrences in the course of their daily studies. Usually, it was objects swimming in front of their eyes and textbooks going missing. Not women being swallowed by masonry.

Having considered my own question for a while, I decided to opt for 'mad' and knocked on the patch of wall, because that's what a mad person would do.

When the wall rippled like a curtain of liquid, I nearly shit myself.

And when the *head* poked through, I was only one spoonful of sugar away from blacking out. Thank Christ I'd had a cup of tea that morning.

'What do you want?' said the head, which appeared to belong to a bald man with a scraggly goatee. His lips turned up in a scowl when I didn't reply. 'Hurry up, sonny. Can't hang around with normies about.'

I struggled for words, blinking repeatedly as my brain made the connection with my mouth. 'I'm with the girl. The girl who just . . . went . . . through . . .'

He squinted at me, unabashedly scrutinising my faded jeans and *Counting Crows* T-shirt with the hole in it. 'That Cora,' he muttered, 'she sure picks 'em. Come on then.'

The head withdrew, leaving me staring at the undulating wall. I glanced about me again, but still there were no other witnesses to this madness.

'Come *on*, boy!' came his voice from the other side.

I stretched out my hands, let my fingertips sink into the wall – a strangely gloopy texture – and then, eyes closed, took a big step forward.

It felt like walking through a curtain of chilled goo. When I opened my eyes I was shivering, but thankfully not covered in goop.

'First time?' said the bald man. 'Can get you like that, stepping through something unreal. Body don't know how to take it. Come on, let's get you a drink before your soul buggers orf.'

I was certainly lightheaded. I felt as though I could simply float away. 'Who are . . . ?' I trailed off, trying to comprehend the space I was in.

It was huge, yet quiet and library-esque, like an echo of the museum space I'd just come from. Tall bookcases – so high I couldn't see where they ended – lined the walls. There was a vaulted ceiling overhead, maybe, but it was too distant to pick out the details.

The bald man pushed me down into a wingback armchair and handed me a glass of amber liquid. It swam in front of my eyes.

'Wha's thiss?' I slurred.

'Whiskey. Drink up.'

He disappeared from my field of vision, which was just fine because I was having trouble focusing on him anyway. I gulped down a measure of hot spirits and suddenly plummeted back to earth.

Voices behind my head appeared to be arguing.

'Why'd you let this shit-head in? I don't know him, Arnold!'

'He said he was with you!'

'And you believed him?'

Angry footsteps reached me, heralding the appearance of a skinny goth girl with a bird's nest of dark hair and heavy eye make-up. She slammed both hands onto the arms of my chair and thrust her face right into mine.

'Right, mister! Who are you, and why are you following me?' she demanded.

'Um.' My thoughts were still putting themselves back into the right order, and the first thing they came up with for this situation was: 'Why do you smell like oranges?'

Her face twitched. I think maybe some colour flowed into her cheeks. 'You're imagining it.'

Behind her, the bald chappie smirked. 'Told you so, didn't I? Don't use too much, isn't that what I said?'

'Shut *up*, Arnold,' she hissed at him.

'How's your skin feeling? Any peel yet?' He took a seat at a large oak desk. It was strewn with open books, displaying yellowed antique pages.

'I'm not going to turn into a fucking orange!' the girl said, throwing her hands on to her hips.

'Hmm. Well, it hasn't made you any sweeter, that's for sure.'

She strangled a curse into a half-scream in her throat, then rounded back on me. 'You think you're funny, shit-head? How about I turn *you* into an orange? Tell me who you are now or I'll . . . I'll do something drastic!'

I shrank as far back as the chair would allow. 'I'm Jack. Please don't do something drastic.'

'Why are you here, Jack? Are you a Vagrant? Did Seven send you? I told him I'd pay back the debt next week! He knows I'm good for it. Or is it the Shamanic mob? I'm done doing runs for them–'

'I'm not anyone!' I blurted. 'I'm just Jack! I'm a student here! I study Classics!'

The following silence was heavily punctuated by the scrape of an oak drawer, and the metallic clunk of an iron rod being placed on a table.

'Don't mind me,' said Arnold, polishing what looked like a sharp fire poker. 'But be warned that I'm not keen on liars.'

I scrambled out of the armchair and pressed my back to a bookcase. I couldn't tell where I'd entered the room from. It was a long rectangle with no doors I could see. No way out.

'Obviously I'm somewhere I shouldn't be,' I stammered, edging along the shelves. 'They should put a sign up, you know? 'Private: Incorporeal Wall', something like that. Um. Didn't mean to disturb you, so I'll be going . . .'

Something nibbled at my fingers. I glanced down. It turned out to be a book, wriggling forward on its shelf. A papery tongue poked out of the pages and lapped at my palm.

I screamed.

It was the only sensible reaction, in the circumstances.

I flailed and knocked into one of the impossibly tall ladders that lined the bookcases. It wobbled and then, very slowly, toppled. Books were dragged from their perches on its descent, creating a chorus of rustling shrieks and howls that sounded horribly like children falling over each other.

The dust settled, and I looked numbly over a large mound of quietly whimpering literature. 'Um. Sorry . . .'

The girl grabbed my arm and shoved me towards a spot between shelves. 'Let's go!'

'What–!' I caught sight, for a split-second, of a hideous creature where Arnold had been standing. A grizzly tower of hair and teeth. It looked *very* angry.

And then cold substance glooped around me, and we re-emerged back in the Petrie Museum.

The girl was grinned at me. 'I love Arnold, but that was funny as *hell*. We need to run though, because he'll also be mad as hell. Nice one, Jack.' She laughed at me over her shoulder. 'I'm Cora. C'mon!'

* * *

Running through the streets of London is rarely a good thing. It usually means you are being chased, or you are running for fun (and neither of those are good things).

Yet there I was, running through the streets of London with Cora, for the first time. I was vaguely aware that I was meant to be in a lecture hall somewhere, reciting some passage from *The Odyssey* before quietly falling asleep on top of my textbook.

And it rather felt like running was the better option.

We ended up on Waterloo Bridge, huffing and laughing our exertion into the Thames.

'So you really just walked in after me?' Cora asked through tears.

'I knocked first.'

'No!' She fell back into giggles, hanging off the railing while other pedestrians shot us odd looks as they passed by. 'Why would you knock? Who does that? What were you expecting?'

'Definitely not . . . whatever it was that happened.' I was sobering up fast and struggling to find sensible explanations for any of it. 'Who was that guy? Beast? Man? What was that place?'

Cora waved a hand like she thought they were dreary questions. 'Most people just call him The Librarian. He's got the biggest collection of magical books in England. That's all.'

'That's all,' I echoed. 'And what about you?'

She drew herself up haughtily. 'I'm a witch.'

At this point, one might be tempted to do the standard up-down look followed by an arched eyebrow and quippy remark, but I felt my survival was dependent on my ability to go with the flow. So I responded with, 'Okay.'

'Okay? *Okay?*' Her hands flew wildly into the air. 'Is that it? Met many witches, have you?'

'. . . No.' I held back from saying that she didn't look like a witch. Because honestly, how would I know?

I was careful to keep my gaze level with her face, but it was at risk of sidling downwards. I felt she wasn't going to be at all flattered by my attention, so I'd been doing my best to observe her haltingly from my periphery. She wore a simple black crop top and cargo pants, exposing her navel with a piercing that I was definitely *not* looking at even if you paid me, and a pair of great stomping boots that could easily crush someone's skull if needed.

The black clothes ticked at least one of my internal checkboxes for 'witch', so I left it there.

She'd been observing me, too. Her eyes narrowed. 'You said you're a student, right? From that university?'

'Yeah. Classics.' I winced, wishing I'd picked something cooler to tell her.

She dipped a hand into one of her massive trouser pockets and withdrew a transparent ziploc bag. Inside was a dried-out, moss-like mixture. 'I reckon you'd like this.'

'Is it drugs?' I said doubtfully.

Cora scoffed. 'Don't be boring. This is a *spell.* Or it will be, once it's had an infusion of filtered moonlight. It's a charm for success. To help you pass those exams or whatever.' She hesitated, dangling the bag in one hand. 'I can only get it to work for multiple-choice questions, though. Because that's just a matter of balancing the probabilities to find the best outcome. I haven't figured out how to make it work for essays yet. I really thought orange peel would do the trick . . .'

Tentatively, I took it from her. 'You sell this stuff?' I held the little packet of herbs up to the light. 'Do you smoke it or . . . ?'

'*No.* Don't be stupid. It's not weed.' She snatched the bag back, then brightened up. 'But I do have some, if you're buying.'

'Some what?'

She allowed me to continue staring stupidly for a good long moment. 'Some weed,' she said slowly.

'*Oh.* No, thank you . . .'

She stuffed it back in her pocket. I felt that she'd expected a more impressed reaction – and inwardly, I was very impressed, though not by the little bag of herbs. I was still reeling from the implications of the whole situation.

I turned back to look over the muddy brown waters of the Thames. A tourist boat emerged from under the bridge, full of unsuspecting people who had no idea at all about the secret magic room in the Petrie Museum, or about this girl beside me who was probably a witch. 'So. What you're telling me. All this stuff, with you, Arnold, those herbs. You're saying it's . . . magic?'

'Yes. *Obviously.* You must've had your eyes closed to not figure that out yet.' She leaned comfortably over the rail and bent her head to catch my eye. 'You've really not met anyone like me before?'

'Never,' I said honestly.

'But you saw me walk through the wall?'

'I did think you were a ghost, at first.'

Her lips pursed into a little black triangle of thought. 'Maybe you just have good eyesight.' A slight flutter of lashes as her eyes widened and I caught the edge of a grin. 'Here, come with me! I'll show you something cool.'

I found myself running after her again, off the bridge and down into the darkness of a graffitied underpass. Once we were halfway in, and sure no one was watching, she held a sultry finger to her lips. Then she melted, like a smudge being rubbed away, into insubstantial shadows.

I waited several seconds before a nervous laugh got the better of me and forced its way out of my throat. 'All right. Very funny. Where are you?'

Enough light filtered in that I could see the scrawled graffiti on the walls, all the way to the end of the tunnel. Cora was nowhere. She'd vanished, somehow before my eyes.

'I'm here,' said her voice.

My eyes strained to find her. 'Where?'

A snigger. 'This way, shit-head.'

A shape unpeeled itself from the graffiti. The black and purple contours of an *S* became her hair and face, the stains on the wall solidified into her body. And then she was just there, standing in front of me again, beaming wickedly.

'Cool, huh?'

'How did you do that?'

'It's called unfocusing,' she said excitedly, bouncing on her toes. And then, as if to reign in her own enthusiasm she became flippant. 'Everyone I know can do it. Only normies that can't. People like you.'

'Can you teach me?'

A pause – a pretence. 'I suppose. If I wanted. Though I don't see why I should.'

Without thinking, I grabbed her shoulders. 'Please teach me. I want to know everything about all of this! About witches, and magic, and The Librarian, and unfocusing! It's all incredible. *You're* incredible! I've never met anyone like you before.'

Suddenly self-conscious, I let go and stepped back. I cleared my throat. 'Um, sorry. But I can't *not* be excited about the idea of magic being a thing that actually exists.'

She didn't seem perturbed. Her smile was impish. 'More than magic.' She leaned forward. 'Hey, do you want . . . to see a unicorn?'

'You're shitting me.'

'I'm absolutely not.' Her hands fluttered as she talked. The words ran into each other like she couldn't hold them back. 'Someone brought it all the way from Scotland! There's an auction happening tonight. Deep underground, I don't think even the Regulators know about it. I only know because Blind Ruth had a vision and Soggy No-Toes heard it from Jittery Bob who says he saw it being moved into an iron-clad stable and I swear I heard Seven mention it too though he doesn't know I heard him . . .'

She finally stopped to draw breath and found me hanging on her every word. She tucked a strand of curly hair behind her ear. 'That's what I've heard, anyway.'

I had to keep from nodding like an idiot. 'So how do we find it? This unicorn?'

Her lips pursed again, hands and fingers fiddling with the air in front of her. 'You're serious? Like I said, it's real deep Black Market stuff.'

'You asked if I wanted to see one.'

She left an exaggerated pause before answering. 'Do you think you can handle it? You don't even know how to unfocus.'

It's an overused metaphor to speak of the fire in a person's eyes, but

Cora's really did *burn*. They burned right through me.

'I can handle it,' I said.

She exhaled, and her fluttering movements calmed into still conviction.

'I think I know a guy.'

* * *

Cora pulled me onto the tube at Waterloo Station. Twenty minutes later we stepped off at Clapham North. There was nothing overly exciting this end of town that I knew of, but Cora clearly knew better. Clapham was a bit run-down in places, though all its messy, ingrained character was gradually falling victim to gentrification as wealthier families moved into the prettier Georgian houses in the neighbourhood.

Cora and I dodged commuter crowds as she led me around the corner onto the high street which, although busy with shoppers and traffic, still exuded a tired sort of atmosphere. Moving furtively, Cora pressed me toward a nondescript, drum-shaped building set back from the road and somewhat separated from the shops. Spiked railings topped the walls around it.

'This doesn't look friendly,' I said.

'It's not supposed to. Follow me.' She took me through a gate and out of sight of onlookers behind the wall. She ignored the door to the building as we passed it, and instead pointed me at a blank stretch of white-washed wall.

'This is the hard part,' she said. 'But you've already done it once by accident, so I reckon you can do it again.'

'What's that I'm doing, now?'

'Unfocusing.'

I stared at her. 'That disappearing trick of yours? I can't do that!'

'It's not about disappearing,' she said, less than patiently. 'It's just about being less *there*. So you can see the other things that aren't quite there, as well.'

'How can something be 'not quite' there? Things don't only half-exist!'

'Fallen through many totally-there walls, have you?' she said sharply. 'Seen many completely-real books that can bite your fingers off? No? Then maybe you should shut up and listen to the expert.' She grabbed my hand and placed it on the wall. 'Start with this, and close your eyes. Sometimes the brain just gets in the way and keeps insisting it can see what it wants to see.'

I shut them obediently. The brick was cool under my palm.

'Now just . . . sort of . . . relax.' It was clear this wasn't an instruction that she was used to giving. 'Try to imagine yourself spreading out. Like your edges are getting really thin, like . . . like . . .'

'Like a piece of jam on toast.'

A pause. 'Yeah. Whatever works for you, mate.'

I did not feel like a piece of jam on toast. But I did feel like maybe a part of me was unwinding. I recalled the brief sensation of madness when I'd seen Cora walk through the wall in the museum, and the sinking feeling that some of my reality was coming undone. I could feel my stomach sinking now, leaving me lopsided and strangely heavy.

Cora moved my hand over the wall. 'You got it yet?'

'Got what? What am I looking for?'

'Stop concentrating and just accept what your body is telling you. What can you feel under your hand?'

'Nothing. Only wood.' I opened my eyes, and saw the door.

Cora seemed amused. 'Not *terrible*, I guess. Only took you forever to find it. This way.'

She shoved the door open, hand still tightly gripping mine, and we plunged inside. The door closed with a slam.

'Hang on! What *is* this place? Where are you taking me?'

'No need to panic.'

'I'm not panicking!'

I could just make out her smirk in the low light. This circular room was windowless, and it took me a while to realise the faint light source was coming from an orb clutched in her fist.

'I thought you were holding a torch,' I said faintly as she pointed down a steep spiral staircase. It formed a double helix, so another staircase mirrored it on the opposite side of a caged column that filled the void between them.

Cora flexed her fingers and the light strobed outward. 'This is nothing. Practically a toy. Just some sunlight that I picked up earlier.'

She tossed her hair in ambivalence – but I caught the surreptitious glance for my reaction.

Unfortunately, I felt I'd misheard. 'Did you say sunlight?'

'Yeah. I like to collect it.'

'What, in a bottle?'

She flipped open another of her trouser pockets and slid out a glass bottle that was *definitely* too long to have fitted inside. I couldn't spend much time thinking about this however, because the light from it seared my retinas into blinking black and purple spots.

'You can put your arm down now,' Cora said. 'I've put it away.'

'Could you warn a guy before *blinding* him?'

'You asked about it,' she replied petulantly, and snuffed out the meagre glow in her hand.

I must have looked comical, flapping my arms into empty space, hoping not to fall down the stairs. 'Now I'm really blind. Doesn't this place have lights?'

'They took all the electrics out after the war.'

'What war?'

'*What war?*' she repeated sarcastically. 'Do you pay attention *at all?*'

'I would if you explained anything!'

There was more acid in my voice than I'd intended. I felt the air sucked down the staircase like a vacuum, leaving us with a hollow, sullen silence to breathe in instead. The metal floor clinked slightly under our weight as we shifted anonymously in the dark.

Cora spoke first, quietly.

'We're in an old air raid shelter. Deep shelters, they're called. They go way underground. There's lots of them, all over London.' A soft intake of breath. 'I live here.'

I found myself chuckling. 'You really have a bottle of sunlight in your pocket?'

'Yes.'

'This is stupid. And I love it. Can you show me again? I'll be ready this time.'

'Okay. Don't look right at it.'

I shielded my eyes as the room flared into daylight again. Cora took my hand and placed something warm in it. Everything dimmed again, and I looked down to see a shimmering ray of sunlight dancing in my palm.

'Woah,' I murmured.

'Right?'

She turned away from me and bent over, passing items between pockets. There was another flash of light, quickly smothered by a woollen rag, and then she pressed the small parcel into my free hand. 'A gift, right?' she said matter-of-factly. 'I've got plenty more. Keep it covered, unless you want to 'blind yourself' again.'

I explored the shape of the thing with my fingers. Something like a small jam jar, small enough to slip into the pocket of my jeans. I looked between it and the floating mote of light in my other hand. 'Why doesn't it burn? How do you control how bright it is?'

The downturn of her mouth told me her patience was running thin again. 'Magic,' she said, plucking the light out of my hand. 'Some things you've got to figure out for yourself, you know. Now you've got your own piece of sunlight to play with.'

I carefully stowed away the wrapped jar, hiding my smile. 'We're going down?'

'Yeah. This way, shit-head.'

The steel stairs creaked under our feet. It was a dizzying descent, maybe four stories down, maybe more. I had heard of these places, the deep shelters, and I knew they were often right next to London Underground stations. I vaguely recalled lessons about the Blitz and the Battle of Britain – some of the more exciting portions of high school history – and found myself imagining I were a resident escaping into this shelter. In a manner of speaking, I suppose I was.

The muted sunlight from Cora's hand gave me impressions of peeling walls, flaking strips of metal and crusts of rust encroaching on the whole structure. When we reached the bottom, a long, pitch-black tunnel stretched ahead.

'So no one's been down here since World War Two?' I whispered.

'What makes you think that?'

As if tuning into a radio station, my ears abruptly caught hold of the sounds that had been there all along. Distant chatter, the rustling of feet and bodies, followed by crackling and a faint smell of meat-drenched smoke.

We entered a new tunnel, and I struggled to take in everything at once.

This tunnel was a semi-circle, like a pipe that had been cut in half: the walls and roof were formed from giant cast iron rings fitted together to make a tube. It was tall enough that I didn't have to fear hitting my head even where the walls curved down, but it still felt claustrophobic. This was, in part, because of the amount of furniture and people stacked into it.

Bunk beds were arranged down one side of the passage; makeshift walls of plywood and cardboard separated some of them into units. People sat and slept in them, reading, talking, playing cards. In one section there was no bed, but a campfire cooking what could have been rabbit, or a large rat. (In London, it's hard to tell.) The men turning the spit paid us no mind as we walked by, but I couldn't help noticing one of them looked rather slimy and smelled like the Thames on a dank evening.

The other half of the tunnel was like a road, stretching into the subterranean distance. More people mingled there, filling the hot space with the breath of their conversations. Fluorescent strip lights blinked on and off occasionally over their heads, and when I followed the trail of wiring I realised they seemed to be hooked up to an array of crystals on the floor.

Cora led me down this strip. 'Keep your eyes to yourself,' she warned.

'I wasn't planning to give them away.'

I brushed shoulders with someone – or, it occurred to me much later, some*thing* – with eyes that glinted yellow, who wore a velvet coat that seemed to swell and then crumple as I made contact. I suppressed a shudder and stuck tighter to Cora.

'You said you live here?' I stepped around a luggage trunk jutting out from the end of one bunk bed.

'Yeah. Mine's a bit further on, but we're not stopping there.'

'Are your family here, too?'

She stopped short and I nearly barrelled into her. 'Don't have one. I'm a Vagrant,' she said proudly. 'You know, societal misfit, or whatever. We live outside the bounds of normality.'

She opened her arms at the same moment as the fluorescent light began flickering, lending her an ethereal quality. 'You're not in Kansas any more, Jack. The people here? We don't play by your rules upstairs. Our world is dark and strange and full of the kind of surprises that can get you killed. It's easier to live somewhere like this, out of sight, so we don't have to put up with all of your–' she twirled a finger at me, '–mundane crap.'

There was a chortle down by our knees. A grey head spoke from the nearest low bunk. 'That's as may be, deary, but I wouldn't 'arf kill for a good hot shower and proper light to read by. Them crystal's are gammy. When're you replacin' 'em?'

Cora didn't exactly deflate, but her shoulders dropped a little. 'Soon, Ruth. I've got my eye on some at the market.'

'Good girl. Who's your friend?'

'No one,' Cora said, pushing me onward.

The old lady's voice followed us down the passage. ''Ansom, is 'e?'

My memory tickled at what Cora had said earlier. 'Was that . . . Blind Ruth?'

'Yes.'

'So why does she need light to read by?'

Cora gave me a sidelong glance. 'You picked that up quick. It's an ironic name, I guess. Because she has visions of the future. Her eyes work perfectly fine.'

She guided me to a very narrow set of concrete stairs in the floor. 'We're heading to the Lower Deck.'

I just about squeezed down them, nearly tripping on the last steep steps. 'Oh wow, it really is just a pipe cut in half,' I said. In this lower half of the tunnel, I could see where the iron rings continued from above, curving down the walls and disappearing under the surface we stood on.

Cora emerged next to me, ducking her head slightly. 'Yeah, I guess it was the easiest way to make them. Come on.'

I'd felt the upper deck was claustrophobic, but the bottom deck was far worse. The floor was raised to account for the curve of the tunnel underneath, so it meant there were only inches between the top of my head and the flat ceiling. Even the light felt more hemmed in, as though it couldn't travel as far around the odd angles and the thin metal pillars which supported the mezzanine above. They gave the deck a prison-like atmosphere as I strained to make out how far the row of vertical bars stretched into the distance.

This passage was also divided in two, but not by bunk beds. Instead, the left-hand path was taken up with what I guessed were market stalls. Some tables, but most spread on blankets, displaying a weird variety of wares. I tried to stop at one which displayed odd, pale creatures quivering in cages – but Cora hastily pulled me away.

'Trust me, you don't want to get their attention,' she said. 'And we're on business, so let's keep moving.'

Frankly, the prospect of the unicorn auction had flown well out of my head back when she'd shown me the invisible door into this place. With a bazaar full of bizarre and unearthly goods now right in front of me, I wanted to stop and look at *everything*.

'What was in those cages?' I said excitedly as she dragged me forward. Every few steps another shadowy trader beckoned with peculiar goods.

'Ask me later. Look, get a hold of yourself. We're going to meet–'

A booming voice stopped us in our tracks. '*Cora Tomaras.*'

It belonged to the figure of someone who really ought to fit the image of a 'jolly fat man'. He had the paunch, and the fluffy beard, and even the pink-tinged cheeks and reddish shine to the nose. However, his mouth was creased downward so firmly that I had to believe this was its default resting position.

Cora smartly crossed her arms and tipped up her chin. 'Hello Seven,' she said. 'How's business?'

'The answer is no,' he replied brusquely. 'I am all out of favours for you, until you have repaid what you are currently owing. What trouble are you trying to get into today?'

Cora thought about it, just for a second, and lowered her voice.

'Okay then, let's cut right to it. There's something big going down tonight, right? Something . . . equestrian? And I hear where maybe you want a piece of it, and I'm here to say I'm your girl. Don't send Skuzzer or Mitts. I'll do the run for you. No tricks. It'll be payment toward my debt.'

Seven regarded her in the slivers of clandestine light. I could just about tell that his suit was a dark, shabby green. He didn't seem to be paying me any attention yet.

From an inside pocket he withdrew two dice. 'I see. And what do you imagine your odds of survival are?' Without leaving pause for Cora's reply he threw the dice onto a table next to him. His lips tightened around the frown. 'Hmph. Snake eyes, sister.'

Cora surveyed the dice critically. Her fingers drummed her elbow. 'That's only probability. I might get lucky.'

'Chances are low. You're not doing this job.'

'You can trust me with this! Not everything is up to luck!'

'Sorry,' I piped up in the back, 'but what's going on right now?'

Seven's bulk turned slowly to fixate on me. The frown strained so low it threatened to fall off his chin. 'Who is this?'

'I'm Jack,' I said before Cora could stop me. I held out a hand, which Seven ignored.

'He's a friend of mine,' Cora said quickly. 'He's all right.'

Seven grunted. 'Well, Jack. I'm a dealer in luck and chance. And I like to measure the probability of success for my investments *before* I invest in them. These dice,' they flashed between his fingers again, 'help me do just that. And the dice say *no*, Cora.'

'Um,' I said. 'So did you roll for both of us, or just her?'

There was a long pause, in which I caught a glimpse of glee on Cora's face.

'He'd be going with you?' Seven rumbled, low and doubtful.

'Yes,' said Cora.

'Then, if it will convince you . . .' He rolled the dice again.

We craned over the table. I wished I knew what the results meant.

Cora grinned. 'Lucky seven.'

'It's only average,' Seven barked back. 'Sixes are what you want.' He stroked his beard, eyeing me up and down. 'You a good liar, kid?'

I shuffled my feet. 'Um. How would you know if I was telling the truth?'

'Ha!'

He turned his back on us, obscuring the table, and rolled the dice again. And again. The results seemed to leave him disgruntled. 'Very strange. But it's still not worth the risk, Cora.'

'*Please,* Seven!' she burst out, and suddenly I caught a hint of childish petulance that threw her relationship with this intimidating man into a different light. She was only a pouting lip short of stomping her foot. 'I'm ready for this! And I'll even have back-up. Even the dice agreed – seven's not a bad score, you know that. Jack might even make the difference on your investment.' She leaned in earnestly. 'Go on, roll on your investment! Roll on the probability of losing it in our hands. How likely are we to fuck it up completely?'

Seven gave a begrudging huff. 'If it will persuade you otherwise.'

The dice clattered onto the table. He stared at them in disbelief.

'Snake eyes on *that!*' Cora shouted, punching the air. 'See, we're a sure bet!' My neck prickled as eyes around the tunnel landed on us. Cora simmered down and addressed Seven solemnly. 'I can do this. I won't draw attention to myself and I'll stay out of trouble. It's only an auction, right? I'll take the goods, place the bids. If we win, we win. If we don't, we don't. I've got to learn to move in these circles someday. Right?'

Seven picked up the dice and glared at them as though they'd betrayed him. 'And him?'

They both looked at me.

'He notices things,' Cora said. 'He'll be a good lookout.'

'You've grown up too bloody fast.' Seven became absorbed in the dice in his palm for a moment. Pensive wrinkles lined his brow. 'You look after yourself, Cora Tomaras. And you, Jack lad, you look after her too. This is no circus affair. It's serious business. Deadly business, if you piss off the wrong people. Understood?'

We both nodded, though I was feeling lightheaded again. What, exactly, was I agreeing to?

Seven drew Cora away and muttered instructions to her. A number of small, shining vials were transferred and placed in her bottomless pockets. The exchange finished with Cora throwing a lopsided hug around his neck. 'You won't regret this,' she said.

Seven caught me by the collar as we turned to leave. 'You've got an average streak about you, lad. Don't underestimate its usefulness.'

I hurried after Cora back through the grim tunnel. 'What do you think he meant by that?' I said, turning over the words.

'No idea. I'd say being average is a bit of a handicap in a world full of weirdos, though. Come on.'

I took care not to bang my head as we climbed the narrow steps again and wound a path through the strange denizens of the upper deck. I stepped over two kids playing a game with knuckle bones on the floor, and danced around a skeleton-thin man meditating two feet off the ground. Cora remained two steps ahead as I tried to elicit more answers from her. 'What did Seven give you? In those small bottles?'

She tugged me into an empty bunkbed section and obligingly pulled a bottle out for me to see. It was only as long as my thumb, and the liquid inside was clear. Cora winked and said, 'Luck,' before dropping it back in her pocket.

I stifled the 'What?' that so desperately wanted to escape my mouth. I'd learned from the sunlight incident. 'Do you mean,' I said carefully, 'that's a bottle full of actual, liquid . . . luck?'

'That's what I said.' She sat comfortably on the lower bunk. The top bunk was piled with junk: piles of clothes and dog-eared books and tacky ornaments, the kind street hawkers sold to tourists with clumsy likenesses of Big Ben and red London buses. Then I had to double-take as Cora began rummaging under the bed – and felt guilty as I realised it was *her* junk I was looking at.

I picked up one of the souvenir fridge magnets, a cartoonish caricature of the Queen done up in a lilac coat, mouth as wide as her face, with a little crown perched on top of the curly grey hair. 'You collect these?'

'They're easy to swipe.'

'You mean you steal them?'

She stood up with a scowl and yanked the magnet from my hand. 'It's not hurting anyone.' She tossed it back on the pile like she didn't care, and it slid out of sight. But looking around this small compartment, I saw there was not much of anything else in terms of possessions.

What she'd pulled from under the bed was a long grey knitted cardigan. Slightly tatty, and a bit grandma-esque, so it was somewhat at odds with the trendy clothes she was already wearing. As it slipped over her shoulders, it struck me that personal treasure could be as simple as a fashionable item you've scrimped and saved up to buy, or a reliable cardigan to keep you warm on a cold night.

She pulled the cardigan closed – self-consciously? – and I realised I'd been staring. 'Seven says it won't start til three AM,' she said, looking off to the side. 'Traditional, you know? We've got a while to wait.'

There was a stiffness in her shoulders and in the way she didn't quite look at me. I guessed she was uncomfortable with me seeing her home so up close. Had I offended her with the souvenir magnet?

I tried to lean against the plywood partition, then quickly jerked away as it wobbled under my weight. 'Um. I'm happy to hang out here. If you are?' I stood awkwardly in the small space, not quite sure what to do with myself.

Cora's hands fidgeted in her lap for a moment. Then she shuffled over and patted the spot next to her on the bed.

Sinking onto the thin mattress, hard springs poked into me and I had to hunch forward so as not to hit my head on the top bunk. But still, I couldn't think of a place I'd rather be right at that moment.

I wanted to ask her entire life story. Where did she come from? How long had she known Seven? Had she always been a Vagrant? These questions and more paralysed me.

Luckily, Cora made the first move, like she often did.

'So . . .' She kicked out her legs and turned to me with a smile that quirked at the edges. 'What brought you to London, Jack?'

Episode 8: The Unicorn Auction

I learned a lot in that afternoon I spent with Cora. We talked for hours.

She'd lived in London nearly all her life. Abandoned by her parents, perhaps, as she'd been found wandering the streets as a child. Residents from the Clapham North Shelter had found her, offered her a semblance of a home – and now they were the closest thing to family that she had.

She did 'runs' for people, she told me. Carried out collections and deliveries for the likes of people like Seven (as well as some shadier characters, I surmised) and errands like fixing lights or fetching odds and ends for people in the shelter. Her business selling supernatural solutions to desperate university students appeared to be a relatively new side-gig, and I got the impression she was itching to stamp her own name on a corner of the underworld she inhabited. Preferably in really BIG letters.

Eventually our growling stomachs prompted us to go in search of food. We left her paltry living quarters behind and ascended from the depths of Clapham North, navigating the double helix staircase by another mote of sunlight.

When we breached the door to outside, the real – grey, British – sunlight looked pallid in comparison. It was early evening, and the smoggy sky ironically seemed to bring us both back down to earth.

The particle of light in Cora's hand dissipated in the air.

'Chips?' I suggested.

'Definitely,' she said. 'I know a place. Follow me.'

We ambled down the high street, which was still busy despite the time of day. The transition from underworld to overworld had caused a break in our conversation, and I noted the way Cora held herself differently up here. Her shoulders were squarer, jaw slightly clenched, and her stride was fast and purposeful. 'Don't touch me,' said her body language. 'Or you'll regret it.'

I was afraid this new silence might calcify into permanence, and sought to break the ice again. I pulled up another question with a chipper tone, to chip it away. 'That bottle of luck, then. What happens if you drink it?'

Cora glanced at me, eyes narrowed with a hint of exasperation. 'You become extremely lucky. For a very short period.'

'Wow,' I said, with real enthusiasm.

Bottled luck. And bottled sunlight. Was there anything you couldn't bottle?

She'd been coy on the details of the auction we'd be attending later – Seven had trusted *her* with the information, not me. How exactly you used luck to bid on a unicorn, I wasn't sure. Were we supposed to drink it? Was it meant as payment?

'The problem is the aftermath,' Cora continued. 'Once you've used up more than your usual quota of luck, the universe sort of has to rebalance itself. So it's like you're borrowing luck, from yourself. Seven's still working out the formula, you see.'

'That sounds like it could be dangerous.' I fell into step with her as we rounded a corner. I didn't know where we were going, but I was definitely going, all the same.

'Oh, it is,' she replied, chewing her bottom lip. She probably didn't know the black lipstick had smudged a little in the corner of her mouth. 'We've had some nasty accidents from it. One of Seven's other guys didn't listen to the warning and drank a whole bottle. Went to a bookies and bet a lot of money on a horse. He won, of course.'

'That doesn't sound so bad.'

'Sure. But he died on his way to pick up the money.' She led us away from the high street, heading north back toward the Thames.

'How?'

'A piano fell on his head.'

I stopped dead in the street. 'That's a joke.'

'Nope.'

'It must be. I mean you'd have to be *stupidly* unlucky for something like . . . Ah. I think I see.'

'Yeah.'

I made a mental note to never try drinking a bottle of liquid luck.

We stopped at a curry house to pick up a paper parcel of chips, and then continued winding through residential streets towards the river. An eclectic mix of historic brick-built townhouses was interspersed with the occasional high rise flat or office building, until eventually we were skirting along the edges of Battersea Park.

Cora talked as we walked, and I was happy to listen to her ramblings about the mechanics of magic which I didn't understand.

'What do you owe Seven for?' I asked in the middle of her explanation of probability-distillation.

Her face scrunched up. 'Weeeeeell. I might've borrowed an ounce of luck without asking him. I was *sure* it would cement my success spell. Literally no luck, though. The guy who tried it passed his exam, but then got kicked out for plagiarism.' Her cheeks tinged pink under the make-up. 'Turned out he'd written word for word the same answers as another student. And of course no one's going to believe that was just because he was really lucky . . .'

We reached the riverside promenade and followed the path into

Battersea Park. A park bench gave us a welcome spot to rest and eat, while the setting sun cast long arms over the Thames and fingered the autumn branches over our heads.

'Maybe it shouldn't be about luck,' I mused, and dropped a chip on the ground for a pigeon that was nosing at our feet. 'What if you could attack it from the other direction with a memory potion, or something? Does that exist?'

'What do you mean?' said Cora.

'Well, if you can make it so they automatically memorise the notes beforehand, that's half the battle, right?' The pigeon cooed as if in agreement. I gave it another chip. 'And then if you, I dunno, could amp up a person's critical thinking for an hour – is that a thing? A spell for a logical argument?'

Cora straightened up. Her food lay forgotten. 'No. But it *should* be.'

We brainstormed an entire catalogue of magical products as dusk fell around us. I was joyfully unhampered by any knowledge of what was or wasn't possible, and Cora seemed thrilled to have someone ready to entertain her drive to try absolutely everything.

The water glittered beyond the promenade as streetlamps and other artificial lights began to light up the banks. The Thames, rarely a source of inspiration to me with its murky waters and garish tour boats, now took on a sublime kind of appeal – because it belonged to the city that Cora called home to all of the astounding things she had shown me.

'I want to do stars, next,' she told me excitedly, after we'd discussed applications for her bottled sunlight. Turns out she had a portion of moonlight in her pocket, too. 'Seven keeps telling me it's impossible, but I'm sure it can be done.'

She'd capture an entire galaxy in a bottle, if she could.

We left the river and walked to the bandstand in the middle of the park, still chattering like morons. From inside it, we took turns pointing out the few stars that were visible in the cloudy night sky.

I rubbed my eyes, leaning back against the cold iron railings, and found myself beginning to nod as Cora's meandering words slowed down. That was where I eventually fell asleep, under the white Victorian canopy with Cora resting comfortably against my shoulder.

She roused me awake in the early hours of the morning.

'Christ, I'm freezing,' I said, hugging myself in my thin T-shirt.

'Don't be a wimp,' said Cora. 'Quickly, we can't stay here now. Over there, in the bushes! We don't want to look like the first ones here.'

I stamped my feet under the trees and huffed into my hands to keep warm. Cora peered intently through the branches, gaze fixed on the bandstand.

'What are we waiting for?' I said.

'The auction.'

'*Here?*' I glanced pointedly at the wide green spaces of the park. 'Out in the open?'

'They lock the park after hours,' she murmured. 'And it means there's lots of escape routes.'

'Why would an auction need escape routes?'

She frowned at me. 'And I thought you were observant.'

I wasn't a complete idiot. I'd got an inkling that we were about to be involved in something so shady that even shadows think twice about showing themselves. But when the moth is dazzled by the flame it's pretty hard to feel the heat at the same time.

Cora had mentioned something about Regulators, and I knew that if they turned up things would go bad. But as for unicorns, and the kind of people who would want to buy one? I had exactly zero frame of reference.

We kept quiet and waited.

The patrons arrived in insidious ways. One moment I was sleepily staring at the scrolled ironwork on the bandstand; the next it was occupied by a huddle of dark figures. The shape of a small tree morphed into a strangely twisted humanoid form before my eyes. In my periphery, an unnerving smudge of gloom advanced until a crowd of spectres waited in silent audience. Before long, there was an obscure horde surrounding the bandstand.

'Three AM,' Cora whispered. 'It's going to start.'

We slipped into the throng. The knot of people in the bandstand untangled, rustling dark coats and lifting a thick blanket, revealing a creature among them.

It did not look at all like a unicorn.

It was about the size of a donkey – and a bedraggled one, at that. A beardy tuft under its chin added an element of goat to its profile. The only unicorn thing about it was the long, thin horn protruding from its forehead, which had a spiral groove running up its length. It did not look magical. It looked quite deadly, and somewhat ugly.

Nevertheless, a ripple of appreciation spread through the crowd. Silently, one figure held up a jar full of quivering moths. The shadows in the bandstand nodded. From across the audience someone else held up a strangely shaped animal skull and shouted a string of words that might have been in Latin.

'Is this the bidding?' I asked Cora.

'Yes. We need to pick our moment.'

I watched another jar of moths go up followed by what was possibly a pitcher full of bats, until the bearer of small winged creatures was outbid by the collection of weird animal skeletons. A new bidder in the middle threw up an ancient looking leather-bound book, only to be outdone by the owner of a jade statue that shimmered in and out of existence under the moonlight.

Cora threw up one of her three vials. 'Luck,' she called over the heads of the crowd. She received a nod from the bandstand and a number of unfriendly eyes turned our way. Goosebumps prickled over my skin.

It suddenly occurred to me that the winners of the auction might not be the most popular people after this was all over.

'Lambton Worm essence,' someone countered.

I breathed a small sigh of relief. But Cora stared at all three vials Seven had entrusted her with, and bit her lip.

'Maybe we should quit while we're ahead?' I said.

'We're not ahead, Jack. I don't think this is going to be enough.' She twitched open another pocket and the glow of sunlight spilled from its seams. 'If I add some investment of my own . . .'

I gently pushed her hand away from it. 'Is that necessary? So what if you don't win this thing for Seven?'

'I have to try.' She wouldn't quite meet my questioning gaze. 'I owe him. Just generally, you know? I want to get this right.'

Her hand shot up again. 'Three luck.'

The man with the fancy worm stuff bowed out. A moment of eerie stillness followed as the assembly waited for a new counteroffer.

'I tender a slice of immortality,' came a lazy drawl from under a wide-brimmed red hat. 'A literal slice, of Promethean liver.'

This drew gasps from all around us.

'Sorry,' I said, louder than I intended, 'does he mean from *the* Prometheus? Stole fire from the gods, Prometheus? Eternally chained to a rock to have his liver eaten by an eagle, Prometheus?'

As yellow eyes turned my way, Cora yanked me to the back of the crowd where my voice wouldn't carry so much. 'Stop drawing attention to us!'

'But–'

'Be impressed later, okay?'

'But it's a myth,' I insisted, while again navigating that lopsided feeling of the world coming undone. Maybe I should have paid more attention in my classes on Greek mythology. It had all seemed so *dull* on paper.

Cora was readying her pocket of sunlight. She locked eyes with me, and I nodded.

Before she could pull out the bottle, a hairy hand clamped over her arm.

Cora whipped round with a fury. 'Get off me you–! Oh, hello Arnold.'

Oh, shite. I sidestepped behind her. Arnold looked human again, the same beardy bald man who had invited me into his secret library. I hoped he wouldn't still be looking to settle his previous score.

'What are you doing here, Cora?' Arnold hissed. He hadn't removed his hand from her arm. 'This isn't a place for sight-seeing!'

'I'm on business. For Seven,' she hissed right back. 'I can handle this.'

'Not any more, you can't. I've just been tipped off. Regulators are coming!' He started pulling her away from the ragged edges of the crowd and I almost lunged to smack him in the face – but Cora yanked out of his grip first.

'What the hell, Arnold?' she said, angry but uneasy. 'You're sure?'

'Better safe than sorry. You want to be hung?' he replied.

'They don't do that.'

Arnold let out a snort. 'Certain, are you? Want to stick around to find out?'

I edged up beside Cora, and Arnold finally noticed me hanging on to the conversation. He glared down his nose at me. 'Get out of it, you nosy fucker. Leave this girl alone.'

'Um–' I said, fighting the urge to retreat.

He peered closer. 'Oh, it's you. Took a shine to him, did you?' This he said while leering at Cora. 'He likes trouble then, I take it.'

'Sorry,' I interjected, 'but what sort of trouble are Regulators? I know I don't want to be hung. Hanged? Um.'

Cora slipped the luck vials away ruefully. Behind us, the bidding was still in full swing. 'They're a bit like police, only less polite. They definitely won't like this auction happening.'

I ran this through a few strands of reasoning in my head. 'So they regulate, like . . . illegal magical things? Stop the dangerous stuff getting out, sort of thing?' I glanced at the sorry looking horned goat in the bandstand. 'What's so dangerous about that?'

'It's not exactly–'

Shouts interrupted her. The crowd was breaking apart.

'Ah, shit,' said Arnold. 'We've dallied too long.'

Yellow torch lights strobed between figures in the throng. At the end of them I could just make out a group of suited individuals, clutching clipboards. One of them was holding out a badge and reciting from a notebook.

'. . . for the attempted sale of critically endangered species, including unacceptable transport and housing conditions, sub-standard para-normal containment measures and reckless endangerment of event participants . . .'

As the speaker continued, her colleagues were walking a perimeter around the bandstand with a very heavy looking net. Purple sparks crackled along its threads.

It was thrown over a small fleeing group who had bunched together – they jolted into the air as if shocked by lightning, and then the net, moving like it was alive, began to wrap them up in itself. My stomach turned as I produced the thought that it looked as though they were being eaten.

'I'd like to run now,' I squeaked.

'This way!' said Cora.

Together, the three of us cut through the stragglers into the depths of Battersea Park. Behind us, someone screamed.

I glanced over my shoulder and saw, in a puddle of light centred on the bandstand, one of the grey-suited Regulators speared on the unicorn's horn. Blood pooled around its hooves. It lowered its head and, with corpse still attached, charged at another.

'You okay?' Cora asked, when I'd finished retching into a bush.

'I might be next week,' I mumbled.

A figure stepped out of the trees ahead of us. It wore a grey pinstripe suit and held a clipboard. Behind it, a lattice of black tendrils hovered eerily in the air like the other net we'd seen. My shock-soaked brain was too overloaded to wonder what exactly they were attached to.

'Cease and desist,' the Regulator said as we backed away. The net advanced toward us.

Fear tingled along my spine, and propelled my hand into my pocket in search of a weapon, keys maybe. Instead, I encountered the small jar of sunlight Cora had given me, wrapped in cloth.

'We won't come quietly,' Cora warned.

The Regulator smiled. 'You don't need to.' The tendrils lunged – and I pulled the sunlight into the open.

Everybody yelled, fighting blazing sunspots on their eyeballs. I dropped the jar and reached out, eyes closed, for Cora and Arnold, and grabbed them both by the arm.

'What the *hell* is that?' Arnold snarled.

'I think we should run!' I shouted desperately.

Cora laughed. A buoyant, exuberant laugh. 'Too right.'

We staggered away, the blind leading the blinded. I felt along with an outstretched hand until I bumped into a tree. 'You can open your eyes now,' I said. I didn't look back, but the beams of sunlight made long shadows out of the trees all around us – until it was suddenly squashed and we were thrust back into darkness.

'Don't stop now,' Cora said. 'We're nearly at the gate.'

The huge Victorian iron rails loomed ahead. We reached the gate to find it fastened with a heavy padlock.

'Excuse me,' Arnold said, shoving past me. He curled his fist. As it swung in an arc it grew bigger, hairier. It smashed down onto the lock and shattered it open.

We ran out into a deserted road junction and followed it south, then flagged down the first night bus we saw.

It was empty save for a couple of drunks propping each other up at the front, and a nurse still in scrubs nodding against a window. Our strange troupe piled into the backseat with hardly a raised eyebrow from the bus driver – she'd seen far stranger than us, for sure.

Cora chattered excitedly as the bus pulled away, her hands flapping in the air. '. . . we showed that Regulator, right Jack? I told Seven we'd work well together! And look . . .' She pulled out the three vials of luck. 'The dice were right! He didn't lose his investment!'

She cackled as she held them up to the obnoxiously bright bus lights. I thought it was a good look for a witch, or a vagrant, or a peddler of magical recipes . . . or whatever else it was she decided to be in the moment.

Arnold quietly chuntered to himself. 'Stupid, all of it. Don't know what I even would've done with a unicorn.'

'I would have bred it,' Cora said confidently.

'With just the one, would you?' said Arnold.

'I'd find another.'

'Ha! It's that easy for you, is it?'

'How rare are they?' I asked.

Arnold harumphed. 'Let's say that'll be the only one you see in your entire lifetime, lad. Regulators will've snaffled that one up, no doubt.'

'Where will they take it?'

'Who knows. Us common folk ain't privy to that sort of information.'

I reflected briefly on what 'uncommon folk' must look like in this world, if Arnold considered himself to be common.

I shifted my weight against Cora, noticed her eyes were closed and gave her a gentle prod. 'Cora?'

'Hmm?' Her eyes fluttered open. 'I'm awake. I was just thinking about how you'd tame a unicorn. They say it's supposedly to do with virgins, but I'd argue there's no such thing . . .'

'Ah?' I crossed my legs. Cora leaned comfortably into me, head resting on my shoulder. I wanted to enjoy the moment, but too many questions were dancing on my tongue. 'Seems like a lot of people wanted to get a hold of that unicorn. Are they magic? Apart from being, well, unicorns? Why have I never seen one in a zoo?'

Cora's mouth scrunched up, and I could see she didn't want to admit she didn't know the answer. 'Well, they're rare. I don't think they're easy to catch. Um. I think the horn has some magical properties . . .'

'They can cure anything,' Arnold interrupted gruffly. 'There's your answer, mate. They were hunted to near extinction centuries ago. Got the plague? Get a unicorn. Leg fell orf? Get a unicorn. Been poisoned? You get the picture.'

'I see,' I said. It rang true. *Everybody* wants a magic cure-all. Whether it's to cure disease, weight loss, poverty – or to pass some arbitrary exams.

Exams which, come to think of it, suddenly seemed extremely pointless. They were a long way away from my new vantage point at the back of a London night bus, sandwiched between a probably-witch and a beast-man librarian, on the way home from a unicorn auction.

I nudged Cora again. 'Can I come with you, to tell Seven how it went?'

'Sure.'

'And I don't suppose . . . is he hiring?'

Her mouth flicked into a smirk. 'You want a job, Jack?'

'People keep telling me I should think about my career options.'

She laughed. 'Think you can handle it?'

'Yeah,' I said. 'Yes. I think I can.'

Episode 9: Safe-Keeping

As my reminiscences drew to a close, I fell back into itchy silence and tightened my grip on the steering wheel.

Ang had been quiet for a long time. My tale about Cora had waffled on and dwelt too much on unnecessary details with nary an interruption. Perhaps Ang knew that I was just avoiding the real story.

Rain pattered on the windscreen. I stared past it and the squeaking wipers, concentrating on a too-familiar route to our destination. I'd probably approached it from every angle of the country, by then.

Ang's fingers drummed on the door; a crisp packet rustled as she shifted position. Eventually she sighed and said, 'So what happened to her, *gwas?*'

'Hmm?' I pretended to be absorbed in the road ahead.

'Ye didn't finish the telling. Still in the dark, I am, about where we're going and what trouble it's for.'

'I thought you preferred the dark.' My headlights illuminated the distorted shapes of tree branches and overgrown verges that obscured my view through the rain. I was guided more by the diamond glint of reflective cats' eyes in the tarmac than by a true sense of where the road ended and began.

Ang tutted. 'Not the time for quips, *twpsyn.* You an' this girl were *cariadon,* aye? Sweethearts?'

'Mm.'

'Not still, I'm guessin'. But she's in trouble, and you wants to help?' Ang pressed. 'How'd you know she'll be happy to see you, *gwas?* Does she even want your help?'

'Ha!' The noise that broke from my mouth was bitter. 'No, she won't be happy to see us, Ang. Because she won't even *see* us. Because . . . it's all . . . it all went wrong. And I don't want to talk about it.'

She continued to mutter. 'Dunno how ye expect me to be of any help if ye won't even tell me what we're walkin' into–'

'You'll see when we get there,' I said flatly. 'It'll be pretty fucking self-explanatory, all right?'

I could see a rebuke on the tip of her tongue, but she held it. Instead, very quietly, she said, 'Language, *gwas,*' and turned to face the window.

My skin burned. Sweating with nerves as much as shame. I should have taken my coat off before the long drive. My pride stopped me trying to shrug out of it now.

'She's in the hospital,' I said to the steering wheel. 'She did something . . . really stupid. And I didn't stop her.'

Ang nodded, with half-lidded eyes in her reflection. The ominous shape of dark hedges and moon-edged clouds flitted by the window. After a little while, her snores wafted over the dashboard.

My knuckles remained gripped tight on the wheel, following the flash of cat's eyes in the road ahead.

'I should have stopped her,' I whispered.

* * *

I called it 'the hospital' out of habit. Or perhaps because calling it a nursing home felt like too much reality to swallow.

The Parkview Residential Home was tucked into an area of social housing in the London borough of Lambeth. It wasn't far from North

174

Clapham: our former home, when we'd wanted one.

Grey blocks of flats surrounded it in a neighbourhood of dying concrete. Mildew stained the cheery little welcome sign that was partially hidden by tall weeds. Once, it was probably quite a grand Georgian house, but now the stucco was cracked and paint peeled in ribbons from the narrow sash windows. A squat, modern brick extension bolted on the side evoked the same feeling as the council flats – one of grim uniformity.

I passed Ang the floppy kid-size sunhat. 'You know the drill.'

She stuck out her tongue in disgust. 'Not the dress, too.'

'It's for the best.'

Ang shrugged into the pastel green pinafore which had been made to fit a three-year-old. She gave me a sour frown. Plastic sunglasses – in the shape of yellow flowers – completed the look. It was just enough to fool the eye into skipping over the greyish hair that poked out from under the hat, and the deep lines in a face far older than any human looking at it.

She refused to remove her trousers though, and her chunky work boots stuck out sorely in the ensemble. I had a mind to buy some pink stickers next time to camouflage them.

The nurse at the front desk looked up as we pushed through the heavy double doors of the home. She regarded me with an initially wary expression (my crumpled coat and uncombed hair didn't do me any favours), which then transformed into recognition.

'Oh. Hello, Mr Hansard,' she said pleasantly. 'It's been a while since I last saw you. You well, are you?'

'Yes, thank you, Mavis. Don't usually see you on reception?'

Her smile faltered, for just a second. 'We're a bit short-staffed today. Wearing many hats! You know how it is, hands needed elsewhere and everyone's covering for everyone else–'

I interrupted her wittering, gently. 'Can we go through?'

'Just sign in here first, lovie. And *who's this darling?*' Mavis crooned. She craned forward to get a good look at Ang. 'What a dear! Those are very pretty sunglasses. Oh and I love those boots, petal! Proper stomping boots, aren't they?'

'*–nks,*' said Ang, in the smallest possible voice.

Mavis' eyes twinkled worryingly. 'Is she your–'

'My niece,' I said, hurriedly scrawling my name on the visitor sheet. 'Yes. I'm just looking after her for today. Come along now . . . Emma.'

There was a near imperceptible shift in Ang's stance and for a heartbeat I didn't think I'd get away with it. Then she said primly, 'Comin', Uncle Pickles,' and trotted after me.

'Pickles!' I heard Mavis exclaim into her hand behind us.

'All right, you got the last laugh there,' I said. 'But how am I supposed to explain a name like Ang?'

''Tis short for Angharad,' Ang replied sulkily. 'Perfectly good Welsh name, that.'

'I'll take your word for it.'

I exchanged a smile and a pleasantry with a few of the care assistants as we traversed the stale green corridors. An unusual tension laced their greetings and haste filled their goodbyes. It put me on edge.

I stopped one of the porters as he tried to rush by. 'Is something going on?' I asked.

He brushed me off with a thin smile. 'Nothing to worry about. Just an agitated resident. You know how things are. Excuse me.' He sped off around a corner. Two nurses followed him. In a distant part of the building, someone screamed.

'That don't sound good, *gwas,*' said Ang, stepping closer to me.

'I know,' I said with a heavy exhale. 'But it's how things are, sometimes.'

'What kind o' hospital is this, then?'

Our feet squeaked on the scuffed vinyl as we continued walking. It was tattered in places where it met with skirting board, and the ugly brown geometric pattern looked like it could have been dredged from the seventies.

'It's not really a hospital,' I said. 'It's a . . . Ang, when coblynau get too old to care for themselves, what do you do with them?'

'Their family looks after 'em.'

'Right. And if they have no family?' I avoided looking at the walls, which were a washed-out kind of sage green. They sported paintings of wrinkly puppies and chubby children in scenes of play. Clearly meant as cheerful decoration, they only served to heighten the depressing atmosphere of the home.

'Then their friends will take 'em,' Ang replied.

I pinched the bridge of my nose. 'Okay. Now suppose there's no one left who knows them, or who can take care of them. Do you have a place where all the oldies can be looked after together?'

'No, *gwas*.' The sunglasses obscured Ang's expression, but her mouth contorted with a note of puzzlement. 'Some family'll always take 'em in. There's a whole clan lookin' out for them, anyways.'

'I see. No coblyn left behind, is it?' I led her up a flight of stairs. On the upper floor our footfalls were muffled by a deep and age-stained carpet. 'It's not that way with humans, I'm afraid. Well, you might say we're all one big clan, and the good ones try to look after our own and– well, not for free of course, because there's also often a price and– I'm butchering this explanation.'

I stopped by an open door and nodded inside. A frail-looking chappie with a ring of white hair on his otherwise bald head appeared to be listening to music from an armchair. He sang along in a reedy voice, though his head was tipped back and eyes were closed. After a moment's listening it became apparent he was singing the lyrics to an altogether different song than what was playing.

'Sometimes, a person needs a little too much help – more than a family can give – or they have no family to give it,' I said, moving on down the hall. 'That's where places like this come in. This home specialises in people whose brains have gone . . . well. Maybe just 'gone".'

'Ah. Your Cora's brain ain't workin' right, then?' said Ang.

'You might say that,' I replied through gritted teeth.

We came to Cora's room. I halted outside, straightened my coat and smoothed down my hair – for no real reason, except perhaps I hoped one day it would make a difference.

The door swung open with a push. Cora was silhouetted in the window, slouched in a high-backed armchair staring out over the grounds. Faded red paper pennants hung like tired bunting around the window frame, lending a cheerless mood to the scene.

'Hello,' I said softly. 'It's me.' There was no response. 'I've brought a friend this time. This is Ang. She's a coblyn. I think you'd get on.'

Ang followed me to the window and took in Cora's vacant, unblinking stare. Her ink-black hair was combed almost straight; face devoid of the zany make-up she loved so much. Dark rings under her eyes made her look exhausted, as if perpetually in need of sleep. Yet she stared forward, relentlessly.

'Disturbing, that is.' Ang said. 'Does she hear us?'

'I want to think so.'

Peering around the edges of furniture, I tried to make a surreptitious check of the room. No monsters hiding under the bed or behind the curtains. No Baines and Grayle assassin waiting to spring from the wardrobe. What danger had Quiet Eyes sent me here to find?

'Ye lost somethin'?' said Ang.

'No. Just making sure she's . . . safe.'

The hairs on my neck prickled.

Ang swivelled abruptly and glowered up at the ceiling. 'What's your game, ye ugly *basdun?* Yeah, I sees you!'

There a shadow curled outward, unfurling a sense of gangling limbs and a multitude of eyes. Ang looked torn between fight or flight as it reached down toward us.

I pressed my hand to the wall and muttered a simple incantation. A blue spark raced along the plaster like lightning and struck the creature in its middle.

It released a sigh – like the sound of air escaping a corpse – and collapsed in on itself. The shape folded inward, shrinking smaller and smaller as it backed into the ceiling, until finally it was only a dark speck against the plaster. A corrosive smell accompanied the final *pop* as it disappeared entirely.

A pattern of glowing sigils flared briefly on the walls, then faded.

I shook the pins and needles out of my hand. 'Reckon it needs recharging. Doesn't matter what I do, I can't seem to keep them out.'

Ang recovered quickly. 'What was that, *gwas?*'

'Protection ward,' I said, dusting off my hands. 'I pay a guy called Seb to install them. A bit of magic to keep the creepy buggers out.'

'I meant the monster, *twpsyn.*'

'Oh. 'Monster' is probably right. Horrid things, like nightmares. I don't know exactly what they are, but they keep appearing around her.' I moved to check on Cora. She looked untouched. I'd never found evidence of any harm, but who's to say it would be visible?

'No one's been able to identify them for me,' I said. 'I had a medium in once who declared this room was a well of negative energy and then promptly ran away. Then I tried a priest for an exorcism. He was certain they were demonic entities, but his tricks only seemed to piss them off. So now I put as many wards and charms around her as I can, and hope it's enough.'

Surely Quiet Eyes hadn't been referring to these monsters? They were run of the mill, in Cora's current state. The one I'd just dispatched may have looked nasty, but it was a weak little thing compared to others I'd seen.

Ang pulled down her sunglasses and peered solemnly into Cora's eyes. There was not a flicker of lashes nor a twitch of muscle. It was only by careful observation that you might notice she was breathing, slow and shallow. Eventually, with sluggish effort, the eyes would blink. And that would be all.

It was a good room that Cora had, despite the general agedness of the décor. Spacious and high-ceilinged, like a lot of these old houses were built to be. And the staff were kind, and devoted to their residents.

I knew Cora was fed, and bathed, and all-told looked after very well. But I never asked the specifics (Does she chew when she eats? Does she seem to enjoy the warm water? Is she ever uncomfortable?) because frankly, I was scared of knowing the answers.

'What were the stupid thing, *gwas?*' Ang asked, piercing my melancholy. 'What she done to end up like this?'

I perched on the end of Cora's bed. It wasn't much of a view from the window: the top branches of a wall of trees, with grey concrete flats poking out behind them. Cora had always been looking to escape, and it was the worst kind of irony that she'd ended up a prisoner.

Wearily, I began. 'She was obsessed. Not with any one thing, but with whatever the next 'big thing' could be. Obsessive, maybe that's the word. Cora always needed to reach one step higher, one score greater, one level beyond whatever she was capable of. And at that time, she was obsessing about bridges.'

I paused, rolling the details around in my mind. Outside the room, a mild clattering marked the passage of the tea trolley making its way down the corridor.

'When I say bridges, I obviously mean the kind you and I use,' I said. 'She was practically an expert on finding them, and *building* them, that's what was amazing. She could do what your coblynau did – create pocket dimensions, with temporary bridges in and out. They never lasted very long, though. We had a few hairy escapes where a dimension nearly collapsed with us still inside.'

Ang frowned. 'Ain't surprised. Takes a mighty amount of effort to do somethin' like that. We had a whole crew and the flames of the furnaces, and a human bridge that were already built!'

She climbed into the chair that was positioned opposite Cora's, having realised this would be another long story, and made herself at home amid the paisley.

'Right,' I agreed. 'Cora was definitely one for taking risks. Is, I mean.'

Ang rolled her eyes as she plumped a cushion. 'Can't guess why ye liked one another.'

'She became particularly obsessed with trying to make a bridge to the fairy world. The fae realm, whatever you want to call it. The place piskies and their ilk come from.'

There was a picture frame facing Cora's bed that the nurses had hung. It flaunted an idyllic meadow of blue flowers, and put me in mind of the piskey glen at Mên-an-Tol.

'Piskies had just turned up again around that time, you see, and all the gossip was about how they got here and what might be on the 'other side'. Cora wanted to be the first to find out.'

Ang's brow crinkled. 'Fairies ain't nothin' new, are they *gwas?*'

'Well, no. But I guess they'd been gone a long time. Those piskies sure caused a stir on the Black Market, anyway.'

I remembered trawling through old fairy stories with Cora, turning the pages of heavy tomes in Arnold's library, trying to trace back their origins in true history. We never got very far. I came away with a good knowledge of fairy tales, and little else.

'The old stories about fairies are . . . well, *old*,' I went on. 'So people thought maybe the fairies all went away for a while. And Cora wanted to know where.'

'*Why?*' Ang implored.

I sighed. 'Why not?'

A rattling trolley interrupted us, and Mavis entered the room. Ang hastily threw her sunglasses back on.

'Hello again, you two,' Mavis said. 'Cup of tea, love?'

'No, thank you,' I replied.

'No trouble, no trouble. I'll just give Cora her pills and be on my way.' Mavis consulted her clipboard and popped two tablets from their packaging. I turned away while she administered them. I knew Cora would hate the indignity of it.

My eyes wandered over the contents of the trolley, tried and failed to decipher the tangle of handwritten notes on the clipboard.

'All done, love. I'll get out of your hair,' Mavis announced.

I was about to open the door for her when alarm bells clanged in my head – to the rhythm of footsteps pounding down the corridor toward us. They were followed by desperate shouts and radio chatter.

I threw out an arm to stop Mavis and opened the door a crack. A blur ran past, a brief impression of an older woman in silk pyjamas and only one slipper. A porter intercepted her and they both tumbled to the floor in front of the next door along.

The other staff caught up, red-faced and sweating in their pastel-coloured scrubs. Clearly, the pyjama'd lady had given them quite the run-around. They tried to shush and calm her. The porter radioed for more hands and for someone to bring sedation.

All the while the woman screamed. 'I won't take them! I won't take them! They're made of people! *They're made of people!*'

'What's happenin',' Ang whispered at my hip.

Mavis gave her a fawning look and drew her away from the door. 'Nothing to worry about, lovie. Sometimes people just get a little bit confused, and we have to help them back to bed, that's all.'

'She don't sound confused,' said Ang.

'Don't make me!' the woman still shouted. 'It's not right! They'll make me hurt you! Do you understand? *They'll make me hurt you!'*

Mavis gave Ang a bright smile, as if trying to drown out the sounds with sheer cheerfulness alone. 'Julie here is a little worried about her pills,' she said in a sing-song voice.

'What's wrong with the pills?' I murmured.

'Nothing, love,' Mavis said. 'She just has problems. You know how it is here.' She gave a wobbly laugh. 'Poor thing thinks her meds will turn her into a werewolf. Can you imagine? She's needed extra supervision all day.'

The voices outside grew more frantic, now punctuated by obscenities and the sound of ripping fabric. And soon enough, more screams.

I slammed the door shut.

'Hey Ang,' I said shakily, 'I don't suppose you have any silver on you, do you?'

'No *gwas*. But our life depends on it, I expect.'

'Probably.'

Mavis stared at the door in horror. I assumed she'd glimpsed the same scene as I.

I steered her to the bed where her mental functions could shut down without fear of collapse.

A quick scan of the room confirmed the obvious – no one's going to display anything of real value in a residential care home, and it's not like Cora owned very much to begin with. There was one thing I could hopefully count on, however.

'Hope you don't mind,' I said to Cora as I pulled open her bedside drawers. The nurses knew I left her 'gifts' and they generally humoured me by leaving them wherever they were. The bunting around her window was a series of *omamori* charms I'd purchased, to dissuade unfriendly things from trying to enter. And in her drawer, assuming no one had half-inched it . . . yes!

I held up the necklace and the pendant caught the light as it spun. A simple pentacle, for protection. Crucially, it was made of silver.

'What's that gunna do, *gwas?* Ye don't mean to give the beast a present, do ye!'

I found Ang hiding under the bed, peeping out between Mavis' stockinged legs. 'I've got an idea. I want you to stay with Cora while I lead our hairy friend away.'

'Suits me, *gwas.*'

I stole up to the door. Snarls and snuffling sounds came from the other side. No more shrieks, I noticed. Hopefully it meant the staff had all run.

Or it could mean the opposite.

From an inner coat pocket, I withdrew a small bottle. The glass was slightly cloudy now from the friction that came with age – and from existing within an item of clothing subjected my often-distressing lifestyle. But the contents still shone as brightly as the day I'd been given it.

Cora had enjoyed bottling moonlight just as much as sunlight.

The soft white glow enveloped my hand.

'Well, I hope these stories are true,' I muttered.

I nudged the door open a crack and peered into the hall. The snarls had morphed into whines: an unsettlingly canine keening that brought to mind a lost puppy.

It would have to be a *big* puppy.

This one was human-sized, and curled into the foetal position on the floor. To my relief, there were no bloodstains surrounding it.

Cautiously, I stretched out my hand with the silver chain . . .

Its snout shot up, catching my scent. The werewolf unfolded, finding more space for knees and elbows than I had accounted for. Long limbs, lean and muscled, opened up until it stood at least eight feet tall. It towered over me. Saliva dripped in globules from the jaw of a true carnivore and splattered on my cheek.

'Meep,' I said.

The beast didn't seem to know what to do with me, however. The head bobbed up and down in a muddled sort of way, and the savage mouth opened and closed like it was trying to form words.

Moving as slowly as I dared with my other hand, I lifted the bottled moonlight in front of its face.

The pupils dilated, transfixed.

'Goood dog,' I said under my breath. 'Now, just follow the pretty light...'

I edged into the corridor and began leading the creature down the hall. I wanted to at least get it away from Cora's room before my next play, just in case things went wrong – as they usually did.

But this brute of a canine was unnervingly docile. It seemed almost grateful to be under the guidance of someone else.

I waited until we were in the stairwell (at least two directions to run, I figured: up, or down). My back pressed up against the black metal banister, while the werewolf took up most of the landing.

Now I'd have to reach the bloody thing.

I steered its head to one side with the moonlight, and the predator's gaze followed calmly. It crouched as I lowered my hand, sitting almost like a dog on its hind legs. I shuffled forward until I was level with its head, and then reached . . . ever . . . so . . . tentatively . . . over its ears with the pentacle.

As the silver touched flesh the werewolf jerked – *screeched* – and yanked me on top of it. I struggled, caught in a fetid knot of hair and claws. I would have been a goner if those claws weren't busy tearing at the creature's face, trying to snap off the chain. The silver burned into its skin with a smell like putrid bacon.

I slipped out of the werewolf's erratic grapple and stumbled away. Already, the form was changing, shrinking. I heard bones cracking as they remoulded in their sockets. Hair fell away in clumps onto the carpet. Claws too, pushed right out of their recesses and replaced by new keratin. Finally, the teeth: they dropped wretchedly out of sore gums, where new white buds erupted underneath.

I watched all this numbly. Shapeshifting wasn't exactly new to me, but this was the most visceral transformation I'd ever seen.

Carefully, I set my bottle of moonlight down in a safe corner, and draped my coat over the quivering body of the woman named Julie.

'Someone will be along soon, I expect,' I said, feeling abruptly useless.

She was more or less naked, having shredded her silk pyjamas. My itchy fingers considered picking up one of the ejected werewolf teeth.

I'd seen a whole set once, for sale on the Black Market. On Edric Mercer's table. He'd hunted a werewolf, or so he claimed, by using moonlight to enthral it. Now I wondered how he'd really gotten them.

It was a lot easier to be amazed by an otherworldly prize when you weren't faced with the person it had been taken from.

A sorrowful groan emanated from under my coat. '. . . Betty?' Julie's voice was weak and croaky.

I leaned down and gently tugged the fabric away from her face. 'What's that?'

'Where's my Betty? She'll know . . . she'll know what to do . . .' The eyes snapped open and a veiny hand lunged for my shirt. 'Don't make me take them,' she growled, an edge of the wolf suddenly in her pallid features. 'The pills. There's something wrong with the pills . . .'

Lucidity faded from her eyes and the hand grasping me fell limply away.

'Betty,' she moaned, like a wounded animal.

'We'll take it from here,' said a voice by my shoulder, making me shoot a foot into the air. 'Sorry to startle you. I've radioed the others.'

The chap was a nurse. He didn't seem fazed by the strange excretions of hair and teeth, and set straight to covering Julie with a warm blanket.

'Does this happen often?' I said as he handed me my coat.

'No,' he replied brusquely.

'Is she being looked after?'

'Yes.'

'She was asking for Betty.'

'She always does.'

I was about to snap when he altered his tone.

He put a hand on my shoulder. 'Look mate, I understand. It's difficult to see someone in this state. Betty was Julie's wife, and she died three years ago.' He stooped to the ground and began collecting up the debris of hair and teeth. He moved fast, stuffing them into his pockets. 'A little help?'

I joined him on the floor. 'Is this the best place for her? For a werewolf, I mean.'

I watched his expression carefully. There was no surprise or disbelief.

'Where else could she go?' He cast one last glance around to check we'd picked up everything. 'Julie doesn't remember. About Betty. Or about her . . . condition. Dementia is cruel as anything.'

Some peculiar bitterness in the way he said this made me pry deeper. 'Did you know Julie before?'

His shoulders slumped and he ran a hand through his coarse brown hair. 'She's my mum.' He held his hand out to me and I shook it. 'Name's David. Thanks for catching her. It's not her fault–'

He bolted upright as other Parkview staff arrived by the stairwell. They carried more blankets but hovered cautiously on the threshold.

'She's had a psychotic episode,' David told them. 'Worse than last time.'

An assistant in pink scrubs said shrilly, 'There was a . . . thing.'

'She's quite calm now, I promise,' David assured.

'No, I mean, it was a creature . . .'

David blustered past this, using a tactic of distraction which I liked to employ myself. 'I know it can be frightening when a patient has an aggressive episode. Quick, now, she needs more blankets. Look, she's shivering. Has someone brought fresh clothes? Wheelchair? Well, why not! Come on folks, we all know what we need to do . . .'

Julie was slowly crowded with caring hands and soothing voices. I hung awkwardly on the edge of the activity, waiting for David to be free again. I had questions for this man.

Finally, a passive and perplexed Julie was wheeled away. David, perhaps having sensed my gaze tracking him the entire time, joined me in leaning against the stairwell railing.

'I know what you're going to say,' he said.

'Do you? I was thinking about chips,' I replied airily. 'I haven't had anything to eat today.'

David patted his trouser pockets, checking he hadn't spilled any of his mother's tell-tale remnants. My fingers flexed guiltily. A small handful of werewolf teeth had made their way inside my coat during the hasty clean-up.

'I can't look after her by myself,' David said. 'I work long shifts and I'm hardly ever home. It makes sense for her to be where I work. I can look after her better here, you see?'

'I wasn't judging.' I looked up at the ceiling. The stairs stretched for another three flights. 'It's not a full moon, is it? What caused her to transform?'

'I don't know. She isn't unsafe,' he was quick to add. 'I know she isn't all there but . . . She doesn't usually transform of her own will, these days. And I can handle the regular ones by myself. They're in the calendar, like.'

'Could something be wrong with her meds?' I asked. 'She seemed very against them.'

David rubbed his brow, and I could feel the exhaustion coming off him in waves. 'Maybe she had a bad reaction to them. I'll definitely get her prescription changed, just in case.'

He pulled out a small white box and turned it over in his hands. 'We had such high hopes for her with this. New wonder drug, you know. They're saying it might cure almost anything.'

'Surely not lycanthropy.'

'Goodness, no. I'm talking about the dementia.'

Some sounds began to filter up the stairwell: gentle but firm instructions accompanied by soft chatter. I gathered that with the excitement of Julie's 'episode' being over, the staff were ushering some of the other residents to the TV room for elevenses.

David turned to look down the stairwell, to the source of the noise. He tapped the tablet box again. 'This has been amazing for other patients. Really life changing. We might be able to bring people back to themselves, you know.'

'Oh?' Of course, Cora flashed to the forefront of my mind, even though I'd long ago lost hope of conventional medicine being the answer to her problems.

But it was almost absent-mindedly that my gaze lingered on the box, and finally saw what I hadn't seen before, a glaring detail in Cora's room that my eyes had passed right over.

I snatched the tablets from his hand.

All trace of affability evaporated. 'You need to give that back. Right now,' David said. Just a hint of growl in his voice told me that his mother's condition was likely genetic.

I placed the box back in his palm and gingerly pointed to a logo in the bottom right corner. 'What's this?'

He relaxed. The suggestion of teeth retreated. 'Oh, that's just the name of the pharmaceutical company that makes them.'

'I see. Excuse me. I have– There's something urgent–' I hobbled past him, knees twinging where I'd taken a blow from Julie's flailing werewolf limbs.

Mavis was right where I'd left her on Cora's bed, being tended to by Ang, who had apparently poured her a cup of tea from the trolley.

'There's no milk, *gwas*,' Ang informed me. 'An' only a coupla them plain biscuits. Could do wi' some chocolate ones when you get a minute.'

I ignored her completely and strode to the trolley where Cora's pills still lay on top of Mavis' clipboard. There, the same red logo branded the box. 'Ang,' I said sharply. 'Look at this.'

She joined me and regarded the box. Her sunglasses dropped to the floor.

'What's this mean?' she said hoarsely.

'I don't know.'

Glaring up at us, so blatant as to be obscene, were the words *Baines & Grayle*. An Egyptian wedjat eye was emblazoned underneath to complete the emblem.

I cleared my throat to get Mavis' attention. 'How long has Cora been taking these?' My voice sounded hollow.

Mavis swayed as she broke from shocked reverie. 'The panaceatemol? The doctor switched her onto them about a year ago now, I think.'

'Why?'

'Thought it was worth trying. I feel they're doing some good, love. We've seen improved muscle control. She can sit for longer and she's better at swallowing.' Mavis sounded hopeful, but her face fell as she took in my expression. 'What's wrong, love?'

It was hard work, keeping the hysterics out of my voice. 'You take her off them. Right now, you hear? You don't give her this drug any more.'

Her eyes crinkled in sympathy. 'I don't decide that, Mr Hansard. And you don't, either. You're not a family member.'

'She has no family,' I hissed through my teeth. 'I'm as good as she's got.'

'Believe me, I wish it could be that way. But there's paperwork.' Mavis retrieved her clipboard and tapped it meaningfully. She'd clearly regained her senses, having been offered familiar, solid ground to reason with. 'Lots of paperwork. Why don't you want her on these pills? I promise, I think they're making a difference.'

I glanced at Cora, where I saw no difference at all. 'Please Mavis. Can't you put a word in?' I thought suddenly of Julie. 'Tell the doctor she's suffering bad side effects! That's why I'm worried. She could even be allergic . . .'

Mavis clacked her teeth and gave me such a look that I knew I must have sounded pathetic. 'Jack, in all these years, you've never once mentioned anything about Cora having an allergy.'

'Please.'

She sighed, her composure softening as she absorbed the tension in my face. 'If it's really worrying you, I'll see what I can do.'

'I can't overstate how much this means to me,' I said.

Taking hold of the trolley, Mavis rattled out the door. 'No promises, love.'

'We could steal 'em,' Ang said, when she was out of earshot.

I paced the room. 'The tablets? No. They'll only get more. How many other residents are they treating with . . . with . . .'

I could barely bring myself to say it. The words whooshed out of me in a frothing mouthful of rage. 'Bloody *Baines and Grayle!* Pharmaceuticals? Ha! Are we supposed to believe they're – what, scientists? *Doctors?* There's something awful going on here, Ang, and I have no goddamn clue what their game might be. None at all. None at *all!*'

'Aye, *gwas.* I hears ye.' Ang sucked her teeth. 'Why ain't we heard this before, you think? Seems right brass o' them, t'be doing business so openly.'

'Maybe it's not their real business. Maybe it's a front,' I hazarded wildly. 'It can't be as simple as . . . this. Except, obviously it can.' I slumped into the chair opposite Cora. 'We've been asking in the wrong circles, Ang. We should've just gone down the bloody pharmacy.'

I rubbed my face. I'd been expecting to find some presence of Baines and Grayle here. But not *this*. Not horribly entwined with Cora's care.

'I expected an assassin,' I said under my breath. 'That's what Quiet Eyes made it sound like . . .'

'Whassat, *gwas?*' Ang said sharply.

'What?'

'You was muttering. About the quiet-eyed *ast.*' Ang's grey eyes drilled into me. 'How's it that she said somethin' to you?'

'Oh, Christ.'

She flung off her disguise, clearly intent on having this barney in more accustomed attire. I briefly wondered if she could throw a punch, and how much it would hurt if she did.

I held up my hands. 'All right, you need to hear me out,' I said. 'And the most important thing is that I was definitely going to tell you.'

'Tell me what?' Ang's grey curls bounced as she visibly seethed. 'Secrets, is there? What was it we agreed *gwas,* about keepin' secrets!'

'It would've complicated things!' I shouted back. 'Quiet Eyes came to *me–*'

'When?'

'At Mên-an-Tol. Yes, hardly any time at all!'

Ang scoffed, hands striking onto her hips. 'We were there a good while. Were this before or after the mess wi' the piskey dust?'

I forgot how well Ang could read my expressions sometimes – and that a good poker face can be the biggest giveaway of all. She went very quiet. 'Say, *gwas.* What happened to all our piskey dust from that business? 'Cuz I feels like I only ever seen one jar go into the stock.'

'You need to listen. Quiet Eyes made a deal–'

Ang cursed vividly. '*You* listen. You makin' deals with our enemies, *gwas?* What were you thinkin'?' She headed off my attempt to interrupt. '*I don't care what it were for!* Ye shouldn't've done it, least've all without talkin' to me! Ye should've told me. That's what business partners do. That's what *friends* do, *gwas.*'

'I'm telling you now,' I persevered. 'And you have to listen. Because what Quiet Eyes exchanged was the location of your missing friends!'

This didn't have the effect I'd hoped for. Ang went quite rigid, and stared at me as though I were a stranger.

'Say again,' she said, in an oddly strained voice.

I exhaled, summoning patience into my tone. 'In return for the piskey dust, Quiet Eyes told me where to find your coblynau,' I said. 'She more or less confirmed Baines and Grayle were behind it, too. I don't know if she's turned tail on them or what, but she gave me an address, Ang. So now we know exactly where to go.'

Her eyes narrowed. 'When were ye gunna tell me this?'

'I'm telling you now.'

'Only because ye let slip. Which it feels like ye didn't mean to.'

I winced, caught out by the texture of a lie. How could I make her understand? 'I thought Cora was in danger–'

'*I would've still come with ye,*' Ang said ruthlessly. 'If ye'd said. If only ye'd *said,* Hansard! Why'd you paint me as a deserter? Or were you afeared I'd demand that we leave your lass behind? Ye thinks that of me? Partners, we were s'posed to be.'

Words, usually so pithy on my tongue, utterly failed me. Ang's anger dulled into a despondent monologue.

'Yer good at leavin' out details,' she said. 'Because no one else is important enough for the details, aye? An' so ye drags people along without concern. Bottom line, *gwas:* your matters were more important than mine, an' you didn't think I was worth even consulting on it.'

She held out a slender, work-worn hand. 'I wants what's mine. Write down this address o' yours, so's I can find mine kin.'

'I'll still help you,' I mumbled, though my ego was busy licking its wounds.

'I *paid*,' she snapped back. 'Give me what you owe, and be on yer way. I don't wants your help.'

'Ang,' I implored, 'hang on a minute. Let's take a breather. We'll be laughing about this tomorrow . . .'

'Ain't nothin' funny about betraying a friend, Hansard.'

'I didn't–' I stopped, because I recognised the warning in her eyes. The sparks of a wrathful furnace glinted in their steel grey depths. 'If you really insist. Here.'

I handed her the crumpled slip of paper that Quiet Eyes had given me. Ang read it coldly and shoved it into her waistcoat. 'Done, we are. Debts paid. If I sees your face again, I'll give it a cuffing.'

She turned and walked to the door. Without even a farewell, she was gone.

Just like that?

I was stunned.

You fucked up.

'Shut up,' I said under my breath. I looked at Cora and blew out a leaden breath. 'I think I really have fucked up.'

Why didn't I tell Ang as soon as Quiet Eyes appeared? Because she wouldn't agree to the terms of the deal, I'd kidded myself. But why not? Why couldn't we have plotted together, outsmarted her somehow? Why couldn't Ang have been in on the plan?

Because I wanted it all to myself.

That rush of adventure. A roll of the dice on who plays the game best.

I was starting to get the feeling that the dice were loaded, and Quiet Eyes always rolled sixes.

I thumped the window sill. One of the faded red *omamori* charms fluttered to the ground.

'She played me,' I said to Cora. 'She fucking played me. It's all mind games. I wonder if Baines and Grayle even know who you are? Who I am? What's it matter if a couple of nutjobs are trying to investigate them? They're a whole goddamn company! We could've looked them up on a register!'

We thought they were master sneaks. We peered deep into shadows when we should have been staring at the light. They say the best hiding place is in plain sight.

I was suddenly desperate for something to occupy my hands. I made myself busy tidying up Cora's room. I straightened her clothes and brushed her hair. I dug into the recesses of my coat for a charm, a trinket, something to replace the pentacle that I'd taken from her bedside drawer. My hand came up with a fistful of costume jewellery containing various Celtic symbols. All cheap pewter and glass. Fakery. A pale imitation of the real magic I was constantly grasping for.

'It was never far out of reach for you,' I whispered. 'I would've followed you, if I could. But then we'd both probably be stuck, wherever you are.' I closed my eyes. 'I wish you'd told me.'

It still stung. Ang didn't know how deep a barb she'd shot.

Cora had also made a deal. With a fairy.

It was supposed to give her a way to the 'other side'. She'd already made up her mind by the time I found out. I should've been able to stop her from going through with it.

'You weren't good at being held back, though,' I said. I swept her dark hair behind her ears.

She'd said, 'Wish me luck, Jack!' and grinned. And then the light in her eyes was simply gone.

Quiet Eyes wanted to mess with me. To let me know she knew far more about me than I about her. Why? I was barely a threat, that much was clear.

Perhaps it was just amusing. Amusing to show me that the grand enemy I'd been tracking was even further out of my league than I could've imagined. Amusing to break down my delusions of grandeur and the novelty of actually having a purpose, for a change.

What had I even been doing, before I met Ang? Drifting. Distracting myself with one mildly interesting oddity after another. Pretending at being a bigshot Black Marketeer, while every one of my supposedly artful schemes backfired.

Ang had taken the phoenix egg with her, I realised. It was still safely ensconced in her bluecap. Not that it mattered any more. Maybe it could have been my truly big score on the Black Market – but a score to what? To impressing gaudy braggarts like Edric Mercer for all of five minutes? Most of the time I scored so low, no one else even knew I was competing.

I sank into the chair opposite Cora.

I'd once entertained the idea that I might hunt down a unicorn for her. The horn could cure anything, they said. But the last time I'd heard even a rumour of one, it was for a single gram of powdered horn supposedly being smuggled by a mafia somewhere in Europe – before it was confiscated by Regulators. If the stuff ever turned up, which by all accounts it hadn't, then every corner of the supernatural underworld would be on top of it.

I folded my hands into Cora's and rested them in her lap.

'I'll stay awhile,' I said softly. 'I know I never stay.'

I turned my gaze to the window and watched the sun climb high into the sky, untethered and free.

Episode 10: Lost and Found

That lyin' *basdun.* I knew Hansard weren't exactly the loyal type, but I never thought he'd scorn a friend so.

To know the whereabouts of mine kin, and not tell me! Even worse, to make a deal wi' that invisible hellion. She that stole Goron's knockers away, and those from my clan as well. She that works for Baines and Grayle, them that we'd agreed were evil! Had they not killed a man wi' a demonic parasite? Had I not nearly died of the same? What were ye *thinkin'*, Hansard?

This an' more I wanted to shout at him. Why would ye trust *her?*

This is what I'm stewing over, while sat at the back of a cross-country bus. Snuck on, I did, and hoping I won't be asked for fare. I've buried myself right in the corner, feet up on the tatty blue seats, while the bus clunks and swerves over potholes in the road.

I stares moodily at my lantern. Bluecap curls towards me against the glass, seeking to offer some small comfort. Still she holds the phoenix egg, safe in her embrace. I daren't remove it, in case I throws it against a wall in anger.

'Shoulda known,' I mutters. 'Business partners. Ha! Ye weren't one fer keepin' promises.'

'You all right there, kid?'

'Tis a man, leaning over the back of his seat on the bus. My new kiddie costume ain't as tawdry as Hansard's pick, but now I'm wishing for a wider brim of a hat to hide under.

'Fine, mister,' I says, and cross my arms around my lantern. He looks dubious, but turns back round.

Took me the best part of the day, it did, to prepare for this journey. Had to swipe the new clothes from an open market stall, and then find the place where buses gather. Turns out there are lots of them, in London. But I made good time.

The light is turning orange out the windows. Doesn't feel like only this morning that I were half-alseep in Hansard's car . . .

I strain for snippets o' conversation in the other passengers, especially any mention of our destination. Think I've picked the right bus, I have. All that map reading for Hansard's got to have had some use.

Some lasses are chatterin' about their shopping plans in Manchester, and I relax. That's what the slip o' paper said. That's assuming Quiet Eyes gave Hansard the right address, and not some nasty trick.

I scribble a letter to Goron while I sit. Include where I'm headed, everything I know, which ain't much. Hansard was right shocked seeing *Baines & Grayle* on them tablets. Think I knows why. It's easier to deal with monsters when they ain't human. For him, anyway.

For me, it's all the same. I've been out of the world so long, it don't matter who sits where in it. I has to scurry through shadows, regardless.

But it had been nice, feeling seen, for a little while.

I fold up the letter carefully. I'll find a rat in the city to carry it for me.

Until then, I doze in my seat.

An advantage of being a coblyn – or any uncanny creature by human standards – is that oftentimes human folk are blind, so I'm not worried about my nature raising any eyebrows.

The same goes for when the journey ends, and I slip quietly off the bus with the rest of them and into the evening crowds. People don't

expect to see a coblyn, so they don't see one. And people hate seein'
lost or beggar children, so the best solution is not to see 'em at all

I sees, though.

I drop coins into the cup of the woman begging at the bus station.
'Can ye tell me where this is, please?' I says politely, showing her the
address.

She squints at it, scrunches up her mouth. 'Hm. Long walk. It's in
one of the industrial parks.'

'If I pays, can ye take me?'

She gives me a long look. 'Where's yer mam, kid?'

'Long gone,' I says. My hand rests on my lantern. *But also not far.*

She nods recognition, as one lost soul to another. 'You need a warm
meal? These fuckers won't pay you any attention.' She spits at the
passersby and cackles when they show disgust.

'No thanks.' I hold up a ten-pound note from my meagre shares o'
Hansard's profits. 'Is this enough?'

'Keep it, kid. C'mon, I'll take you.' She gathers up her things: the
sad cup and a sleeping bag she carries over her shoulders. 'My name's
Minty. What shall I call you?'

'Ang.'

'Nice to meet you, Ang. You got people waiting, where we're going?'

'That's right.'

She cocks her head. 'Friends?'

'Some of 'em.'

We amble easily through the streets. I'm doubly invisible, I realise,
with her as company. People swerve round us, as if repelled. Their
eyes stare fixedly at their mobile phones or the paving slabs as they
pass.

'S'it drugs, kid?' Minty asks.

I startle. 'How'd ye know?'

She stops us, lays a hand on my shoulder. 'If you're mixed up in something bad, we got folks who can help.' She spits again, this time at the pavement. 'Fuckin' despicable, using kids as mules.'

'Ain't nothin' t'do with donkeys,' I says with uncertainty. I sound out the word Hansard had used. 'It's farm-a-sutikals.'

'Opiates?'

'What're them?' I shake my head. 'Thanks, but I don't think ye can help. I'm goin' to find my family, is all. It ain't some criminal dealings. Not on my end, anyways.'

She smiles, showing yellowed teeth with a few holes in, but it's still a nice smile. 'If you're sure, kid.'

The sun is well past setting when we arrive at a gated estate of modern work buildings. Some are plain and boxy like warehouses; at the front is a tall glass one, all windows. There's a sign over the door, an' it boils my blood to see *Baines & Grayle* advertised so brazenly.

'Thanks Minty,' I says.

'You want me to wait for you?'

'Dunno how long I'll be, lass. Don't worry about me.'

I'm about to squeeze through the bars when she touches my shoulder again. 'Careful,' she says seriously. 'There's weird stories about this place. We don't go near it usually.' She looks t'be deciding whether to say more – whether to scare me, I suppose.

'Any screams?' I say flatly, to draw it outta her.

'More like . . . ghosts,' she says. 'Strange lights. Trucks that come and go at weird times. Just be careful, you get me?'

'I do.'

I leave her behind and steal through the parked cars up to the glass building. There's a reception area but it's all locked up, no one inside. A cold breeze blows through me, and my nose picks up sharper notes of petrol and fumes. It provokes a thought: that I miss the leafiness of Goron's Cornish country. The scent of spring is far away from the mechanical, concrete smells of the city.

My ears prick at the sounds of activity. Work sounds, men hauling and cussing. I follows it to the back of the box buildings, where men in overalls are unloading white supplies from a van.

I'm nippy, and well-practised in avoiding the gazes of people fixed on labour. I skirt round their peripheries and into the loading bay. I dodge between plastic-wrapped pallets – masks, gloves, and syringes – until I find a door at the back and slip quietly through into the bowels of the building.

It ain't a warehouse, like it looks from the outside. Or at least, no warehouse I've seen. The walls and floor are cream and white, with mirror-shiny linoleum and fittings in sleek chrome. A sterile smell fills my nose. Reminds me of my mother's ointment for cuts and scrapes.

Arrows on the walls point each way down the corridor.

Biolabs and *Containment*.

I don't know the meaning of the first, but the second sounds closest to 'captured'. I follows it down the left corridor. It's lined with white doors, spaced far apart. No windows anywhere.

I'm not far down the corridor when my ears start fizzing. I thump the side of my head, but it won't go away. Feels like a wasp is holed up inside, a horrid tickling buzz hopping around in a panic saying, 'Look out! Tread careful ahead!'

I has a better feel than humans for the weight of the world around me, and I got the feel that somethin' is pushing down *hard* on it nearby.

I focus on it, attune to the eerie vibration. (Always struck me as funny, it has, that Hansard calls this *un*focusing. Shows you just how wrapped up humans are in their own heads.) It beckons me to the second door down. I tries the handle. 'Tis locked.

Well, I'm invested now. I release the bluecap and retrieve the phoenix egg from her core. 'I'll keep this safe awhile,' I says. 'Can ye get this door open?'

There's a quiver of uncertainty. This ain't the usual work of bluecaps, but she's been doin' more and more unusual tasks of late.

'If I've picked a lock before, so can you,' I say reassuringly. Not a trait of which I am proud. Lockpicking is more've a side-effect of hanging around Hansard.

She drifts to the door, moves up and down its seams in search of gaps. There's not a single crack for her to slide through. No keyhole either, I soon realise. A number pad blocks the way instead.

She comes back to hover in front of my face. There's no words between us, but I sense distress in her flickering edges. Whatever's behind the door don't feel like anything good to her.

I click my teeth. 'Can ye feels the whereabouts o' coblynau nearby? Other bluecaps?'

Her flame shudders. Then she flares in the direction we've come from. Back towards the sign marked *Biolabs*.

'Should've asked you first, shouldn't I?' I says.

I opens my lantern and beckons her inside – but she don't come. She's jittery, dancing in the air with anxious energy.

I extend a hand to stroke her flame, calm her a little. Normally I'd heed her warning. But I already know we're in for some danger tonight.

'Keep low, then,' I says, closing the lantern. She follows, and I starts creeping back down the hall.

The Biolabs corridor looks the same as the other one. More white, tightly sealed doors. More number pads for locks. I gives each one a push as we pass, but none yields. Bluecap stays by my ankles, hangin' onto me almost. I gets the feeling that she don't want to go any further, but when I stop she applies a gentle pressure to my leg, urging me on.

A sudden noise has me pressing my back into the wall.

Further along the corridor, a door swings open. A man steps out, wearing a white coat and surgical blue gloves. A cloth mask and visor cover his face – all the easier for him to miss me, and I'm lucky he's heading in the opposite direction as well.

He ain't closed the door properly.

'Catch it!' I hiss to bluecap.

She races along the wall, catches the door half an inch ajar. I breathes a silent victory as I catch up. We let the door close behind us as we slip inside.

The lights come on automatically, but there wouldn't have been any need. There's a blazing blue glow all around the room; even a non-coblyn would see well by it.

The glow is coming from all manner of curious tubes and containers. All the counters are white, just like the floors and walls, so the whole room absorbs and reflects the ghostly blue of the stuff filling the strange glassware. Long pipes connect beakers to drippy upended flasks, and curious sieves with pumps that work like bellows in some kind of cylindrical filtration system. Flowing along all of them is this eerie blue . . . not liquid, not light, nor smoke.

I'm searching for a stool to get a closer look when I notice the change in the bluecap. She hovers erratically, flames stretched out in taut tongues in all directions like a star. It's as close to a scream as I ever seen.

I dunno if I just didn't want to see it. Like with humans and coblynau, or lost souls. It never even crossed my mind that the blue glow could be exactly what it looked like. That the essence of bluecaps could be so maliciously distilled. That ancestral spirits could be crushed and ground into ethereal shingle.

'Never,' I choke, staring up at the caged blue vapours.

I climb on the stool, pick up the nearest utensil: a pair of metal tongs. Like in a dream, I raise them over my head. I breathe, and bring the tongs crashing down over the nearest web of glass.

Air rushes from the room, knocks me to the floor. One by one all the beakers shatter. Glass sprays into every corner and I throw my arms over my face. Broken bluecaps rush out of their confined hell. Their essence is formless, directionless, all mixed up with one another and vying to separate. Tormented sighing fills every inch of empty air as they expand, grasping for their absent parts. They reach into me, tugging at my soul.

They are in my ears and my nose and my mouth and it feels like I am being split, atom by atom, into my fundamental parts. This here is the part your father gave you; this here from your mother. Here is the same laugh that your great-grandfather had, and here are the working hands of your many aunts. Here are the millions of fragments of your ancestry, overlapping each other like new patches on a worn pair of trousers, holding together your seams with ancient stitching and ingrained discomfort from the prick of many inherited pins.

Where is the soul housed in my body, I wonder? How do you wring it out of the skin? What happens when the soul itself is broken apart?

I'm lost, I think. The many parts of me tangle with the tattered edges of other souls, all fragmented, in immeasurable pain. We are fractals, spiralling into one another, separating and multiplying in infinites, yet desperately trying to cling to one whole before we dissipate, before the splinters of our selves become too small to ever reform again . . .

Suddenly I am me, in the whole. There is a storm raging around outside me, but I am held by my mother. Her presence is warm and calming. I look at my hands and see her fire enveloping them, protecting me from the squall that is our broken brethren and ancestors. It is whipping at her edges. She is fraying.

'No, don't,' I whimper.

There is a memory. Of a hand stroking my hair. A soft lullaby in my ear. Rough palms and a gentle smile. She pulls away.

The tempest of fractured bluecaps roars upwards. She's forcing them away, up through the ceiling. They are spreading too thin and so is she. She's unravelling. Her soul is a fine mist, absorbed by the cloud.

The bluecap storm sputters as it stretches beyond hope of staying whole.

Their flames dispel with a final gasp.

Air fills my lungs again. The room is strangely brighter, all white without the blue glow.

My mother's bluecap is nowhere. A sob escapes my throat in the silence.

I lie on the floor and I wail.

* * *

No time to mourn, even as I spend whole minutes on my back, sniffling at the ceiling. Our chaos has set off an alarm somewhere. All its blaring can't take my mind off've the dreadful sights I just witnessed.

I think myself into iron. One by one my muscles clench; the tears dry on my cheeks. There are pounding footsteps approaching the door and I need to find strength.

I stand, throw the fripperies of human disguise on the floor. I'll be all coblyn if I die here now.

I have the weight of families pressing down on my shoulders. I shall carry them like a strong oak beam lifting up a mine shaft. I shall bring the ruin of earth and fire upon those what done this.

The door opens. People in black uniforms pile in. Shocked, they are, at the devastation. Then they spy me.

I feel so violently full of rage I should be shaking, but I am still as a dead thing, surrounded by sparkling debris.

One of them inches round. They have called for backup into their radios. Their nametags say 'Security' but all I see is four monsters. They have blocked the path to the door, but I do not care.

I bend and scrape my hands through the glass. One fistful of glittering pain, and one large sliver of evil sharpness.

205

I roar a thunder of grief at them and charge. I fling the glass shards into the eyes of the first man that tries to grab me. The second gets a deep slice across the thigh. The third slashes his own hand as he tries to seize my wrist, and my teeth ensure he loses at least one finger.

Then my body sizzles and spasms – a great shock of pain from head to toe – and I'm left motionless on the floor. Another shock and I helplessly spasm again.

'Enough,' one of them pants. 'Don't kill it.'

'Did you see what it did to my fucking hand?'

'Sure. But do you see all this lost product? They'll want this one, mark my words.'

The world is swimming in my eyes. I can't tell what's up or down. My last thoughts are of my mam before darkness closes in.

* * *

I wakes up on hard metal bars. There's a single towel layered between me and the steel, but it don't give any real relief. Sore all over, I am, and feel I've slept crooked. I was dumped in here in an untidy heap, knees and elbows akimbo.

I groan low and ease my throbbing neck into a stretch. Gradually I sits upright, hazy on the size and shape of the cage I'm in. Only just enough room to sit up with my legs out – my boots press against the front bars. There's horrid bright light overhead, reflecting off every surface. It's all blurs, but I can hear breathin'.

'Ye damn . . . evil . . . *cythreuliaid.* Devils, all. I hopes ye . . . I hopes ye burn . . .' My voice is parched for water, lips feel puffy and cracked.

An equally hoarse voice answers, 'Hush, lass. Rest.'

'What hell is this?' I asks in its direction. The shape is fuzzy as my eyes struggle to focus on its owner. 'How long I been here?'

'Hell is right, lass,' it replies. 'A day or more since they pitched you

206

in wi' us, I reckons. But time is hard to track, here.'

His outline gradually swims into definition next to me. We are separated by another wall of bars. 'Are ye coblyn?'

'Knocker,' he says. 'But the Welsh ones are down there.'

My vision is strengthening, and I force my head to turn where his finger points. There be cages all around the room. Some of them are empty.

Near the floor, there are familiar faces.

I shoots forward, press my face into the bars. 'Adda! Lowri! Huw! Hark at me!'

Eyes turn upward, but with grief rather than hope. 'Angharad! Not you, too.'

'What vile purpose is this?' I says, drawing on the fires that still smoulder in me. I gather the embers and will them to burn. 'Where are the others?'

A few more voices I recognise pipe up, but still there are some missing.

'It's terrible,' one coblyn says. His friends echo the cry:

'Terrible.'

'Loathsome!'

'Unspeakable!'

'They wants us for our bluecaps,' he continues.

'*The bluecaps!*' As one, all coblynau and knockers wail with shared grief.

'Some awful magic they wants to wrought wi' 'em.'

'Evil sorcery.'

'Black magicks.'

'*Pharmaceuticals.*'

'We hears them talk of chemical compounds, an' cures an' medicine. But it ain't, it ain't. It's death.'

'*Death,*' the rest echo hollowly.

The key speaker goes on. 'They took our bluecaps off us first. Felt their essences break apart, we did. Then when they ran out, they started to come fer us.'

'Then they came fer us.'

Soft keens rise around us as the collective grief rears again. I join the lament. So many souls lost, old and young.

'Why are ye here, Angharad?' says the first, sorrowfully. 'Have they captured more of us?'

'No,' I says. 'I came to rescue ye.'

The response is only sadness. They would rather not see another join their fate.

'We'll find a way out,' I says firmly. 'There'll be a way.'

'There is no way, Angharad.'

'Let me think on it. There's always a way.'

I gives the room thorough appraisal. These cages are stacked five-high in places, lining the walls. They are small, so we can only sit or crouch within them. There's space for maybe fifty prisoners, but I counts about half that in empty cages.

Pragmatist, I am. But, as I sits trying to work out a plan in this hopeless place, I realise I'm also more optimist than I ever used to be. That's what comes of spendin' too much time with a man who keeps his head in the clouds – oftentimes too high up to see the danger under his feet, yet somehow high enough to see a way forward. Or, at the very least, to imagine one, where none existed before.

They haven't gone through my pockets, I realise. They threw me in a cage like an animal, with no expectation o' my faculties.

I roll my fingers over the smooth surface of the phoenix egg in my waistcoat. There's also two safety pins, already bent for lockpicking, and the crust of yesterday's – or is it the day before's? – Cornish pasty. It ain't quite the tricks of Hansard's pockets, but it's more than nothing.

I stare at the locked cage. It looks like a simple little padlock.

I start chewin' on the pasty, and get to work with the pins.

Pale faces stare up at me forlornly. Why should a coblyn know how to pick a padlock? It ain't our kind of work. My coblynau kin forgot how to be creative when we locked ourselves inside our home.

Some o' the knockers start getting excited, though. They egg me on in whispers. One of them has a Ma who constructs magical locks, an' she tries offerin' advice.

Soon even my folks are jittering with energy. One of them stares at a thick iron nail he'd had about him. 'Hammer it!' someone calls. 'Wedge it on the lock and hammer it!'

'With what?' he says helplessly.

'Your boots got steel in them, don't they?' I says.

He blinks. And takes off his boots. Carefully he places the nail, and hammers the toe against it like a chisel on the padlock.

'Harder!'

'Keep goin'!'

'Yes yes yes!'

My lock clicks just a little before his clatters to the floor. I urgently hush them all, for fret of them cheering – but they don't. They're just watchin' me, expectantly.

I turns to the chap with the boot. 'You take that side. I'll take this'un.'

We work silently together. It takes a long time, but we aren't disturbed. I guess that it's the middle of the night. Knockers tell me the lights stay on in this room all the time, making them delirious for lack of sleep.

But the humans definitely sleep. Even security guards sleep.

I haven't missed the camera that's pointing down on this room. I haven't mentioned it to the others, for fear of alarming them. We may only have minutes more, if someone is watching.

I work faster, and pray tonight's watcher is too lazy to actually watch.

Clink. Another lock falls to the ground.

Soon we are many. Maybe two dozen knockers, and my handful of coblynau. The knockers is from different corners of the country – most know Goron and are his kin. A few say they'd left Cornwall many years ago and travelled around north, until recently when The Woman came, offerin' them work with Baines and Grayle.

'The Woman,' many hiss with venom.

We are at the last cage when we hear the alarms.

'Smash it!' I cry.

Three of us raise our feet and stomp down together on lock and latch. The bars bend but don't break, and the padlock is still uselessly intact, wedged between them. The coblyn inside chitters in panic.

'You lot, get up high,' I tell the others. 'Be ready to jump on 'em!'

I kneel at the lock with my pins. Sweat beads on my forehead. Knockers and coblynau are silent around me. We hears the low chatter behind the door. They ain't rushin' in this time. They're talking on their radios, askin' for our positions.

A knocker climbs on his friend and wallops the camera off the ceiling.

It goes dead quiet on the other side.

'*Clever bastards,*' is all I hears.

Then the door swings open a crack and a smoking canister is rolled inside.

'Quick quick!' knockers cry.

'Get out get out!' coblynau shriek.

'Go,' pleads the one in the cage.

The smoke stings awful in my eyes and lungs; others are spluttering. I tear away and bellow, 'Open the door!'

They fling it open. I boot the canister out into the waiting crowd of guards. '*Shut it!*'

We are red-eyed and still struggling to breathe, but they does me proud. Soon the sounds on the other side match our own.

I see weak smiles. 'They runs away!'

I round the healthiest up for another try at the cage. No coblyn left behind.

We smash and smash at it, until finally we break it off the hinges. The coblyn climbs out and picks up the broken cage door like a shield.

'Y'all ready to run?' I shout.

A chorus of 'Aye!'s meet me.

I'm wheezing, but I grin. 'Let's go.'

We cover our noses with our shirts – some have even taken off other bits of clothing to wrap round their face, so we look a motley gang of thieves in a mix of neon and brown tweed masks. The door opens again and out we rush.

The rotten gas is nearly dispersed. We spy our enemy congregated at the end of the hall. Callin' for more back-up they are. They're a handful, at most.

'As one, lads!' I call.

We charge.

They shoots at us with hooks attached to wires, which drop my companions when they strike and cause them to spasm painfully on the ground. But they've only got one shooter per man and we are two dozen, and when we reach them we bite and kick and wrestle the horrid things out of their hands.

We pull the probes out of our prone friends, and use the long copper wires to tie the hands and feet of the men. I finger the trigger on one of the devices and their eyes widen in fear. 'Don't,' says one, in a strangled voice.

'I ain't like you,' I say, and pull the wires clean away from their housing. I disables the other devices the same, and we quickly scour their pockets. We finds some multi-tools, torches, and keys.

I clap each man round the head as we leave. 'Yer mam would be *ashamed.*'

It's a maze to find a way out. The main lights in the next corridors are off, leaving only green strips of emergency lighting to see by. Low light wouldn't normally be a problem for a coblyn, but right now I'd take total darkness over this disorienting electric glow.

The knockers we're carrying eventually come to. We takes a minute to let them test their knees, and the rest of us to catch our breath. We've passed many doors all labelled with codes. Sound erupts behind the nearest one we're restin' by. The noises are animal, though I can't figure which kind.

I grabs a knocker, whose name is Jago. 'D'ye know what else they keep in here? Have they more've our kin stowed elsewhere?'

He shakes his head to both questions. 'I don't rightly know. Seems they kept knockers and coblyns together – didn't see a difference between us at all – and all the groups that arrived professed to be whole. If they have more of us, I wouldn't know how many or where.'

'Aye. Then we get these folks out first. Number one job. No others.'

As we move onward, I feel a familiar, tell-tale fizzing in my ears again. I excitedly nudge Jago and explain we're close to where I came in.

'Best hasten then,' he says, 'for they're on us.'

They are. It's another group of men at the far end of the hall, and these look far more serious than the others. Two of them hold a net, which looks like a living thing. It reaches out as though grasping for us.

Between us and them is a junction in the corridor, the place where *Biolabs* and *Containment* divide.

'Lead 'em all that way!' I tell Jago. 'Don't stop runnin'!'

'They'll be on us from behind!'

'No, they won't.'

I plants meself in the middle of the crossroads as knockers and coblynau stream past me. The ugly net is creeping forward, looks like it's being held *back* by the men. One of them holds a gas canister and pulls back his arm . . .

I mirror the movement, with the phoenix egg clutched in my fist.

The motion gives him pause, and the egg hits the ground before he finishes the act.

It cracks.

Light blinds me, and an earthquake knocks me off my feet. I spits dust from my mouth and look up from the floor, and am struck by the sight of a god.

Episode 11: Baines and Grayle

After Ang stormed out, I spent a whole day in Cora's company. Something I used to do at the beginning, but not so much in recent years. These days I'd come, drop off my offerings, and go.

This time, I remained sitting in the armchair opposite Cora. The sun was warm in the window. My body, having been stretched to the brink by an all-night drive and a werewolf attack, finally forced the issue of sleep. I rested quite comfortably. You'd think I'd be plagued by guilt-ridden nightmares, but I wasn't. Those came after I woke up.

It was Mavis who roused me. 'Time to go, love,' she said kindly. 'They'll be starting bedtime routines in a minute.'

'How late is it?' I burbled.

'Half past eight. End of visiting hours, dearie.'

My eyes were still horrible heavy, like I hadn't slept at all. I rubbed the sleep out of them and looked at Cora. She'd been moved into a wheelchair, done up in pyjamas and a bathrobe. I was shocked the commotion hadn't woken me.

'Looked like you needed a good sleep,' Mavis offered, noticing my consternation. 'We let you be while we kept Cora's usual schedule. There's a sandwich waiting at reception for you, if you want it for the road, what with you not having eaten all day.'

'Thank you,' I said.

Mavis's face crinkled briefly in concern. 'Your niece . . .'

I hastily tried to think up an explanation for her disappearance, but Mavis beat me to it.

'It was Nelly on reception,' she said, wringing her hands. 'Apparently little Emma said she was being picked up by her mum? Only I didn't find out until after, and no one actually saw her leave and well . . . that is right, isn't it? She was being picked up?'

'Yes,' I said, feeling sorry for the anxiety in Mavis' eyes. 'Thank you for worrying, but she's back with my sister . . . in law.'

'Oh, that's good to hear,' she said, pressing a hand to her chest with relief.

I massaged my legs a bit where they'd gone to sleep, and stood up. My stomach gurgled emptily and my shoulders ached.

I leaned down and kissed Cora on the forehead. 'Take care,' I said. And finally to Mavis before I left, 'You promise you'll try to get her off those meds?'

'I can't say he'll agree, but I've written to the doctor today,' she replied. 'It's up to him.'

This I hated the most: my lack of agency in Cora's care. She was technically homeless, and had nothing to formally identify her with any family, biological or otherwise. And even if I wanted to intervene – what could I do? Kidnap her from the home? How would I even look after her? Feed her? Keep her breathing when the body occasionally forgot? Should I carry her around like a ragdoll in my car?

These thoughts had me detesting myself.

I slumped into my car. It felt wrong to have an empty seat beside me. The absence was mocking.

How long had it been since Ang first took to the road with me? A year, at least. And so much had happened in that relatively short span of time. I finally had someone I could rely on. We'd gotten through so many fantastic scrapes together by just the skin our teeth.

I'm used to gambling with my life – that's safe in its selfishness. Gambling with Ang's trust was a line I should never have stepped over.

I wondered what her next move would be. She'd be travelling to Manchester, obviously. To the address I'd given her. Was she hot-footing it across the countryside at that very moment? Would she think to catch a train instead? She could have arrived there already, if so.

She'd made it very clear she didn't want me to follow her.

So what now? Back to the road, and the next opportunity? Off to another town, tourist-trap, or otherwise profitable mark?

Every part of me ached. I was drained.

I pulled out the map book and stared at it.

My left hand whipped open the glove box. After some rummaging, it closed around my quartz scrying crystal. It wasn't too much trouble to then find a couple of Ang's grey hairs from the passenger seat. I tied these into a knot around the crystal.

With the map book balanced on my knees, I thumbed it open to the page that displayed Manchester's spiderweb of roads. I dangled the crystal from its silver chain and waited.

The chain began to vibrate in my hand. The crystal was tuning into Ang's resonances.

It swung into a wide, slow circle over the map. Gradually, the circle tightened. It tugged on my grip as each swing became faster.

The crystal pinned itself to the map. To a road just outside the city.

I breathed out. She must have hitch-hiked or stowed away on a bus. Within half an hour Ang would likely be in the city proper.

She still had to find the place, I reminded myself. And surely she'd rest up for the night, rather than steamrolling straight in.

I considered this thought, and saw all the little holes poking through it.

A little urgency wouldn't be amiss.

I plotted my route north and started the engine. Probably five or six hours, to reach Manchester. That was if I didn't stop.

I rolled my neck, and settled in for another long drive.

* * *

I had to stop. There was no way around it. Perhaps my body had crashed out of all backup supplies of adrenaline – or perhaps I was now too numb to feel its effects. So I pulled over into dark lay-bys on unlit roads and snatched brief fits of sleep during my journey.

I'd become too used to having Ang nattering next to me. My eyes drooped dangerously as I made it past midnight, with a long way still to go. To keep them open while driving I shoved sugary snacks down my throat, washed down with a flask of Claritea from my stock.

I didn't usually consume my own wares, but the Claritea was an exception because it was one of my own creations: just cold tea, with extra caffeine. (And a crystal at the bottom, because crystals make anything appear magical.) I sold it to punters as a refreshing beverage to provide 'supernatural focus and lucidity of reason'.

I could do with some of that right now, I thought.

When I finally trundled into Greater Manchester, my head thumped with a colossal sugar-caffeine headache. I found a quiet residential street to stop and whimper in for a few moments.

A hint of light in the sky suggested dawn was not far away.

I took a long swig from my flask and spread open the map once again. I had a hazy recollection of the address. It was in an industrial park of some kind. I hoped the scrying crystal would tell me exactly where.

That was, if Ang was already there.

If she wasn't, then maybe I could head her off. Get her to see sense and let me help hatch a plan. We could still see this through together.

As I swung the quartz on its silver chain, a sinking pit in my stomach already knew what the crystal was about to confirm. The quartz settled on a spot south of the canal. I was roughly familiar with the area, having passed through before. Factories, warehouses, and other trade units filled that district.

I hoped I wasn't too late.

The city began to wake up around me. Early bird commuters stepped out to their cars, while night shift stragglers arrived home.

I pulled out of the suburb I'd found myself in, slowly navigating my car around Manchester's convoluted streets. They were already full of crawling traffic, one-way systems, and impatient motorists. A single wrong turn forced me into the city centre, and I again bemoaned my self-inflicted lack of a dedicated map-reader.

As I steered myself back on course, the hip and modern buildings of the centre dissolved into a neighbourhood with far fewer aesthetic qualities, where the industrial bones of the city showed through.

The industrial park, like many of its kind, had an anonymous quality to it. I glimpsed simple, blocky buildings in shades of green and grey, hidden behind tall steel fences. Occasionally a discrete company sign would betray the big brands that held territory there.

I stopped to use the crystal again, to hone in on Ang's location in the maze. It was an inexact art – I needed a more detailed map. But it gave me a better sense of the direction I needed.

It was troubling to see that Ang's position hadn't moved. Maybe she was lying low.

I drove up to the spot and circled the area a few times, searching for any clue as to which cluster of units was the right one.

The *Baines & Grayle* sign winked from behind a tall steel fence. I thumped to a halt as I pounded the brake. The sign was mounted on what looked like an office building. At least, I assumed there weren't many factories that had such trendy glass frontages and potted trees outside their front doors.

I also noticed a line of cars pulling into the gates. It gave me an idea.

Rounding a corner, I found a quiet spot to stow my car – within easy running distance.

As I considered my plan, I reached for my comb and razor and did the best I could to reshape the dishevelled landscape of my face into something more presentable.

Off came the stubble. A bit of spit helped slick back my hair. After adding a severe grey tie and swapping my trench coat for a suit jacket that usually remained bundled up under one of the seats, I almost looked like a respectable salesman. I disliked the inferior pocket capacity, however.

I caught sight of myself again in the rear-view mirror. I could hear Ang's voice in my head. What was I going to do? Just walk in the front door?

Well. If that's what it takes.

I selected a few choice artifices that would fit snugly in the lining of the black jacket. A roll of lockpicks, a small knife, one of Merouda's clockwork monkeys. I turned toward the gates.

They were wide open, but a road barrier was lowered to stop cars entering without first checking in with the little security post next to it. The drivers looked like clean professional types: smart shirts, cup of coffee in one hand, briefcase or smartphone in the other as they got out of their cars.

Off to the side of the entrance, an odd shape sagged against the bottom of the fence that surrounded the whole complex. This shape stirred as I approached, revealing a shaggy head of hair and extremely world-worn eyes peeking out over the top of a dirty sleeping bag.

'Spare a quid, mister?' it drawled.

'I'll spare several,' I said, 'if you know anything useful about this place.'

The shape stretched out and became more obviously female as she replied. 'I know the best place to take a piss round the back.' A cracked but toothy grin followed.

'Okay. Funny.' I flashed some cash. 'Is this your spot? I imagine you see people going in and out, right?'

'Don't know, don't care,' she said in a sing-song voice. 'Don't work for you, do I. Prick.'

I bit back an insult and tried one last time. 'Have you seen a . . . little girl?'

She dropped the cheerful voice and her mouth pressed into a frown. 'Dunno. Have I?'

Ah. I looked closer. The woman's whole stance was defensive, poised for flight despite being buried inside a sleeping bag. The eyes darted all over me, looking for clues to figure me out. She didn't look like she was comfortable in this corner of the city at all.

'Her name is Ang,' I said. 'I'm here to help her.'

The defensiveness didn't change. If anything, she became more alert. 'And how are you helping her, mister?'

I pointed at Baines and Grayle's gated facility. 'I'm pretty sure she's gone in there to rescue some friends. And I'm almost certain she's going to end up in trouble . . . if she hasn't already.' I crouched down, lowered my voice. 'You know something's up with this place, don't you? Did you see Ang go in?'

Her eyes flicked backwards and forward across my face. 'She went in there last night. Getting on close to midnight, I reckon, and I've been up the whole time watching for her to come out again. She hasn't.'

The pit in my stomach deepened. 'Thank you. I need to hurry.'

She called out as I turned, 'Why you'd say rescue?'

'What?'

'You said the kid was rescuing people.'

I gave her a grim nod. 'I don't know what from, exactly. I guess I'm going to find out.'

She shrank back into her sleeping bag, glancing furtively beyond the fence. 'I'll be here a bit. Until they move me on.'

'Thank you.'

I advanced on the barrier.

This was the perfect time to sneak in. The chap in the kiosk was focused on the queue of cars, checking badges and exchanging pleasantries. I waited until he'd leaned fully out the window then crossed through on the other side of the booth, right behind his back.

Most of the arriving cars slotted into a bank of charging points for electric vehicles on one side of the car park. Their owners were as shiny as the vehicles themselves. Glossy black shoes, well-tailored suits. A mix of young men and women – young, hungry professionals, I guessed. Professionals at what, was the question.

I joined the pack. The real trick is to power-walk, not sneak. I marched through them like a Very Important Person who was late for a Very Important Meeting, and for the most part people stepped out of my way or paid me no mind at all.

The crowd was headed for the glass-fronted building. A few other structures surrounded it, but those were square, characterless units. Ang had surely gone for the glass edifice – an HQ, if ever I saw one. The red *Baines & Grayle* signage was underlined with an audaciously elegant flourish which blended into the wedjat eye from their logo. It gave the unsettling impression that the building was watching me.

Est. 1895, the sign also declared. If they'd been in business for so long, then why hadn't I heard of them on the Black Market until only recently?

I caught the glass door before it closed behind someone. With a gracious smile which also avoided any eye contact, I held it open for the next group of oblivious employees, then tagged onto the end of them and slipped inside. There, I discovered a reception area that seemed designed specially to intimidate small-timers like me.

Every surface was a polished one, from the marbled floor to the shining white walls, and the obnoxious mirror sculpture that took up one end of the very empty space. Only a slim desk and two low seats – all matte black and with hard angles in them – made up the rest of the furniture. Employees filed into an array of lifts on the back wall, and the opening and closing of their shiny doors reflected eerily in the metal sculpture.

I pretended to admire this while the lobby emptied of people. Really, I was assessing the environs. Watching for any familiar – or strikingly unfamiliar – faces. I couldn't imagine Quiet Eyes working alongside these office types. But she might be here, nonetheless. Or maybe her acolyte, Vincent. He'd accompanied her last time, during our escapade with the phoenix egg.

An odd reflection in the sculpture caught my eye. The artwork, if you'd call it that, was made up of separate but interconnecting strips of mirror in a nonsense formation. It was strangely at odds with the precise corners of everything else in the room, that this mess of a shape was allowed to take up so much space. As I moved, the shape changed, moulded by perspective into an Egyptian wedjat eye.

There were other shapes, too. As I tilted my head, more symbols emerged on my periphery. Two crossed spears. A pentacle. A triquetra. The solar cross. All of them resulting in a mishmash of what I knew to be protective symbols – because I had placed all of them, at one time or another, on Cora.

'Can I help you?'

The voice made me jump, despite its polite tone. It belonged to a young lady in a slick trouser suit, who I'd seen behind the reception desk.

'Ah, I was just admiring your . . . art piece,' I said cagily.

'Fascinating, isn't it?' She gave me a bright, earnest smile. 'You see the Eye of Horus in there, of course?'

'Your, uh, insignia, isn't it?'

She nodded happily. 'Yes. It represents divine healing, and protection from evil– Are you all right?'

I covered up my shocked choking with a cough. 'Never better. What a wonderful . . . ethos your company has.'

She bade me step to the right. 'Do you see the snake curled around the rod? That's the Rod of Asclepius, the Greek god of medicine. Perfectly fitting, don't you think?'

'Ye-es.' My hands had curled into fists. What kind of distasteful joke was this?

I tried to shrug away the rising outrage. As much as I wanted to reach the bottom of Baines and Grayle's evil purposes – I wanted to *demand* answers about the medication, about Cora – I couldn't get side-tracked now. Ang was somewhere in this place, and I had to find a discreet way of tracking her down.

The receptionist gave me another courteous smile. 'Did you have an appointment, Mr . . . ?'

Quick, time to take control of the conversation. I stuck out my hand. 'Jack Hansard. I *do* have an appointment. With the–' I bit my tongue before saying *boss*, '–sales team. I didn't catch a name, though. I'm pitching a presentation today. Can you show me where to set up? I'll need a projector.' I flashed my business card, thumb carefully placed to cover up the 'Occult' in *Purveyor of Occult Goods*.

She blinked a few times, clearly caught off guard. 'A projector? I don't think we– Hang on, I'll check the diary.'

'I was told I'd be provided with a projector,' I said, following her to the desk. The key here is to be insistent, but very polite. Put them on the back foot, and keep them there. 'No trouble if you can't, but I'll need a little extra time to arrange everything. Can you possibly delay everyone by ten minutes? I appreciate you're on a tight schedule.'

'Everyone?' she murmured, desperately scanning her sleek computer screen.

'I know how important this is to the company, and I certainly don't want to waste anyone's time,' I continued.

'I don't see it on the system. Do you know what room you're supposed to be in?'

'I'm afraid I don't,' I said apologetically. 'I was just told to turn up and it would all be ready for me.'

'Ah-hm. No one's mentioned anything to me . . .' A hint of stress entered her voice. She chewed her lip while her heels tapped intermittently against the floor. Time for the *pièce de résistance*.

I leaned casually onto the desk and put on my most gracious tone. 'I am *so* sorry. This isn't your fault. Look, I do know my way around. I know John; he'll be able to put me right.' There's *always* a John.

She sagged with relief. 'I'll call him.'

'No need!' I said, almost too hastily. 'He's a friend. I've been to his office before. I wouldn't want to trouble you any further. Thank you *so* much.'

I gave a generous smile and strode confidently to one of the lifts. I nearly got away with it. Just as the shiny doors slithered open, I saw her pick up the phone.

'Hi, John . . . ?' The doors closed on the picture of her worried face. *Drat.*

But it didn't spell disaster just yet. I could count on a few minutes of confusion as they puzzled over the details ('Did he mean *this* John? Is there another John? Someone get John from Accounting. Does anyone know about this presentation?') and even once they'd worked it out, they had no idea which floor I was heading to.

Nor did I, for that matter.

I stabbed a number at random. I'd expected there to be a Basement level, for some reason, but there wasn't. Because surely you'd keep your kidnapped coblynau in a basement, rather than next door to your offices?

Next door to your offices . . .

I recalled the squat storage units outside and groaned deeply.

I wasn't *thinking* straight. I'd gone straight to Baines and Grayle because they were at the forefront of my mind. Where Ang should have been.

I glanced at the lift buttons. Of course, it turned out I was heading straight for the top.

Perhaps it was purely a trope absorbed from movies, but I felt that the architects of *Baines & Grayle* – criminal masterminds who had terrified half the supernatural underworld, villains who fancied themselves the superiors of demons and demi-gods – would *definitely* put their most senior offices on the top floor.

I was gratified, in a bleak sort of way, when I stepped off the lift on the fifth floor to be confronted with a sign pointing to the Senior Executive Committee Boardroom.

The halls up here weren't opulent, like I had for some reason expected. Instead, my surroundings carried the same sleek but sensible atmosphere as the ground floor. No frivolous trimmings to suggest the top-dogs lived better than the working mongrels. Part of me wanted everything to be clad in ornate brass and dark oak. Somehow more fitting for a malevolent corporation.

The lift doors slid closed behind me.

I looked down the long hallway to my left. A set of double doors marked the entrance to the Boardroom. A neat placard declared 'Meeting in Progress'.

My palms were sweating.

I could barge in there, I thought, taking a step towards it. Confront them. Find out who the 'them' actually were. Demand to know what their so-called medicine was doing to Cora.

Maybe get torn to shreds by whatever Lovecraftian horror lurked within.

Who'd save Ang then?

I stalled, halfway down the hall.

She was counting on me. Even if she didn't want to.

I felt as though my joints creaked as I forced myself to turn around. My eyes squeezed shut as I pummelled my forehead with the heels of my hands. God *damn* it.

'Are you all right, sir?'

'Fine, thank–' I looked up into a youthful, though slightly rodent-shaped face.

Fucking *Vincent*.

He locked eyes with me.

'*You,*' we said in unison.

Quiet Eyes' lapdog, her special protégé, Vincent!

'What the fuck,' he hissed. 'How did you get in here?'

'I knocked,' I said.

He squared up to me. Shoulders back, fists clenched. But he was on his back foot, as though uncertain of which move to make. His eyes flitted past me to the Boardroom. He was wary of causing a disturbance up here.

'Where's your boss?' I asked.

'What?' he snapped.

'Quiet Eyes on holiday, is she? Or do you call her Rien?'

'Oh, *her.*' He said this with unconcealed contempt. Last time I'd seen Vincent he'd been shellshocked, having just witnessed Quiet Eyes shoot one of his colleagues dead. 'Who knows. Who cares. You need to leave.'

My gut twisted. Could Quiet Eyes have really betrayed them? Left the organisation completely?

'I thought you were her special student,' I said, inching back towards the lift. 'Did she leave you behind? Who's your boss now?'

'I am,' he said, tipping up his chin. He wore a black uniform, and I spied *Chief of Security* on a badge pinned to his chest.

'Congratulations on your promotion,' I said, watching his expression darken.

'Get the fuck out of here, Hansard, or I'll make you.'

A door opened behind him and a woman with spectacles poked her head into the corridor. 'Excuse me, could you keep it down out there?'

'Yes ma'am,' Vincent replied through gritted teeth. 'I'm just escorting a trespasser off the premises.'

'Oh, dear. Another animal rights protester?' she said.

I leaned on the wall by the lift, affecting a roguish grin. 'Oh, I protest all sorts, miss.' My hand slid stealthily over the call button. 'Fake medicines. Evil corporations. Coblyn trafficking. You name it.'

The lift *dinged* behind me.

'Toodle pip,' I said brightly.

I side-stepped as Vincent rushed to grab me. He crashed into the lift as I took off down the hall, past the spectacled lady and towards a flight of stairs. I half-ran half-fell down them, until I encountered a dead end on the next floor.

I went careening down the halls, looking for a fresh set of stairs. Pounding footsteps told me Vincent was hot on my heels. I crashed past stunned employees – at least three cups of coffee and a stack of files fell victim to my daring escape.

Someone rolled a desk chair into my path and I toppled over it onto the carpet.

'Where's security?' one of the staff screamed.

Vincent yanked me up by my collar. 'It's under control,' he barked at the growing office crowd.

'Must be exciting, this,' I chuckled in his grip, perhaps a little madly.

As he opened his mouth again, I stomped on his foot – '*Fuck!*' – and wrenched out his grasp.

My hands snatched for some form of defence from the nearest desk. They came up with a stapler, which I held out pathetically as Vincent advanced.

I blinked and suddenly he was gone. 'Where . . . ?' He reappeared and thumped me hard in the solar plexus. '*Oof!*'

'You have some nerve,' he snarled in my ear.

I swung a fist at his voice, but he'd already unfocused by the time it should've connected. I overshot and collapsed onto another table, sending the immaculate office workers scrabbling for their papers.

'Aren't you a professional?' one of them cried, presumably at Vincent's hidden form. 'Do this decently, man!'

Vincent stepped back into view by the wall, as if he'd always been lounging against it. '*So* sorry,' he sneered. God, I hated that smirk. 'I'll put the trash out of sight.'

I should have remembered that disappearing people was his specialty. But I was too riled up, and instead of backing off I got ready to swing again as he came toward me. He ducked easily under my arm and grabbed hold of my lapels. I got a good whiff of his sugary sweet cologne as my edges involuntarily unravelled, and Vincent pulled me into the background of reality.

A moment later the big, open plan office appeared deserted to my eyes, though of course it wasn't. Papers shuffled mysteriously on the desks; chairs scraped back as the people occupying them apparently straightened themselves as well as the room. We were like ghosts now, who couldn't see the people we were haunting.

'Clever trick,' I said. My knuckles whitened over Vincent's where I'd clamped my hands. He still tightly gripped my jacket.

'Okay, Mr Hansard,' he said evenly, 'we're going to take this nice and slow. Just you come for a walk with me.'

'And if I don't?'

There was a fleeting muddle on his face as he looked from his occupied hands to his trouser pocket.

'You have a gun?' I said doubtfully.

The corner of his mouth curled up. There was mockery in his spiteful rodent eyes. 'What, you think they'd let us carry a gun in here? This isn't America.'

Oh, Vincent. He was clever, and talented – especially at forcefully unfocusing people against their will. But he was also young, and so very lacking in the wisdom that only experience could bring.

I brought my knee up and connected with his groin.

As he let out a high-pitched wheeze I lunged for his pocket. *What's your hidden ace, matey boy?*

It looked a little like a gun, though it was bright yellow. The barrel was square and loaded with something pronged. *Taser*, I realised.

Vincent doubled over, huffing at the ground. I could feel reality flickering around me, like a curtain blowing open in the wind. I bent to Vincent's ear. 'You should have just said 'Yes'.'

I pointed and pulled the trigger.

He flopped on the floor like a fish. It severed his hold on me, and I focused back into the room with a rush of blood to my head. I staggered from the shock of it: that feeling of catching yourself falling in a dream – the jolt awake as your brain and gravity collide.

I didn't know how to reload the taser, so I dropped it. The office yuppies were still in the middle of tidying up their desks. They froze and gaped at me, also rather like fish.

'He might want an ambulance,' I suggested, nodding to Vincent, who had ceased spasming and now lay prone. 'Or perhaps you've got a drug for him.'

I leapt over his body and bolted for the stairs.

People scattered as I came roaring down the last few flights and through the lobby. I burst into the fresh air with adrenaline pumping in my ears. I wasn't being chased. How many office workers would give chase to a madman, I suppose?

Having run a circle around the building and found a dumpster to hide behind, I finally collapsed to my aching knees. A near-maniacal laugh threatened to spill from my throat, but I held it back. How else could I botch up this rescue?

I'd nearly let my own ego condemn Ang. It was a part of me I didn't want to face up to. The part that was only here because of Cora.

What was I thinking? That I'd have some epic showdown with the head honchos of Baines and Grayle? That I'd take on the whole company, somehow? How would that have saved Cora, let alone Ang?

I was blinded – and blindsided – by my fury at discovering they'd had some contact, however distant, with Cora. I so desperately wanted someone to blame. Despite knowing the only people at fault were myself, and her.

My head rested back on the brickwork. I'd have to move soon. There were probably cameras. People would be looking for me. Would they call the police?

And risk inquisitive eyes snooping into their business? I think not, somehow.

Across the car park, a lorry trundled through the security gate and steamed to a halt outside the blocky warehouse building opposite me. There was a loud clattering of steel shutters. I sat upright. They were unloading.

Maybe this would be my only chance.

I searched for a sense of calm. My mind landed on memories of Ding Dong mine; of Ang's rattling snores being swallowed up by the sounds of home and family carrying on at an unhurried pace all around us. Of late nights with Cora in the deep shelter, listening to snippets of conversation and quiet chuckles of friends from the comfort of a bunkbed too small for two.

Forget the present – let the world in the here and now lose focus on you. Breathe out, and unwind as the centremost parts of you blend in with the background noise. As you become the conversation, the chuckles, the snores.

Moving slowly, I walked across the car park and sidled around the lorry. I skipped behind the team unloading, keeping mainly to the walls. Their passing stares skidded off me. I was no more than a blur on the edge of their vision.

Once inside, I stifled a groan. There were too many people here, too much activity. Too many eyes to accidentally snap me back into focus. And my suit wouldn't blend in nearly as well with all these people in green overalls.

I hid behind a shelf, listening. Attempting to glean whatever I could from the conversations that filtered past. I heard longs lists of medical equipment being ticked off as it was unloaded, with plenty of names too long and full of Latin for me to make sense of. The haulers bitched and moaned and laughed and joked. I got a vague sense of an upstairs-downstairs dynamic – the men and women unloading the trucks didn't sound on the best of terms with the people they were unloading them for.

The other people who worked in this building sounded like science types. That fit with the equipment lists. Was this where they made their drugs? A nondescript laboratory?

I didn't want to risk being caught again, but the passing minutes drummed an urgent beat inside my head. At the first sign of a lull – someone was pouring cups of tea – I zipped out of hiding and made a beeline for the back of the warehouse.

There was a door! I rattled the handle. Locked.

I pulled out my lock picking kit and set to work, as quietly and efficiently as possible. It was just about to click into place when . . .

'Oi. What d'you think you're doing?' said a gruff male voice behind me.

I dropped my picks and swept around – affecting a lofty expression and a disappointed tone of voice. 'Well that *certainly* took you long enough. Could you imagine if this hadn't been a drill?'

'What's that supposed to mean?' The man was probably in his fifties, and looked world-weary enough to not be taken in immediately by a confidence trick.

So I upped the stakes. 'I'm here for the security audit. Did you know I was able to just walk in here without anyone stopping me?'

'Who–'

I interrupted before he could his question out. 'I'm on a tight schedule, so let's get this done, shall we?' I breezed past him and picked up an errant sheet of papers that had been left on a shelf. We'd attracted the attention of the other men and women in the warehouse, who now watched me flourish the blank pages in my hand.

I addressed the room. 'If I could have your full cooperation, please. Your friends next door took forever to complete the audit, so now we're running extremely behind. I don't want this to reflect badly on you in my report, you understand?'

Their faces paled.

There are certain Words of Power that the universe acknowledges as indomitable, and 'audit' is surely one of the most powerful. You don't always need a string of incomprehensible Latin to bend people to your will.

Several folks hurried after me as I trooped round their shelves, rattling off the names of equipment I'd heard earlier. 'Where's your PPE store? How many surgical masks? I want to see all the petri dishes and volumetric flasks. Did a spectrometer arrive today? What's this mark on the box? Any damages? Who keeps track of inventory? No, this won't do.'

I tutted loudly at a disorganised shelf of half-piled stock. 'I'll need to speak to the building manager, please.'

'We're just in the middle of unpacking that, actually,' said someone from the worried crowd.

The man who'd first stopped me stepped forward, burly arms crossed over his chest. 'I'm the manager.'

'Ah,' I said as briskly as I could manage. I sensed things were about to go downhill. 'And you manage . . . ?'

'The warehouse.' His eyes narrowed. 'No one told me about an audit.'

I attempted a congenial smile. 'As a rule, we don't give notice for surprise audits. Listen, I'd like a word.' I beckoned him to one side and he begrudgingly followed. The rest of his staff threw us wary looks, but sheepishly got back to unpacking boxes and hastily tidying shelves.

'I'll be honest, mate,' I said, conspiring to appear as though I'd thrown off my formal façade, 'your section is far from the worst. I'm harsh because I need to be, but your chaps don't have anything to worry about. Between you and me, someone upstairs has really stuck their foot in it. This mess could cost the company millions if they don't get on top of it, sharpish.'

I jerked my thumb at the door he'd caught me rattling. 'Did you know there was a break-in recently?'

His bushy eyebrows shot up. 'They caught the bastard, though.'

It had been a complete guess on my part. As much a ruse as anything else. But this confirmed my fears – Ang was probably a captive now.

I tried to keep my tone light, unaffected. 'Unfortunately, there have been . . . repercussions. What can you tell me about the break-in?'

He shifted uncomfortably. His arms unfolded just a little. 'Just some idiot protestor, wasn't it? It wasn't on my watch, anyway.'

'I'm not saying it was. But there's some very sensitive information on the line. You must be aware of what goes on here . . .' It was a dangling line, a fishing hook looking to snag any errant gossip, any hints for myself as to what actually 'went on' here.

The chap's beefy arms closed ranks again. 'Nah, mate. I just count and unpack things. The labrats keep their business to themselves.' He glanced at his crew, and the furrow in his brow betrayed some anxiety. 'What kind of sensitive information?'

'I've said too much. My apologies, I shouldn't burden you. But–' I skimmed my gaze over the loading bay as a lorry drove off, directing his attention to the glass office building, '–between you and me, I'd start looking for new employment. You know how these types like to find a fall guy.'

His jaw tightened and he spared me a nod. 'Thanks for the tip.'

'I'll let you go,' I said. 'I can finish up here by myself. Tell your team not to worry. Or, you know. Maybe to worry a little.'

I turned back to 'inspecting' a towering shelf of syringe packets. He kept an eye on me as he returned to his staff, so I wasted a little time pretending to check things off on a list. When his back was turned, having hopped into a forklift truck, I dashed back to the door and wiggled the pick still in the lock. The final gratifying *click* felt like a cry of relief.

I shoved the door open and stole inside. It closed softly behind me.

Episode 12: Panacea

I found myself in a hospital-like hallway, all plain and clean with a lingering smell of disinfectant. It fit my internal idea of what a lab could look like.

I eased some of the tension from my shoulders as I looked around. Unlike the warehouse, there was no sense of bustle. As I reached the first T-junction, where the corridors apparently split off towards either *Biolabs* or *Containment*, I saw a line of white doors offering the only distinction in the blank walls.

I started cautiously into a section marked *Containment*.

After a few steps in, goosebumps pricked on my arms and neck, followed by a tickle down my spine. A familiar kind of buzzing sensation filled my head. I was close to something unreal – or to something more real than real. Could it mean coblynau were nearby?

I traced the feeling to a particular door sealed with a keypad. Beyond my traditional lockpicking skills, then.

However, humans can be a bit predictable.

I started with *0 0 0 0* on the keypad. It blinked red and reset.

Hmm.

1 2 3 4

Still no good. Perhaps I was being a little optimistic. These were smart people, right? Scientists, and whatnot. They could probably be trusted to remember a security code.

Even smart people get lazy, though.

What was that date on the sign?

1 8 9 5

It flashed green and I grinned. There was a clack as the door opened and I stepped inside. The buzz intensified and turned into a whistling in my ears, like wind in a tunnel. It was difficult for my eyes to adjust to the scene in front of me.

A transparent tube reached from floor to ceiling. Thick cables attached to its base and cap. They snaked across the walls and into ducts where they disappeared from sight. A few wires connected the tube to a computer terminal which displayed a series of metrics over three screens. They seemed to be capturing data about the thing inside the tube. I skulked forward and stared.

If a whirlwind could look humanoid, this was it. Fine dust particles zipped along air currents to give the vague impressions of human shape – the contours of a torso, the line of a squared jaw – constantly shifting and reforming with every frenzied gust.

This was the source of the buzzing sensation in my head. The droning of it now filled the room.

'What are you?' I said into the ethereal hum.

The wind stilled suddenly in the tube. Dust motes collected into more features: a wave of hair and the hollows of eye sockets, but no mouth. Instead, it spoke through the air around me, entering my ears like a whisper of wind.

I AM SHU.

I AM THE DRY AIR OF DESERTS. I AM THE COOLING WIND OF THE OASIS. I AM THE FATHER OF GEB AND NUT. I HOLD APART THE EARTH AND THE SKY SO THAT LIFE MAY PROSPER.

'My god,' I said, and reiterated the thought to myself. 'You're *a* god, aren't you? I'll bet you're what hatched out of that phoenix egg of theirs.'

I HAVE BEEN IMPRISONED FOR MANY EONS.

'Looks like you're still imprisoned now. Or are you here by choice?'

Shu's form exploded against the glass. I stumbled back, expecting it to break. But it remained contained, now a furious squall within the tube.

THEY MURDER ME.

THEY DRAIN ME.

THEY FEED ME TO THEIR MACHINES.

'Yikes.' I inched away. I wasn't totally sure I was safe, despite the containment measures of Baines and Grayle. They must be mad, thinking they could incarcerate a demi-god. Thinking they could *use* it to their own ends. 'What's their purpose?' I asked. 'Do you know?'

If a breeze could sneer, it did so.

THEY STUDY ME. THEY FUNNEL ME. THEY SEEK TO CONTROL WEATHER WITH ME.

I shook my head, feeling for the door handle behind me. 'Utterly mad.'

FREE ME.

'Sorry pal. Above my pay grade.'

FREE ME

The words battered against my ear drums as I ran from the room and tore down the corridor. Whatever Baines and Grayles' nefarious plans might entail, I wasn't here to rescue demigods or other supernatural beings. I was here for Ang and her friends, and I couldn't afford to get side-tracked.

If only I could *find* them.

I spotted my next opportunity around a corner. A team in white lab coats stepped out of a lift, wheeling a trolley. It supported a large cage containing . . . some kind of monkey, maybe. They were moving away from me.

I puffed a long breath out my nostrils and unfocused again. The mental exertion was taking its toll on me.

I crept after the trolley, following as they turned another corner – a real labyrinth, this place – and waited as they keyed in a code to open another door.

I slunk inside behind them, and had to stifle a gasp as I took in the dreadful spectacle of the room.

It was huge, a good twenty metres across. And it was filled with steel cages. The off-putting stench of faeces mixed with bleach assaulted my nose.

I got a brief glimpse of something furry and shuddering in the cage nearest me, before I hurriedly crouched behind it, out of view. The people in the lab coats shunted their cargo onto one of the stacks. They talked conversationally, about the weather and weekend plans, as they swivelled the trolley around and strolled back out of the room with it.

The door closed with a heavy thunk, followed by a brief *blip* noise from the external keypad.

I rose from my hiding spot.

The room was dimly illuminated by strip lights on the floor. Turning in a circle, I gained a sense of neat aisles formed by the cages, which were stacked at least three levels high. And inside them, a mishmash of animalistic shapes.

Some I recognised: a few three-legged crows, at least one jackalope. A reptilian creature that might've been a young wyvern.

Bipeds and quadrupeds, fur and scales. I thought suddenly of coats, and then of children escaped from cages. Buck and Sable.

Heat rose in my chest. 'What are they doing with all of you?' I said.

How was a pharmaceutical company tied up in Black Market poaching. . . and on such a *massive* scale? Was this their real operation? Were the drugs just a front?

I approached one of the lower cages. It was as tall as my shoulder, and probably the same in length. Its lone, goat-like occupant reclined on four bent legs, and glared outwards with feral intelligence.

I gave a low whistle. 'Never thought I'd see another one of you.'

The unicorn tossed its head. Its scruffy mane was matted. The tip of its spiral horn had been shaved off, exposing what could be raw pink tissue inside.

I stared at the unicorn and it stared right back. I wondered if it knew that I was, once again, weighing up my own moral fibre. If it weren't for Ang, I could find a way to free this unicorn, or take a bit of its horn for myself. For Cora.

If it weren't for Ang . . .

I shook myself sensible. 'Ang? Are you there?' I hissed into the gloom. No one replied.

I marched up and down each stack, inspecting the contents of the cages. No coblynesque shapes resided in any of them.

'Crap,' I muttered, stamping my feet on the floor. The room was a chill temperature. Some of the creatures shivered against their bars.

I strode to the door, ready to quit this nightmare room for another.

The door didn't budge. I stared at it in mounting horror.

There was no keypad on this side of the door.

Fuck.

I smashed my foot into it, to no avail. It was made of metal, hermetically sealed. I ran another frantic circle around the awful creature warehouse. There were no windows, no other doors.

I was trapped.

I wanted to slam my head into the wall.

'Well, you've gone and done it,' I announced. 'Fucked it *right* up now, haven't you?'

I pounded my anger out onto the door with my fists. Some of the cages erupted with grunts and squeals. If anyone heard the ruckus, they didn't come running.

I slumped into a heap next to the unicorn's cage. 'When's feeding time?' I asked it.

The unicorn snorted at me.

'You're right,' I said wearily. 'I am an idiot.'

I felt around in my jacket. There was a single digestive biscuit stowed in the inner pocket. It had been hours – felt like weeks – since I'd last eaten anything.

The unicorn champed next to me, eyeing up the biscuit. It was a scrawny beast. Ribs poked painfully under its flesh.

'Go on then,' I said, breaking the digestive in half.

A sandpaper-rough tongue snatched it from my hand. The unicorn stood up, turned in a half-circle, and flumped back down.

'You're welcome,' I said to its tail.

I rested against the bars. Sometimes, when there is no other option, the best thing you can do is rest.

So I chewed my biscuit slowly while staring at the door, and hatched a plan.

* * *

I was locked in that hellish room for hours. I alternated between sitting and pacing, exploring every inch of wall space and even the non-existent gaps around the door. The dim light gave me a relentless headache from constantly squinting into shadows.

For a while, I allowed myself to be distracted by the spectacle of it. I studied the trapped inhabitants in their cages, identifying or guessing at the names of creatures I'd only heard of in wild Black Market gossip.

'You're a miracle,' I told a scrawny griffin. It gave me a yellow-eyed glare before tucking its eagle head back under a wing. In the cage next to it, a scaled, amphibious thing with fins and a tail could have been some form of merfolk, though it looked painfully dried out. Withered for lack of water.

Most of the occupants huddled into themselves. They didn't move, I noticed. They slumped in their cages like already dead things.

My interest turned steadily to nausea. Hadn't I wanted to see such wonders?

I considered trying to break them out, but I'd dropped my lock picks back in the warehouse. I didn't know how I would deal with a room full of loose mythical animals, anyhow.

My morale, the little I'd re-mustered, began to drain away. Surely they fed these creatures? Not often, if the state of the unicorn was anything to go by. How often did they need to add or remove one, like the cage I'd followed inside? Were there other storerooms like this one, taking up all of the attention?

When the door finally opened, I almost wasn't ready for it. Lucky for me, neither was the guy who entered.

It was another man in a white coat. He sipped coffee idly from a mug while staring at a data on a tablet in his left hand.

I emerged from the shadows and pressed my knife into his back. My other hand gripped his shoulder. 'Put down the tablet, and don't make a noise.'

He startled, sloshing coffee down his shirt. 'Wh-what are you–'

'Put it down, or this gets messy,' I said.

I could feel the way he tensed. Fight or flight, or cool-headed compliance?

Slowly, his knees bent, and I followed as he placed both tablet and mug on the ground.

'I suppose that's a knife?' he said in a very nearly calm voice.

'Bloody sharp gun, if it isn't.'

I wasn't proud of this stunt, but I'd run out of options. The slim blade was an athame from my stock, a ritual knife inscribed with mystical symbols on the handle. The blade was also, to my concern, extremely blunt.

'What do you want?' He tried to turn his head to look at me, exposing a square jaw and prominent brow, along with bushy sideburns that led into a neatly trimmed beard of grey stubble. He was in his fifies, I guessed. The hair on the back of his head was flecked with strands of white.

'Tell me where the coblynau are,' I said.

'The what?' Genuine puzzlement marked his voice. Either that or he was a very good actor.

'What do you do here?' I tried instead.

'I'm a scientist.'

'And what do you *do?*'

'Science.'

I didn't quite push the knife, but I did turn it against his back as a reminder. 'Listen, my good fellow. If you don't give me some useful answers this is going to go *very* badly. So you'd better change your attitude, sharpish.' It wasn't strictly a lie. Things would go badly – for me.

'I take samples from specimens,' he replied.

I let the breathy sounds of the caged animals fill the air for a moment. 'Specimens,' I repeated numbly. The knife bit in a little harder than I intended. 'What do you make here? What's all this *for?*'

His hands flexed wildly at his sides. 'Drugs! Medicine! Exactly what a pharmaceutical company does!'

'How are you using a god to make medicine?'

This elicited a sharp intake of breath.

'That's right. I know a thing or two,' I said. 'What kind of arcane magics are you trying to work with a goddamn *deity* in your control?'

He squirmed. 'That's not . . . The Preternatural Power Source is part of the bigger plan.'

'Bigger plan?'

'What do you want? Are you with the animal rights people? These aren't like animals, you know. They're preternatural quantum constructs!'

'You'd better start speaking English, pal.' I caught the way his eyes darted to the door. I added another not-quite lie. 'I've got friends with me, elsewhere in your lab. So even if you got away from me now, you'd run straight into them. Your best bet is to answer my questions.'

'And then what?'

'I'll probably let you go,' I said generously. 'You can mosey on home and claim back compensation for a stressful work environment. Hazard pay, right? They'll give you a few weeks off to recover, I should imagine.'

He exhaled. 'We're helping the world, you know. I don't know what your agenda is, but you're on the wrong side.'

'Ha! I know there's something wrong with your medicine,' I hissed in his ear. 'I know it made a werewolf turn against her will. What's that about, huh?'

This seemed to honestly stump him. A note of curious concern entered his voice. 'The Panaceatemol? It shouldn't . . . Well, it's not *made* for werewolves. But I suppose it might cure them.'

'What the hell does that mean? You can't cure lycanthropy!' As if to punctuate my point, a low, pathetic howl rang out from one of the higher cages.

My hostage remained aggravatingly calm. 'We might. We're still improving the formula. What happened to the werewolf, exactly?'

'She–' I caught myself. 'No, I'm asking the questions. This pana-whatsit, what does it do?'

'It cures people,' he said sourly. 'Have you heard of medicine before?'

'But what does it cure people *of*?'

'Everything!' Then he corrected himself. 'That's the aim, at least.

The trials are going very well. We might be able to make a public announcement soon. Look . . .' He slowly raised his hands and inclined his head to the side, trying to look me properly in the eye.

'Can you imagine, finally, a cure for cancer in all its forms?' he said. 'To do away with childhood leukaemia, with Alzheimer's and HIV, with diabetes and liver failure and heart disease – and all the rest? We're on the cusp of all this. That's what panaceatemol is.'

I'd forgotten about the knife as I tried to process this. He must have noticed the lack of pressure from it, as he carefully stepped away and turned to face me.

'You didn't know this, did you?' he said.

I found myself staring blankly at his lab coat. An employee badge hanging round his neck declared his name was Rupert and he was a lab technician. 'Rupert' wasn't the right name for a maniacal villain, and his motives didn't sound like the machinations of an evil corporation. It was all wrong.

'And the . . . Egyptian demi-god back there?' I said, stilted. 'What's that grand plan?'

His eyes gleamed with a fervour that I found unnerving. 'Climate change. It's not there yet, but we can find a way to save the whole world. Do you see?' He stepped closer – the knife had dropped to my side. 'We might be able to adjust the very temperature of the earth. Control weather patterns to redirect storms, to end draughts. This is the way humanity survives. Are you so sure you want to destroy that future? To impede the cure for all ills – just in the name of saving a few anomalous organisms?'

I was sucked in, for a moment. Humans could be gods, I thought. We already very nearly are. We've taken reality and bent and reshaped it until the world suits us, multiple times over, pushing all other creatures out onto the fringe in the process.

Ang's people hid themselves away because humans took over their landscape; they couldn't keep up with modern machinery and the technology that took work away from them. Goron's knockers lived in abandoned mines because we'd farmed out all our mining needs to other nations: we created our own dearth of purpose for them to exist. The kind of creatures, people, beings, that make a living on the Black Market were now irregularities, striving to make a path for themselves in a world that's steadily leaving them behind.

Is Ang an anomalous organism?

This thought punched my heart into my throat – and it was the wrong time to choke, because my science friend had thrown himself out the door and pressed a button on the wall.

'Security!' he said urgently into an intercom. 'Armed intruder in the C9 Specimen room! I repeat–'

'Shit.'

Rupert tried to swing the door back on me, but I knocked him backwards with a punch and shoved through. I cast one last look at the hopeless prisoners before the door closed, and legged it.

I was halfway down the corridor when the lights cut off and an alarm began blaring. I stumbled the last few steps and banged a knee as I hit the floor in green-etched darkness. Urgent shouts echoed down the corridors, but it was impossible to pinpoint their direction. I was utterly disorientated anyway, so it barely mattered.

'This feels like overkill,' I said to no one. But then again, I had threatened a man with a knife and claimed to have multiple comrades infiltrating the building. Hopefully this panic would keep them busy.

I ran to the end of the hall; stopped short as I spotted flashlights hurrying past the corner. They didn't see me in the dark and ran on, barking orders into radios.

'Seal the doors.'

'Coming past Biolab 4 now.'

'Check cameras on the perimeter.'

'*B1! B1! Targets sighted in area B1!*'

Targets? They couldn't be referring to me.

Another crackle of radio and one of the flashlights separated from the pack. It turned back in my direction. '*Say again, Shane? Trespasser where?*'

From my jacket I pulled the small tin monkey. I carefully wound the key and set it in the middle of the floor. Taking several steps away, I pressed my back into the wall and clamped my hands over my ears.

The torch light fell onto the monkey's grinning face. It drew apart its cymbals . . . and clapped.

'Thank you, Merouda,' I said as I leapt over the security guard's prone form. He moaned and clutched his head. I snatched up his torch and followed in the wake of his friends. They were shouting.

'Up ahead, there they are!'

'Hold up, release the koromo.'

The group drew apart in front of me, holding a lattice-like thing between them. Its edges stretched as if it was waking up, and then strained against the men holding it back. I flicked up my torch and saw small bodies hurrying around the corner, further down the passage.

Planted firmly between them and the living net, was Ang.

She clasped something in her fist.

She was winding up for a throw.

I ducked as it hit the ground and was spared a collision with anyone's hard bits as a seismic wave threw us all off our feet.

'Bloody hell,' I murmured, though the words distorted into drunk slurs in my ears. I rose amid a sea of groans and saw Ang also lurching to her feet. Her eyes locked with mine. 'Run,' I mouthed.

A brief hesitation – she wanted to say something. But her window of escape was closing fast. She gave me a curt nod and slipped away.

That just left me, all these sore security guards at my feet, and one Egyptian deity calmly staring me down.

Episode 13: Lady Of The House

She looked, to my surprise, quite human.

Despite the darkness of the corridor, she was perfectly illuminated by a soft internal glow. Long, straight dark hair framed an oval face with red-bronze skin. The walnut brown eyes blinked slowly, doe-like, as they skimmed over me, and a petite mouth pursed in something like uncertainty. She wore a simple red linen dress, with gold bangles fixed on her upper arms and wrists. No shoes on her feet.

Feathers rustled as she shifted position. At first I tried to work out if they were part of a cloak. But as she raised her hands palms out, it was plain the feathers were attached to her arms. They sprung from wrist to elbow to shoulder blade, and were a soft mottled brown, like the wings of a hawk. The longest feathers reached to her knees.

'HELLO,' her voice boomed.

It was so loud that I clapped my hands to my ears against the auditory assault. Unlike the voice of Shu, the sound entered the usual way, travelling from her mouth into my eardrums – painfully.

She cocked her head. 'Hello,' she said again, volume muted. Her palms remained open in a gesture of greeting.

Dark shapes stirred on the floor between us. A few grunts indicated the dazed security team had recovered from the shockwave of the broken phoenix egg. Now they stared up at the heavenly body before them. One man wrestled with the black net that they'd been advancing towards the intersection of corridors. I was pleased to see that neither Ang, nor any other coblyn or knocker, was in sight. A siren still echoed the alarm through the facility, but it seemed faraway now.

I turned my attention back to the god, and sought to give Ang and her friends more time to escape.

'Which one are you?' I asked, desperately trying to recall my limited knowledge of the ancient Egyptian pantheon. An uncanny prickling sensation – like I'd experienced around Shu – caused my brain to itch as I looked at her.

'I am Nephthys,' the glowing deity replied, her voice now soft and willowy. She spoke again, and it was tremendously calming. 'I am the Lady of the House, Mother and Protector. Come, let me carry you safely.'

My feet propelled me forward of their own accord. I stepped over the men still on the floor. They seemed entranced by the entity before them. She was so magnificent, and so very welcoming.

A light switched back on in my head as I registered my hand already outstretched to grasp hers. I snatched it back. Her warm eyes still held me, projecting a sense of deep love and unending empathy. 'It is time to go,' she said tenderly.

'Go where?' I croaked.

I registered the movement of a security guard. He was crawled toward her on all fours, expression slack with rapture.

Nephthys knelt to embrace him. She cupped his face like a lover, and he shivered under the graze of her wings on his neck. Her forehead met his. Not quite a kiss, but certainly an intimate act. 'You are safe,' she told him. 'I will guide you.'

He gave a long, contented sigh, and closed his eyes.

Nephthys lowered him to the floor. He was no longer breathing.

I should have gone cold, but instead I was filled with warmth. He looked so serene. I longed to taste that kind of peace. And her eyes were so inviting. This was the natural end to all things.

'She *killed* him!' someone cried.

It broke the spell on me. I faltered, inches away from taking her hands, as two of the guards behind me pulled up their demonic net. The rest of their colleagues decided deity-nabbing wasn't in the job description, and bolted.

Koromodako, if I'm not mistaken, I thought woozily as oily black tendrils slithered over my shoulder. Squid-like creature. Notoriously hard to control. Regulators used to employ them in their work, until too many of their own handlers got eaten by the damn things.

Teeth pricked my arm. *The rumours are true, then. The tentacles do have teeth.*

Nephthys approached. Her fingertips brushed the unctuous appendage. It pulled away from me and curled around her bare flesh.

She wore it on her arm like an alien accessory, gazing at it in what appeared to be wide-eyed curiosity.

Its handlers hissed amongst themselves.

'Why isn't it attacking?'

'Don't look at me. It wasn't fed this morning. It should be starving!'

'What *is* she?'

A small, disturbed laugh broke from my mouth. 'She, gentlemen, is a demi-god, rather like the one you've got locked up in a tube elsewhere in this building. I don't know how she's going to take that news, by the way, so you might want to start rethinking your immediate career choices.'

I was rethinking mine, too. The last time I'd encountered a deity from a phoenix egg, Quiet Eyes had reasoned with it and struck a bargain. It would have gone with her willingly, if it hadn't been for the phoenix itself showing up and blasting the goddess to smithereens. What would happen if Baines and Grayle tried to reason with this one?

In a suddenly breathless silence, the limbs of the koromodako shrivelled up on the goddess' arm. The rest of its limp bulk weighed down my shoulder. There was a dull slap as its handlers let go, and the tentacle slithered off me onto the floor.

'Oh,' said Nephthys faintly, gently shaking it free. 'I didn't mean to do that.' Her gaze moved back to me. 'Are you next?'

I stumbled hastily backward. 'I don't need to go anywhere, thank you! I'm quite happy in the land of the living!'

The frantic thud of footsteps marked the fast exit of the remaining guards. Nephthys didn't seem at all interested in chasing them. She was more absorbed in her surroundings, still lit only with green emergency lights, and the slight illumination from the yellow glow of her own skin.

She turned in a slow circle, momentarily unconcerned with me, peering at the high ceiling and smooth white walls. Really, I should have taken the opportunity to run. But I didn't want to risk letting this chaotic entity cross paths with Ang. If I could stall a little longer – maybe call Baines and Grayle's full attention to the new divine power source in their midst – then surely Ang would be able to get clean away.

'What kind of temple is this?' Nephthys asked.

It wasn't clear whether this question was directed at me or the universe, but I answered it anyway. 'Not a temple, actually. Though I can see your confusion, what with being a god, and all.' I heaved in a breath, trying to draw courage up from my diaphragm. 'Are you Death?'

She seemed almost startled by the question. 'No.'

I gestured to the two corpses she'd caused, while carefully taking another step back. 'Excuse me. But it seems like us mortal folks are somewhat allergic to you.'

'You needn't be afraid. I will keep you safe.' She stretched out her arms again.

'*No,*' I said firmly. I wagged my finger as if to a misbehaving puppy. 'No more of that hypnotic nonsense, thank you!'

'Why am I called here, if not to carry souls?'

'Where do you carry them *to?*'

She motioned vaguely into the distance. 'Across. Through. Over the divide. From life to oblivion.' Her face became crestfallen as she glanced at the desiccated tentacle monster. 'I am a little out of practice.'

'Ha!' I spluttered.

'Where is the temple? Where are the priests?' she said mournfully. Her glow dimmed. 'Where are the souls in need?'

I tried to slide further along the wall. It looked like the corridor beyond was deserted.

'Bear with me,' I said. 'I hate to be the one to break this to you, but . . . you're somewhat irrelevant now. Times have moved on since you were last, well, here. Which I'm guessing is a good few thousand years or so. Um. There, there.' I curbed the impulse to reach out to pat her shoulder. The distant alarm had stopped blaring and one by one the lights flicked back on.

'I'm afraid I don't know what happens to gods after people have stopped believing in them,' I added, a little madly. 'I don't have much experience in this area.'

'Nor do I.' She folded into a neat sitting position in the middle of the floor, knees bent underneath her. 'Do I still have a place in the world?'

'I don't think I'm the one to say either way.' An image of the captive Shu sprang to mind. I was aware of the little dome-shaped cameras dotted along the ceiling, and wondered when more security forces would descend on us. No doubt they would be more heavily armed, next time. Perhaps they would call for reinforcements. 'I suspect if you don't decide on one for yourself, there are people here who would decide it for you.'

The silence in the halls unnerved me. I wanted to make my own escape, before Baines and Grayle commenced their next onslaught.

I edged closer to the pensive goddess. 'Listen. If I come past, will you promise not to accidentally carry my soul off its mortal coil? Only, I want to get to that door down there. If you don't mind.'

She roused from some deep meditation. 'Why do you leave?'

'Because this is a dangerous place to be. You should probably leave too, by the way. Just in case you were thinking of staring into space from that spot all night. You'll be captured, mark my words.'

'A god cannot be captured by mortal hands,' she said.

'Tell that to your mate Shu.'

She lifted her head. 'Shu?'

'He's one of your lot, I believe.' I started sidling around her, casting furtive glances each way down the corridors. 'They've got him locked up here.'

'Take me to him.'

'Would love to, but I need to be going–'

'Take me to him.'

It wasn't a matter of obeying. The command yanked at my very nerve endings, bypassing my brain all together. My legs swung out and turned me around. They marched me back, deeper into the facility. Nephthys rose and followed.

'This is the opposite of where I want to go!' I shouted.

'You will show me first.'

Her footsteps were silent behind me. I had awful visions of her simply touching the back of my neck, causing me to fall down dead.

I recognised the door concealing Shu by the increased ethereal buzzing in my head as we drew nearer. Nephthys inspected the metal door blankly. Before I could tell her the passcode for the lock, she simply extended a hand, and pushed.

Steel shrieked as it tore from its frame. The door landed with a teeth-knocking *clank* on the other side. The goddess stepped over it gracefully. She surveyed the cables and blinking computer lights with a beautiful but impassive face. 'Father of my father,' she said softly. 'What binds you?'

The contained cyclone that was Shu awakened at the sound of her voice.

LEAVE NOW, it bellowed like a gale. **DO NOT BE TRAPPED BY THEIR ARTIFICES.**

'How do they imprison you?'

WITH VILE MAGICS.

The way Nephthys' head turned from side to side was quite bird-like. She seemed to hone in on the computer console hooked up to Shu's tube, and glided towards it. She bowed over the monitors, her long feathers sticking out at an acute angle behind her.

I couldn't help myself. The invisible puppet strings had fallen away, but now an internal force compelled me to follow her into the room. Like a moth to flame, I needed to see how this played out. I craned my neck to see what Nephthys was inspecting.

A shiny black USB stick protruded from the console. Nephthys' trained her hawk-eyes on it, as though it were a quivering rabbit frozen in a wheatfield. The transient form of Shu was also transfixed. Swirling dust particles revealed the shape of a head staring level with Nephthys.

REMOVE IT.

A tremulous voice intruded. 'I wouldn't touch that.'

'He means stand the fuck back,' sneered another, all too familiar one.

Silhouetted in the doorway was Vincent, holding Rupert the lab technician roughly by the shoulder in his left hand.

In his right hand, he held a gun.

I don't know guns. But I knew this was a large one, some kind of rifle with sights and a long stock to fit into the crook of the shoulder. Vincent held it awkwardly, like he wasn't at all comfortable with the weight or the shape of it.

The barrel tilted askew as he shoved Rupert forward. 'Do the thing!'

Science guy wasn't at all happy with this. 'That's against procedure. We would normally try to reason with an entity of this scale first . . .'

'Fuck your procedure! Do you see there's a deity loose in the room? Put it in a goddamn bottle!' The rifle waved in a disturbing arc as Vincent yelled. I hoped the safety was on.

'You're not authorised to make that order–' Rupert protested.

The rifle swung in his direction. 'I'm making the orders right now,' Vincent snarled. 'Because you people are too stupid to deal with these things on your own.'

Rupert froze up. The eerie glow of the monitors made clammy rictuses of all our faces. The human ones, that is. Shu had become an indiscernible storm within his tube, while Nephthys remained quiet and curious as she regarded the scene, as though she was merely observing a play.

Although Vincent now had both hands on the rifle, I noticed it twitch in his grasp. He could barely hold it steady. *I could rile him,* I thought. *He's not actually going to fire it.*

'*Now* you're allowed guns?' I said, stepping forward. 'This is more Quiet Eyes' style, right? Like when she killed your pal, a while back – just to prove a point?'

Vincent lifted the barrel level with my face, perhaps to hide the edge of terror in his. Sweat beaded on his forehead. 'Don't fucking try me, Hansard.'

A cold trickle coursed down my spine. I hadn't actually considered what it would feel like to stare down the barrel of the gun itself.

I splayed my fingers and made sure to keep them in full view. It took more effort to keep my tone conversational. 'These guys are mad, right? Do you think they know what they're dealing with, trying to harness the power of gods? And who knows what else, besides.'

There's something quite terrifying about a totally calm voice in the middle of a desperately dangerous situation. I could see Vincent hated it; his face locked into a contorted grimace. So I shrugged, for added effect. 'I suppose you knew about the coblynau though, right? And the magic pills and whatnot. Are you saving the world, Vincent?'

'I'm getting paid,' he growled. *Not enough,* said his eyes. 'It's adapt or die, Hansard. I'm not going to lose sleep over a few ugly beasts who couldn't keep up.'

'Ah. Would you also be classed as an anomaly, do you think?' I said this with a chipper smile, glancing at Nephthys and Shu. 'If you weren't useful to your employers, I mean?'

Vincent's pupils flicked from the tube and the wires to Nephthys and the computer console, to the glossy black firearm still pointed at my nose. His gaze hardened. *'Press the damn button.'*

Rupert jerked, and I realised, too late, that he was clutching a remote of some kind. His hand shook as he pointed it. A thin beam of red light projected outward, landing square in the middle of Nephthys' chest.

She stared at it with pleasant interest. 'What is this, please?' she said.

'Subject marked,' Rupert stammered. 'Initiate containment protocol Xi3– um, hang on. Let me get this right . . .'

There was a low scurry of movement behind Vincent.

Oh no.

Ang's beady eyes flashed briefly in the doorway. She was alone.

My jaw seized up. My eyelids strained as they were forced open by instinctual dread. Ang should have been far away by now.

Vincent saw. His head snapped round, followed the trajectory of my stare, and the gun pivoted. He led with the barrel without looking, and had already fired a panicked shot before it was level with the doorway.

Ang stiffened, inches from where the bullet had bitten into the floor. Vincent's lip curled. 'A rat,' he hissed.

I jumped on him. Arms around the neck, pulling him backwards. The rifle rolled up, shot another round into the ceiling. And then Vincent slipped free, reached out to grapple me–

My ears rang before I heard the shot.

I was suddenly loose, swaying slightly as Vincent backed off. His face had gone positively white. Behind him, Ang looked to have been in mid-lunge for his knees, but now freeze-framed in shock. Rupert too, his mouth gaped open around a half-formed syllable.

I looked down. A vivid red stain spread quickly across the middle of my white shirt. It was accompanied by a deep throb of pain in my abdomen.

'Oh dear,' I said.

Nephthys looked up from her inspection of the laser dot. 'Time to go.'

I slithered gently to the floor. My eyes closed as everyone exploded back into action.

* * *

'I really need to get out of this habit,' I told the grey world. My voice shook slightly. 'Of slipping out of reality, I mean.'

The words echoed strangely in my ears. I stood in the same room of wires and blinking lights, though a loss of colour gave a washed-out pallor to the otherwise dramatic scene. Vincent, Rupert and Ang were all statuesque, paused halfway through motion.

Ang hung in the air like some frightful fairy mid-flight, as she leapt past the gun to bite Vincent's wrist. The slimy bastard himself recoiled, tilted the gun up and clearly pulled the trigger once again, judging by the hot flash of light forming at the tip. Rupert had dropped his little remote: it, too, hovered eerily in the middle of its downward descent.

Wait, the tableau wasn't frozen at all.

I peered closer and observed sluggish movement: eyes slowly widened, mouths formed laborious vowel shapes. The sounds themselves hung in the air as a low, uncomfortable drone, the way a slow motion video distorts noise into an oafish parody of itself.

Glancing over my shoulder I saw Shu also stuck in slow-mo, giving an elastic effect to his vortex shape within the tube.

I waved my hand in front of Vincent's face. He didn't react. Or at least, not fast enough for me to notice.

'They cannot see you,' said Nephthys.

I would say I jumped out of my skin, except I suspect this would no longer have been a metaphor. She'd simply materialised beside me in full blossom colour, her crimson dress stark against the background grey.

'Where am I?' I said. I felt, in a giddy sort of way, that fear ought to be raking icy claws across my flesh. Instead I was curiously detached, like nothing much really mattered now.

I looked down before Nephthys answered, and discovered my own body sprawled on the floor, leaking a dark pool from my stomach onto the tiles. 'Oh,' I said dully.

The goddess' voice had a dreamy quality. 'We are in the space between life and death.'

'. . . Limbo?' I stooped to inspect my body. It looked like it was still breathing. For now. 'Is this how it ends for me?'

Nephthys drifted away, back to the computer console. 'When you wish to go, I will carry you,' she said. 'You needn't be frightened. This is my realm. It is where I am supposed to dwell.' She bent over the USB again. 'What is a protocol?'

It took a moment to realise she was asking me. 'No idea. An instruction of some sort, I suppose. That's called a computer.' I said this as she fingered the screens hooked up to Shu's tube. 'It's like a . . . a mechanical brain. Calculates things.' I bit my tongue to stop from describing it as 'like magic', but Nephthys did it for me.

'Modern magics,' she murmured.

'You don't seem all that bothered. That your friend is being held captive here, I mean.'

Her eyes passed disinterestedly over the glass. 'I have duties to tend to. The phoenix will reclaim Shu soon enough. As for this . . .' Her finger brushed over the USB. 'Speak.'

A disgruntled, yet familiar and windy voice filled the space.

'*I am Zawba'ah, The Eternal Whirlwind.*'

I started. 'Bugger me.'

The jinn I'd stolen off Steve! How did it get into the hands of Baines and Grayle?

I remembered the handover of the data stick to Seb, my go-between. *Ah. I never ask where the goods are going, do I?*

Nephthys' forefinger remained in contact with the device. 'You are caught in a space between,' she observed.

'*Free me,*' the jinn demanded.

'I can only take you one way. To oblivion.'

'*No.*'

'So be it.'

She made to pull away, but I cried out, 'Wait!'

She tilted her head at me, questioning. I danced on my toes, feeling a trace of living fervour re-enter my soul. 'I just want to ask it something,' I said.

She nodded graciously.

I leaned down to the USB as though I was talking into a microphone. 'What are they using you for here, mister genie?'

The breathy reply contained a rumble of loathing. '*Containment. They outwit my wishes with algorithms. They harness my power to imprison that which they should not.'*

'I see.' I didn't. But it made a certain twisted sense. Perhaps a computer could calculate the perfect way to phrase a wish? Had they created a fancy shortcut for 'I wish this god were locked up tight'?

'Free me, mortal!' the jinn screamed. *'I will make it worth your while. You will reap my rewards. I am made to grant wishes, not protocols!'*

I waved my translucent hands, though I was unsure if the jinn could see. 'Sorry pal. I'm not in a state to help anyone right now.'

Nephthys pulled her hand away and the jinn fell silent. She glided away from the console, heading towards the wall, and abruptly disappeared through it.

'Hey, wait!' I scrambled after her, stopping dead (ha!) at the metal panelling. It looked solid enough. It *was* solid. By contrast, I was not.

I plunged head-first into the wall.

It revealed a dark lab room, strewn with funny-shaped glassware and other incomprehensible chemistry gear. I caught sight of Nephthys disappearing through the wall on the opposite side of it. I ran to catch up, following her through another two empty lab spaces, and then into what must have been a staff break room. Two white coats, a man and a woman, sat huddled around a table clutching mugs to their chests, while the door was apparently guarded by members of the security team I'd tangled with earlier.

I slowed my chase of Nephthys to examine the scene. I wish I knew what they were saying. The lab techs didn't seem happy to be held here – fearful, even. The guards clasped their tasers with white knuckles as they stared into the hall. I spotted Rupert's name tag carelessly tossed on the floor. Lost, I guessed, when Vincent had grabbed him to initiate his god-catching protocol.

No time to study more. I rushed to follow the flash of Nephthys' red dress through the wall, grasping – and failing to grasp – her arm as we both emerged on the other side.

'Where are you going . . . ?' my question dwindled away

I knew this room. I'd spent several long hours in it.

Cages towered over me. Their occupants were indistinct in the ashen shadows of limbo.

The unicorn was stood up at the front of its cage, head trained on Nepththys' position as though it had been expecting us.

The slit pupils followed me, ever so slowly, as I kneeled in front of it.

'You see me,' I murmured.

The unicorn blinked, a motion that took nearly half a minute. My gaze lingered on its butchered horn.

'Are you an ingredient in their magic cure-all?' I asked. Not that it could answer.

But damn. Wouldn't I do the same? I'd entertained the thought to hunt a unicorn once, for that very reason . . .

Ang's voice resonated in my head. *Yer a good man, Hansard.*

With a jolt, I felt I was beginning to wake up. As if my brain had been in a dopey stupor – except of course, my actual brain was several rooms away where my body was bleeding out, so it's not like I could blame it on physical chemistry.

I leapt to my feet. 'I can't die yet,' I said, whirling round to look for Nephthys.

She was bent by a cage at the end of the aisle. She cupped something small and softly glowing in her hands. As she stood, she released it. It fluttered away into the air like a bird.

I drew close and saw a creature with ragged bat wings sprawled inside, unmoving. What had it been called? Did it have a name? Who would know, now?

I looked up at Nephthys. She seemed much taller than before. 'Did you hear me?' I said. 'I need to get back to the land of the living.'

Her face turned away, an unspoken shrug. Her black hair now had a strange sheen as it caught the light, reminding me more of polished glass than organic tresses.

'There's too much I need to do,' I insisted as she began to walk away. 'There are people . . . there are people *counting* on me, you hear?'

Anger tinged my voice as it landed on her retreating back. I marched forward intending to grab her shoulder, but instead I barrelled right through her. It felt like running through a heavy, ice-cold waterfall. I stood shivering, expecting to be drenched, but remained bone-dry.

Already she was walking past me again. Clearly, I was of no consequence.

But as she brushed by, I noticed another subtle change: the way her dress no longer flowed naturally. Though it still shifted as she walked, it was in a rigid, unbending way. The cloth refused to crease or furl, merely stretching with the bend of each knee. She was like a moving statue, keeping its smoothly carved outlines even while in motion.

What had she called herself?

'Lady of the House,' I announced. She halted. Perhaps the title had pulled her attention. 'Great Lady, won't you carry me back to the land of the living?'

'I have other works to complete.'

Her voice thudded down my spine like a heavy ice cube. No longer the warm and motherly tones she'd first greeted the world with.

She turned to face me and I held in a gasp, horribly unnerved by her eyes. They had become a pair of shining onyx pebbles.

'I must find my new place here. Humans do not speak the name of Nephthys any more. There are many new words.' Her head tilted to the side. She appeared to be listening to something. **'Grim Reaper?'**

Lightning flashed across her face, and for the barest second it was replaced by a grinning skull. Then it was her human visage again, though now it turned as hard as the rest of her, like cold and pale marble.

'Looking for a career change, are you?' I said, shuffling out of reach.

'**I must find my new purpose, else the phoenix will come for me again.**'

'You're not on the best of terms, then.'

Her arms spread wide, and the feathers dropped from them one by one. They crumpled to dust as they hit the floor.

'**We came from the primeval mound, birthed by the phoenix in creation. This is the myth humans gave us. When we are forgotten, we must return to the mound, to our birthplace.**'

The scarlet threads of her dress darkened to midnight. A cowl folded up around her head. '**I have lain dormant for millennia, waiting for my name to be spoken again. I awaken to find it is a new name. And I accept it.**'

A scythe formed in her hand. It was the gentlest *clink* as it tapped the floor, but it reverberated around all of limbo like the thunderous tolling of a great brass bell.

Above the cowl, a mass of blue light formed high up near the ceiling. It was like a cloud, made up of many shimmering smudges. My ears picked up a tinny wailing sound, as though hearing a crowd of people weeping from along a radiator pipe.

Nephthys' pebble eyes lifted to focus on it. '**I have duties to attend to.**'

Those are souls, I thought numbly. They reminded me very much of bluecaps.

What did Ang's people believe about bluecaps?

That they were the souls of their ancestors. Of people who had once been living.

And there were so *many*.

Nephthys – Grim Reaper, Death – raised her scythe and cut through the glowing cloud.

They dissipated with a long, grateful sigh.

'Are you ready to go?'

Death held out her hand to me.

I thought back to Ang, facing down a mad gunman for me. To Cora, counting on me to find her a way home.

'Hell no,' I said.

Episode 14: Crossroads

I spluttered awake. Intense pain spiked in my stomach, radiating up through my chest. The world was loud and full of confusing colours.

I glimpsed Rupert cowering against the far wall. The rifle lay near his feet, apparently dropped or thrown by Vincent, who now writhed on the floor in a struggle with Ang. She was clever, had made it onto his back where it was hard to reach, and had both arms locked around his neck.

I tasted iron in my mouth, along with an acid sting in my throat. There was no way I could stand. But I could crawl.

The computer console wasn't far.

I dragged myself to it, leaving bloody handprints on the floor. The shouts behind me were incomprehensible, no inkling of who was winning or losing the fight. All I could hope was that this stunt would give Ang a chance to get away.

I hauled myself onto my knees. Swung my arm up. I felt around blindly until my hand encountered the protruding shape of the USB stick. I grabbed and yanked.

It clattered to the floor and wobbled in and out of my blurry vision. I shoved myself backwards against the console so I could stretch out a leg. With an awfully pained grunt, I lifted my foot and smashed the heel down on top of the stick.

The first sensation was of fresh autumn wind, the crispest breeze. It washed over me like a welcome bucket of water.

Zawba'ah's voice whispered in my ear. *'I keep my word, mortal. What is your wish?'*

Think carefully. Never try to be clever with a jinn. Keep it simple, stupid.

Blood dribbled from my mouth as I said, 'Open all the locks in this building.'

The wind swirled about my head and emitted a cruel, cackling laughter.

'It is done.'

Immediately, the alarms blared again. I clutched my head, blind both from pain and disorientation. In the background, other noises quickly built on top of each other. Squawks, shrieks, and grunts. The pounding of many feet and hooves.

Ang's distraught shouts penetrated the turmoil. Her small hands covered mine. I opened my eyes to see her steely grey ones grimly examining me.

The fuzzy dark shape of Vincent clung to the wall, staring dumbly out into the hallway where creatures – precious preternatural assets, no doubt – streamed past in panic.

'Y'should go,' I slurred.

'Don't be stupid, *twpsyn.*' Ang wrenched off her waistcoat and pressed it hard into my wound. 'Yer comin' with me, Jack.'

I looked up. Opposite Vincent, but unseen by him, stood Death. She inclined her scythe towards me.

'Not yet,' I muttered.

Vincent backed away from the door. He seemed ready to dive for his gun, but whatever had spooked him now stood in the way. It clip-clopped into the room.

Ang tried to wave it away. 'Geroff, yer nasty goat!'

Solemn, slit pupils met mine. I put a hand on Ang's shoulder. 'S'aright,' I mumbled.

The unicorn regarded me with that same peculiar sense of intelligence. Perhaps it was taking the measure of me.

It trotted closer and lowered its mutilated horn to my abdomen.

'Psssh.' I was on the verge of hysterics. *Not me!* I wanted to shout. *This isn't meant for me!*

A tingling warmth spread through my torso, like a perfectly heated bubble bath. The pain seeped away, and a red vein pulsed along the spiral groove of the unicorn's horn. It dipped its beardy chin at me and turned away.

To face Vincent, who'd picked up the gun.

'You idiot,' I groaned.

The unicorn snorted and lowered its head.

Vincent screamed at it. 'Get back in your fucking cage!' His chin was flecked with spittle, his eyes bloodshot and wild. '*Scum!*'

'Leave it be,' I tried to tell him, but my voice was cracked. Calm down, I wanted to say. You've still got a way out of this.

But Vincent planted himself in the doorway. He'd forgotten about everything but the unicorn, it seemed. 'It's the cage or death, you revolting beast!' His lips pulled back from his teeth in a bestial snarl. He lifted the rifle.

The unicorn charged as Vincent fired. He missed, though the bullet drew sparks from the console next to my head.

He gagged on his own saliva and looked down at the head butted against his stomach. Blood-soaked horn protruded from the other side. The rifle slipped from Vincent's hands. His knees sagged, head nodding onto his chest, mouth lolling open.

Light glinted off a ghostly blade. The scythe swung across Vincent's neck, and Death faded away with her prize.

The unicorn withdrew and tossed Vincent's body limply to the floor.

It turned back to look at us briefly, a ghastly four-legged silhouette in the doorway, and then trotted out of sight.

'Bloody hell,' was all I could think to say. Had Vincent deserved that? Something in his insane desperation suggested he'd run out of options. I wondered if he'd ever meant to get in so deep.

A whimper from the corner called our attention to Rupert. He hugged his knees, huddling amongst a knot of wires. 'They'll kill us for this.'

Now there was someone who I felt definitely deserved it. I found I had the strength to be angry again. I hurled myself upright, with Ang fussing at me to go easy.

'What were you doing with all of those creatures?' I demanded of Rupert. A juvenile griffin limped past the doorway, trailing blood from its paws. 'Is it really for a cure? How many did you maim?'

'And kill,' Ang added with menace.

Rupert buried his head in his knees. 'It's all for the greater good. When they approached me I– I just wanted to learn. There's so much I never knew still to discover . . . And we're making such a *difference*. We're supposed to be pioneers!'

Ang strode over, yanked his head up by his greying hair. 'People, we are. Murderers, you.'

Rupert's eyes were glassy. 'We were going to save the world . . .'

I stiffened to a noise behind us. A pronounced, multi-faceted cracking sound. As one, Ang and I rotated to observe the tube presently containing Shu.

'Presently' because it was obviously not going to be for much longer.

Shu's tornado form strained against the glass. Three long cracks ran along its length.

'We should run,' I croaked.

'Aye.'

We leapt (in my case, staggered) past Rupert and into the zoological chaos of the corridors. The alarms bellowed overhead and everything had been plunged once more into green-lit darkness.

I was knocked down by something that stank of sewage – Ang booted it off me and screamed some obscenities for good measure. Together we waded through bedlam.

Whatever miraculous healing the unicorn had granted me, it clearly wasn't perfect. I was utterly winded every few steps. Ang led me like a child as I gasped and wheezed through our retreat. Finally she kicked open a door and fresh night air spilled over my face.

I lapped it up like I was thirsty.

'Keep goin', *gwas*,' Ang coaxed. 'Nearly there.'

Nearly where? I could barely see. If there was any moon out, it was obscured by clouds. No streetlamps lit our path as we hobbled into the tarmacked bays outside the grand *Baines & Grayle* office block.

Howls pierced the night as other shapes darted from the lab building and spread through the estate around us. They smashed into the few cars parked up – probably belonging to the night shift I'd spied in the break room. A few human screams cut through the noise, and I guessed those same owners had finally evacuated their posts.

Ang dragged me to the gates and I gratefully collapsed when we reached the other side of the fence.

'How do you think we–' I started.

A deafening roar shook the sky as a portion of roof blasted off the lab. The explosion went up in a whirling column of debris. The twister pulled tight, raking slats off the roof, pulling walls from their foundations. Ang and I grabbed onto each other, and I hooked an arm into the fence for fear of being sucked in.

The giant form of Shu manifested briefly in the centre of the cyclone's destruction. It towered over the whole estate, dwarfing the tall Baines and Grayle office block – and brought a fist down on top of it.

Windows blew out under the pressure, showering sparks and glass across the car park. The building concertinaed, slowly collapsing as each floor gave way.

I shared a taught nod with Ang. We sprang across the road, around a bend. My car welcomed us with its musty smells and homely stains. We lurched into seats, snapped keys in ignition as the wreckage of Baines and Grayle began tumbling our way.

'Fast, fast!' Ang cried.

We screeched into the road. Rubbish dashed across my windshield in the wake of Shu's storm.

In my rear-view mirror, I saw him stretch out high into the sky. Arms wide, like Nephthys had done. Shedding an old form, perhaps.

Shu merged with the clouds, losing distinction. The flotsam and jetsam gradually dropped out of his shape as it diminished. The gale calmed, until finally there was only wind on an otherwise still and moonless night.

I considered being the first to break the silence between Ang and me. She stared intently out the window as I retraced my route to escape the industrial park. There was so much that needed to be said.

'Ang, I–' I started.

'Stop, *gwas!*'

I slammed on the brake, throwing us both forward in our seats. 'Bloody hell. What's wrong?'

'We gotsa passenger.'

I followed her pointing finger to the side of the road, where a bedraggled face grinned at me with crooked teeth. It was the homeless woman I'd spoken to outside the complex. I rolled down the window. 'You've been out here the whole time?'

She gave Ang a thumbs up. 'Said I was watching out, didn't I?'

'Her name's Minty,' Ang said. 'Took my kin to a safe place, she has.'

'Cor, what a dump,' Minty said as she climbed in the back seat. 'Take the next right.'

I followed her directions without question. If Ang trusted her, it was all right by me.

She led us to an abandoned bus station nearby. Half its roof was missing, but at least it afforded some shelter from the elements.

I didn't take too much of it in: I near enough passed out as soon as I pulled up the hand brake. My mind was clouded by pain and fatigue. Several pairs of hands – quite a few small ones – helped pull me from the car and laid me onto a bed of cardboard and bin bags.

I slipped into sleep with a lasting image of many knockers peering out of the darkness, and Ang staring silently down her nose at me.

* * *

When I awoke, it was to a nicely blazing fire held in a dustbin, and I was covered in a mountain of blankets. Chill morning air grazed the many scrapes I'd picked up during the night.

A group of knockers in a strange variety of attire were making cups of tea round the fire. Old-timey Victorian waistcoats clashed with fluorescent safety vests.

'How long was I asleep?' I asked. The words only just made it out. My lips were cracked and dry.

A knocker passed me a cup. 'About two nights an' a day, I reckons,' he said.

'What?' I pushed myself into a sitting position. 'It can't have been that long.'

'Body needs to heal,' he replied. 'Worried ye still had a bullet in you, we was. But looks like it went clean through.'

'How–?'

'Gots a scar on yer back.' He flashed me a wry grin. 'Matchin' pair. Impress all the ladies wi' that, eh?'

With one hand I felt inside my ruined shirt. They'd cleaned the blood off me, and replaced my jacket with a threadbare blanket from the car. The vestiges of the bullet wound were a deep purple bruise under my skin and a lingering throb of pain in my core.

A police siren shrieked down a nearby street. Tea sploshed over the edge of my cup.

'That ain't fer us,' the knocker said, turning back to poke the fire. 'Been left alone, we have.'

I shuffled position. It seemed I'd been laid at the foot of a concrete pillar. As I rested my head back, it knocked into a string of plastic fairy lights. They were looped all around the column. Shapes of stars and hearts and flowers.

'Done our best to cheer the place up,' my new knocker friend told me. 'Least we could do to thank Minty.'

There were two more pillars to my right, similarly adorned, which held up what remained of the bus station's roof. It made for a kind of L-shaped canopy, with a wall sheltering the open side from the road, creating a courtyard effect where the knockers brewed their tea.

In the far shadows by the last pillar, a mound of candles burned steadily. The knocker followed my gaze.

'Fer them we lost,' he said quietly. 'Their souls light the darkness no more.'

A figure detached from the candle shrine and donned a flat cap. My shoulders dropped with relief as Ang's craggy features came into view.

Her face was lined more deeply than I remembered. Her eyes seemed heavier.

'Mornin', *gwas*. Good t'see ye've come round.'

I rolled over a few responses on my tongue. There was really only one appropriate one. 'Listen, Ang. I'm sorry–'

'It's done,' she interrupted. She sat in the pile of blankets next to me, arms folded across her shirt. Blood stains were still smeared across it

– mine, I realised. Her waistcoat was wholly absent. But then, it was probably unsalvageable after she'd used it to staunch my wound.

'I regret betraying a friend,' I said to my feet. 'Especially knowing you would've still had my back, if I hadn't.'

'Why'd ye do it?' she said wearily.

'Ego, I think.'

She snorted. 'That thing'll get ye killed.' It became a rueful chuckle. 'Still, am grateful yer ego led you back to savin' me own life, back there.'

'That was a selfless act!'

'Ye don't know the meanin' of the word.' She gave me a light shove. 'Yer a good man, Hansard.'

'I could be better.' I hoped to draw a smile, but Ang rested her chin on her knees and stared listlessly at the fire. 'Why so down? We finally did it, Ang. Well, you did it. Rescued your kin. Everyone's safe now, right?'

'Aye,' she said. 'Them's that made it out.'

This triggered a foggy memory. Something about a cloud of bluecaps. Had I been dreaming, in that space between being shot and waking up?

'How many were lost?' I asked.

'Too many.' She huddled in on herself. 'My mother's bluecap were one.'

I glanced to the stacks of candles. At least two dozen there, if not more.

'I'm sorry,' I murmured.

'It's done.'

The knocker wandered back over, this time offering a steaming mug to Ang. 'We're heading out soon, lass.'

She nodded. 'Safe travels t'you an' yours, Jago. Give me regards to Goron.'

'Shall do, lass.' He touched his forelock and moved away to round up knockers into packing food and gear into sacks. The knockers in modern clothing separated from their old-fashioned counterparts, bidding warm farewells. The group left over were Ang's coblynau, I realised.

They clustered around some sudden activity at a hole in the wall across the courtyard. Minty emerged carrying a bulging shopping bag in one hand and a knocker on one shoulder. She caught my eye as she dumped out the bag's contents: fresh vegetables and cans of soup, and another string of pink fairy lights.

'Stealthy little buggers, ain't they!' she said gleefully.

I raised an eyebrow at Ang. 'Stealing, are we?'

'Seems more like charity t'me, *gwas,*' she replied. 'Noble cause, right?'

'But people don't know they're providing donations, I presume?'

'Thassit.'

The coblynau set to work chopping vegetables into a pot. They were withdrawn, hushed in their work. When some small conversation led to an unexpected chuckle, it was quickly smothered. They were still learning to feel free again, I sensed.

Ang watched them like a mother. Eyes drawn heavy with both compassion and sorrow.

'So here's the plan,' I began. 'There's what, seven of your lot, all told? It'll be a tight squeeze, but I reckon we can fit everyone in the car. We'll double up on seat belts and some will just have to lump it in the footwells. Won't be long til we have you all back home.'

'Nah, *gwas,*' Ang said. 'You ain't comin' with us.'

'But–'

She shot me a stern look. Then poked me right in the stomach.

I keeled forward. '*Goddamn* it. That bloody hurt!'

'Aye. You need rest, *twpsyn.* No more foolishness for you, fer a while.'

'How will you get home?'

She settled back against the pillar. 'We'll walk. At night, like. And some o' these don't even want to go home. These are the ones that wanted t'leave our mines in the first place, see? Take me time, it will, to see 'em right. Find 'em somewhere safe. A couple have already gone with Jago. Excited about working with piskey dust, they were. The rest don't yet know where they ought t'be.'

Minty paused her happy rooting through stolen goods by the fire. 'You're welcome to stay here as long as you want.'

'Thanks,' Ang said. 'Stay awhile, we prob'ly will.' She sipped from her mug and closed her eyes. The lines fell out of her face, very briefly.

I hated to break into her peace, but I still had questions. 'What happened to Baines and Grayle?'

Minty joined us, chewing on a carrot. 'Police and fire engines have been all over it, twenty-four-seven. They're keeping journalists out, though. Gas explosion, they're calling it!'

'Aha. Of course they are,' I said. 'And no one saw the god explode through the roof, I expect?'

'Freak tornado, I heard,' Minty said. There, I heard the faltering in her voice. If she repeated that lie enough times, she'd end up believing it herself. Funny how the brain can overwrite itself, when faced with something it doesn't want to accept as true.

Like how I convinced myself that letting Ang in on my deal with Quiet Eyes was a bad idea. That somehow chasing a flighty promise of exhilaration was more important than keeping the trust of a friend.

I turned my head to Ang. 'Will I see you again?'

She snorted. 'Reckons I won't have a choice.'

'I've never told you how much you changed my life,' I said.

She met my gaze. I hoped she saw the honesty in it.

'*Twpsyn*,' she tutted, and looked up at the sky. 'Your lass is next. We'll see her right, *gwas.*'

'Cora? I'd never ask you to–'

'Then don't ask.' Ang stretched out her legs and pulled some of the blanket over them. 'I needs to help mine own kin first. But mark me, Hansard. I'll be seein' ye again.'

There was a slight smirk on her features as she closed her eyes once more. 'If only 'cuz you always owes me a pasty.'

A couple of pigeons landed by the cooking coblynau. One of the chefs tossed them an apple. They pecked at it with happy coos.

Sunlight peeked over the station's ragged walls. The sky overhead was a bright, clear blue. A flock of birds turned lazy circles in the air, enjoying true exhilaration – total freedom.

I glanced over, and saw Ang had drifted into sleep.

I massaged the ache under my ribs. There was still so much to do. Still questions to be answered. Would this be the end of Baines and Grayle? I doubted it, somehow.

I itched to know why Quiet Eyes had turned on them. Was she opposed to their evil methods? I doubted that, too.

Had those pills hurt Cora?

Or could they possibly have saved her?

That last one I tried to put out of my mind. Ang was right, I needed rest – for my brain as well as my body. Despite having slept for nearly two days already, I felt I could easily go for another week.

Ang snored next to me. I soaked up the moment.

The sun gradually warmed the concrete. A mouth-watering smell wafted from the coblynau cooking pot. Minty had joined them, and the group seemed to be breaking into easier conversation with one another. They ladled vegetable stew into empty tin cans and drank it unhurriedly. Someone cracked a joke and the group laughed. The sound spiralled into the air with the pigeons.

I smiled at the rhythmic underscore to the scene – the gentle snores of a friend beside me, finally finding peace.

Epilogue: Visitation

Golden summer sunlight filled the rooms of the Parkview Residential Home. Mavis looked up from her desk and smiled at the visitor.

'Sign in here, love. You know the way to Cora's room?'

'I do.'

'Janet will be up shortly with a cup of tea.'

'Thank you.'

Strange, Mavis thought, after the visitor had turned down the corridor. Something seemed off about her, but she couldn't put a finger on what it was.

Soft footsteps fell on the faded green carpet outside Cora's door. Inside, Cora rested in her usual armchair, propped with pillows, staring at the blue sky. Red *omamori* charms fluttered in the gentle breeze where a nurse had locked the window slightly ajar.

Her visitor did not take the other seat. She bent low into Cora's face, grasping the arms of the chair. The muscles in Cora's face didn't twitch, or indeed show any signs of life other than a slow blink and shallow breathing.

'I found him,' whispered her visitor. 'Your sweet boy, Jack. And he is *so* sweet. How ever did you stomach him?'

She fingered a silver bracelet on Cora's wrist. Another silly charm, like all the others in the room.

'I hear Mavis convinced the doctor to take you off the medication,' she continued. 'That's one thing Jack has in his favour. He has a knack for persuasion, don't you think? Could you imagine what might have happened, if you'd been allowed to keep taking them?' Her voice was a mocking, sultry sigh. 'If you'd been allowed to wake up?'

An observer might have gained the impression of a frown forming on the visitor's face, though they'd never be able to describe its nuances. 'I didn't expect him to be quite so successful at stunting the operations of Baines and Grayle, however. That was unfortunate.'

She released her hold and straightened up, became an abstract shadow against the window.

'Still, it won't matter for long. I got what I wanted from them.' She stroked Cora's cheek. 'I'm pleased to find you in the same . . . condition. Do keep resting, dear. *Au revoir. Pas de chance, mon amie.*'

The woman with the quiet eyes slipped easily out of the home.

Cora's room became hushed and still once again. Only the breeze was left to brush strands of hair across her forehead.

The rattling tea trolley passed briefly by. 'Is she gone already? Goodness, that was a quick one . . .'

It clattered on down the hall. Nurses came and went.

The heat of the afternoon climbed, shifting the air from fresh to stifling. Cora's quiescent face remained bathed in rays of liquid gold. The glare reflected in her irises; they contracted tightly, turning her pupils to dots.

Cora's hands rested limply in her lap.

As the sun climbed ever high in the sky and the care assistants prattled their gossip and the heat drew prickles all over her skin . . .

. . . her fingers trembled.

About the Author

Georgina Jeffery is a British author of speculative fiction. Her stories often blend elements of fantasy, humour, and horror, and tend to reflect her penchant for regional mythology and folklore. She writes in frenetic sprints during her daughter's naptimes, and very late into the night.

Georgina's work can be found in a variety of anthologies and journals, including *The San Cicaro Experience, Unbreakable Ink,* and *Copperfield Review Quarterly.*

You can connect with me on:

 https://georginajeffery.com

 https://www.facebook.com/GJefferyAuthor

Subscribe to my newsletter:

 https://www.subscribepage.com/georginajeffery

Also by Georgina Jeffery

The Jack Hansard Series: Season One
https://books2read.com/u/49Mjd0

Jack is used to a life of handling dangerous goods, dodging disgruntled customers, and sometimes running away very fast. But when Ang (a furious Welsh coblyn) buys his help to find her missing kin, Jack finds himself chasing someone even monsters are afraid of.

The Hub
https://books2read.com/u/3yaDqJ

A sci-fi short story with a supernatural edge.

When an app developer accidentally creates a maliciously benevolent social media network, only her girlfriend can save her from what she's brought to life…